THE OMNIFEX CHRONICLES BOOK 2

I0545992

MONTGOMERY'S
Battle with Atlantis

PHIN HALL

Lundarien Press

Published by Lundarien Press, UK
Copyright © Phin Hall 2015

ISBN 978-1-910816-10-3 (Paperback)
978-1-910816-08-0 (Kindle)
978-1-910816-09-7 (ePub)
978-1-910816-11-0 (Audiobook)

For more info and other books: **www.lundarienpress.com**

To David Hall (my son) and Dave Evans (not my son) for hassling me to get this book finished. About time too!

OTHER BOOKS BY PHIN HALL

CONTENTS

LIST OF CHARACTERS

In London:
Montgomery Vane
Pepper - *his mum*
Victor - *his dad*
Gabriella - *his little sister*
Mike Jeffers (aka Jeff) - *not his friend*
Steve McGee - *Jeff's friend*
Julian Poore - *no one's friend*
Mr Pemberton-Drake (aka Trev) - *headmaster at St Kevin's*
  plus sundry teachers

His Lundarien Friends:
Jarfin Farle - *a Watcher*
Marlah Vandar - *a Mover*
Alcott Goye - *a Bardle*
Clovis Waylander - *a Hunter*

The Novaristee:
Wyndham Farle - *of the Watchers*
Berinon Brize - *of the Bardles (The Lord Chapman)*
Catrain Waylander - *of the Hunters - temporary*
Seraphina Ellendrie - *of the Changers*
Bancroft Felding - *of the Movers*
Bryce Goye - *of the Cealers*
Angmar Jarrody - *of the Healers*
Yvaine Morricote - *of the Mansers*

Others in the Underworld:
Vala Stroud - *Montgomery's aunt and magic teacher*
Dalton Stroud - *his granddad (deceased)*
Medway Soames - *a Watchman*
Yedda Vandar - *Marlah's mum*
Favian Vandar - *Marlah's dad*

Rowan Waylander - *Hunter leader - injured*
Dain Cottle - *a Watchman*
Emony Ellendrie - *a Multifex*
Bressalan - *the leader of Dursehaven*
Kolter - *his son, another Multifex*
Destrian - *the leader of Yarnock*
Mildred - *the other leader of Yarnock*
Anselm - *an Arister of Salistra*
Emlyn - *another Arister*
Garrick - *the third Arister*
Lockley - *of the Transak*
Randall Scolland - *also of the Transak*
The Bainard twins - *a pair of bus drivers*
Payton Stroud - *the baddie from the last book*
Merek Bandish - *one of her followers*

The Atlanteans:
Kuruk - *their king*
Rayen - *his right hand woman*
  plus sundry soldiers

LUNDARIEN MAP

KEY

1 TOWN HALL
2 TOWN SQUARE
3 JARFIN'S HOUSE
4 VALA'S COTTAGE
5 THE MELLADIE MAKER
6 RIVER TIMBRIS
7 LAKE ALTIS
8 THE AGRA

A WESTERLY PORTAL
B EASTWISE PORTAL
C MILLERS ESCAPE
D STAG GATE
E FISH GATE
F RIVER RUN
G BREWERS TUNNEL
H THE SLIP

N

The Vines

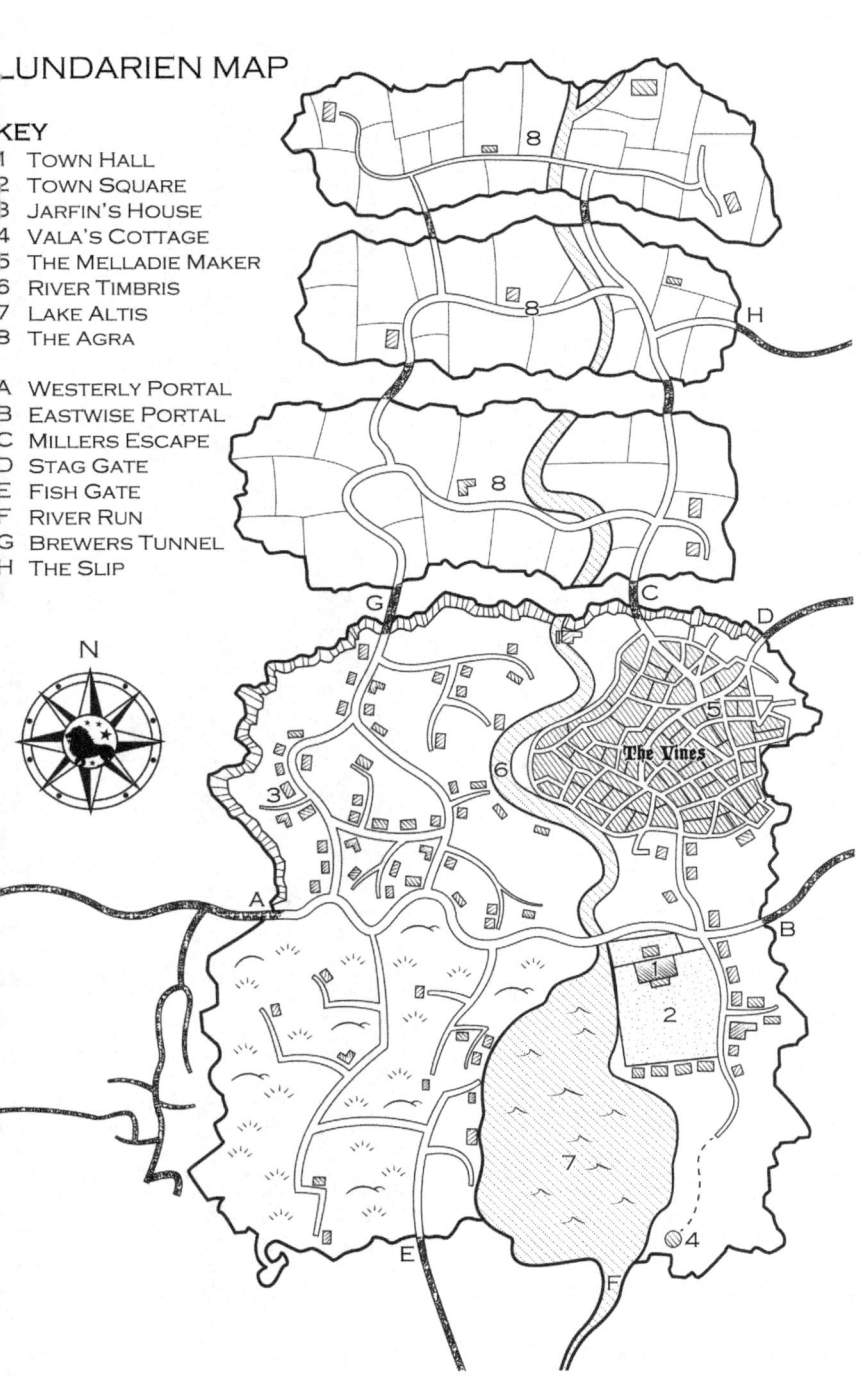

1. "Bend It To Your Will"

There's a monster in the dark. He can't see it, but he feels it all around: its anger, its hatred, its malice. In the blackness of the cave something is stirring and he leans forwards to peer into the shadows, his concern turning to fear as he strains to make out what it is.

And then he realises. There's no monster in the shadows. The monster is the shadows. Around the cave, they begin to shrink and thicken, taking form like smoke in reverse, being drawn back into a fire. But there are no flames here, there is barely the suggestion of light, only the gathering darkness closing around him.

He tries to move, to back away, but there is nowhere to go, no escape, just the bare wall stretching away on every side. Little by little the creature emerges, its arms, its legs, its body, a skeletal form woven from darkness and night, all skull and ribs. It is tall, far taller than a man and, as the last wisps of shadow fall into place, it leans its face down almost touching his own. Its eyes open, two holes red with fire, and then it speaks, its voice an echo from an ancient cave.

Three words: 'I know you.'

'Ow!' Montgomery jerked awake, confused for a moment by the strange surroundings of the small cottage, before he remembered where he was. He was in the Underworld, in Lundarien, the city housed in vast caverns far below London. More accurately, though, he was in his great-aunt Vala's cottage, and he'd travelled down here for his after-school magic lesson. But instead of paying attention to what she was teaching him, he'd been...

'Sleeping?' said Vala, her voice its usual rough growl. The ladle she'd used to wake him up floated back to its hook on the wall above the cauldron. 'What's the matter, boy? Magic too boring for you, is it?'

Montgomery tried to hide a yawn. 'Sorry,' he said. 'I'm really tired. I've only just started at my new school, remember?'

'School!' Vala spat the word and Montgomery had to duck sideways to avoid the flying spittle. 'Filling up your head with all that Maffy-matticks and Jogger-fee.'

'Do you mean Geography?'

'Who cares what it's called? Knowing about oxbow lakes and the capital of Paris - what use is that to anyone? This,' she jabbed a finger at the table between them, on which sat the sort of lumpy-looking clay mug you might make in primary school, 'is what's important!'

'That pot?'

'Magic, you half-wit!' Vala snapped her fingers and the pot rose up above the table, spinning as it did, so the red spots, that had been crudely painted across its bumpy surface, blurred together. Behind her, a stack of rectangular Underworld coins leapt into the air and span off across the room. The pot then started darting around catching them one at a time. This was called Moving, but it wasn't the sort of normal moving people on the Surface do, using their hands or a wheelbarrow. This was Moving with a capital 'M', using magic.

The pot drifted back down to the table, the coins nestling inside. Vala pointed a gnarled finger at it. 'Your turn.'

Montgomery puffed out his cheeks. 'No pressure then!'

'Of course there's pressure! The people of Atlantis are on the move.'

'So you've told me every day for the past week, but so

far nothing's happened. And no one else I've spoken to has heard any news about…' he rolled his eyes, wishing it didn't all sound so ridiculous, 'about Atlantis.'

Vala scowled at him. 'Who've you been talking to? Those idiot friends of yours?'

'If you mean Jarfin, Marlah and the others, then yes.'

'Hah! What do a bunch of whippersnappers know about the important things what're going on in the world?'

Montgomery folded his arms, cross at Vala's comments about his friends. 'If it's so important, why don't you go and speak to the Novaristee? If Atlantis really is on the move, and Lundarien is in danger, wouldn't it be a good idea to tell the city leaders? They'll want to know what's going on.'

'Shows how much you know!' she said. 'The only thing people really wants to know is that *nothing's* going on! I don't get involved in all that politics stuff. Not any more.'

'Why not? Why do you hide away in this old place?' Montgomery unfolded one arm and used it to gesture to the cottage around them. The back of his hand knocked against what looked like, and probably was, a shrivelled up, dead rat that hung from the ceiling on a length of twine, causing its crispy tail to fall off. He ignored it. 'You've got powerful magic that could help the city, so why not use it?'

Vala opened her mouth and, for a moment, Montgomery thought she was about to tell him. 'None of your business, boy!' she snapped and slumped back against the rickety wooden wall. She snatched a pipe from the folds of her dirty clothes and shoved it between her teeth. With a click of her fingers, it burst briefly into flame before emitting a steady stream of smoke.

'I wish *I* could do that,' said Montgomery, distracted by the magic and forgetting he was supposed to be cross.

'One thing at a time,' said Vala, as the coins leapt up out of the pot and landed, in a neat stack, on her outstretched hand. 'I want to see you do a bit of simple Moving first.' She nodded at the pot. 'See if you can get that thing to rise up. Nice and steady, like I showed you.'

Montgomery laid his hands flat on the table and breathed out slowly. He closed his eyes and tried to focus, slowing his breathing and clearing his mind.

'Try not to fall asleep this time,' said Vala.

Montgomery ignored her, concentrating on his breathing. When he felt calm and ready, he opened his eyes, fixed them on the pot, and willed it to raise up off the table.

Nothing happened.

Vala plucked the pipe from her mouth and jabbed it at the pot. 'It's not a staring competition, boy,' she said. 'Remember what I told you, you've got to want it to move. Bend it to you will.'

'That's what I'm *trying* to do,' said Montgomery, through gritted teeth. He narrowed his eyes, his gaze still fixed on the rough surface of the pot.

'That's right,' said Vala. 'Focus.'

'I *am* focussing,' he growled, but he was finding it hard. It wasn't just his great-aunt's constant interruptions. He was tired and cross after his first week at his new school in London, which had not gone at all well, and his concentration was suffering as a result. As he glared at the pot, he was struck by how much the spots looked like eyes - glowing, red eyes. They reminded him of ... What had he been dreaming about just now? His gaze slid slowly away from the pot as visions of darkness and smoke drifted into his mind. Shadows with red eyes and a voice like tombstones being rubbed together. What did it mean? Was Lundarien under threat again? Did it have something to do with...

'Focus!' Vala snapped. 'Concentrate on the pot. Will it to Move.'

Montgomery held his breath and stared at the pot, glaring at it, willing it, forcing it with his mind to Move. To Move.

Move!

The pot exploded, showering them both in clay and dust. He slumped back into the chair, blinking a bit of pot out of his eye.

'That wasn't exactly what I had in mind,' said Vala.

Montgomery waved a hand at the mess on the table. 'It was a rubbish old pot anyway,' he said. 'It looked like something my little sister would make.'

'*I* made it!' said Vala, scowling at him while puffing crossly at her pipe. Realising it had gone out, she snapped her fingers to light it again. 'Not a very successful lesson. And I suppose you'll be off wasting your time with those friends of yours, now?'

Montgomery looked at his watch. 'But I've only been here for fifteen minutes. I-' He was interrupted by a knock at the cottage door.

'Told you,' said Vala, looking smug. 'Come on in, young Farle.' The door creaked slowly open and, sure enough, Jarfin's messy hair peered around the doorframe, closely followed by face. He looked nervous

'Er, hello?' he said, sounding equally as nervous. 'Is Montgomery here?'

'He's sitting right here, ain't he?' said Vala, jabbing her pipe at Montgomery. 'If you can't see him from a few feet away, what hope do have of being a Watchman?'

Jarfin swallowed, ducking slightly back behind the door. 'Er, can I borrow him please?'

'Borrow?'

'There's a … an emergency. And I really need him to come with me.'

Vala puffed on her pipe for a few seconds, narrowing her eyes at him. 'An emergency, you say?'

'Yes?' The word came out as a question in a small, squeaky voice. 'Please?'

'Sure,' said Vala with a sudden smile. She flicked her fingers in a shooing motion at Montgomery. 'Off you go, boy. And once you've dealt with this "emergency", I suggest you practice your Moving. Try it on something that's not too valuable!'

Montgomery jumped to his feet, brushing pot dust from his school jumper. 'Thanks, Vala,' he mumbled as he nipped through the door.

He had to run to catch up with Jarfin, who was already hurrying off along the overgrown track that led back towards the Town Square and the centre of Lundarien.

'So?' he said, as he drew alongside his friend. 'What's this big emergency?'

2. "They're Coming For Us All"

'So what's this big emergency?' said Marlah, as she swept into the Melladie Maker. She stopped in front of Jarfin, flicking her long, red hair from her face so she could give him the full effect of her accusing glare.

'It's not really an emergency,' said Jarfin, handing her a steaming mug of Melladie and gesturing for her to join the others sitting around a table. In addition to Montgomery and Jarfin, there was Clovis, a Hunter girl, able to be magically swift and silent, and Alcott. He was a Bardle, which meant he didn't have any magic, but he did have an impressively broad, muscular body, making him the strongest, if also the youngest, of the group. 'I just wanted to get you all here so I could tell you my news. I only said there was an emergency to get Montgomery away from Vala.'

'A good thing you did,' said Montgomery. 'My lesson was going particularly badly.'

'So what news is *so* important I had to wander half way across the city to hear it?' Marlah, having accepted the Melladie from Jarfin without a word of thanks, pulled out a chair with Moving magic, and sat down.

Jarfin, handing out the mugs to Alcott, Clovis and Montgomery, ignored her. The complex, Christmas-in-a-sweet-shop aroma of Melladie filled the air and Montgomery bent over his drink to breathe it in. As he inhaled the hot steam, he felt himself relaxing, the worries about his lack of magical control slipping away.

'I think you're supposed to *drink* it,' suggested Clovis, grinning over her mug at him.

'So, what's going on exactly?' asked Alcott, his look of confusion amplified by a ring of Melladie froth coating his upper lip. Marlah chuckled under her breath, as Montgomery tried unsuccessfully to point it out to him.

Jarfin, still standing by his chair, cleared his throat importantly. 'As you are all aware,' he began, clearly reciting a prepared speech, 'today is my fourteenth birthday.'

'Whoa! What?' Montgomery's eyes widened at this revelation. '*I* wasn't aware. I would have got you a card or something.'

'A card?' said Marlah. 'Like the eight of clubs or king of diamonds?' Montgomery opened his mouth to answer, trying to work out how to explain about birthday cards, but decided it wasn't worth the effort.

'It's a Sunner thing,' he said. A Sunner was what the Underworld people called those who lived up on the Surface. 'Happy birthday, Jarfin.'

Jarfin gave him a quick smile and carried on. 'As I said, today is my fourteenth birthday and…' He paused dramatically, looking from face to face, making sure he had their full attention.

'Have you forgotten your important news?' asked Marlah.

Jarfin glared at her. 'No, I haven't. I was just building up to it.'

'Building up to what?' asked Alcott, who had just noticed his reflection in the window and was busy wiping his Melladie moustache off on a sleeve. 'What's going on?'

Clovis nudged him. 'Shh. Jarfin's just telling us it's his birthday.'

'I-' Jarfin began.

'I *know* it's his birthday,' said Alcott, looking even more confused. 'You didn't bring us all here to tell us that, did you?'

'No, I-'

'Yes, Jarfin!' said Marlah, evidently enjoying herself, and even Montgomery was struggling to stop grinning. 'Did you drag us out into the Vines just to bore us to death about your birthday?'

'Hang on,' said Montgomery, jerking himself upright and pointing at Jarfin. 'Did you just say you're fourteen? You can't really be older than me.'

Clovis kicked him under the table. 'Shh,' she said, her voice on the edge of laughter. 'Let him speak.'

Jarfin, who looked as if he was about to burst, almost yelled at them, his words tumbling out in a single burst. 'My dad's taken me on as his squire!'

The Melladie Maker was hidden away in the heart of the Vines, an area of tightly clustered houses and alleyways where the Bardles, those without magic, lived and worked and sold their goods. The shop was quite full this afternoon, including the usual couple of elderly ladies, chattering away by the window, but the sounds of conversation and the clink and tinkle of cups and spoons fell silent, and all eyes turned to Jarfin.

He sat down quickly, his face reddening, and pulled a dark-blue jerkin from under the table. 'I got this too,' he said, his voice almost a whisper. Around the Melladie Maker, people slowly returned to their conversations and their drinks. 'I just wanted you to know, that's all.'

'What's a "squire", exactly?' asked Montgomery, who had a vague idea the word had something to do with medieval assistants. 'Is it like an apprentice?'

'A squire is a person who learns their magical skills from someone else, following them around and seeing how they work. It's like one-to-one training.'

'O-kay,' said Montgomery, slowly, pulling the face that says, *Isn't that what I just said?* 'So, it *is* like an apprentice then.'

'What's an apprentice?' asked Alcott. The others looked at him, wondering if this was supposed to be a joke, but it obviously wasn't.

Ignoring him, Marlah turned to Jarfin. 'So, you actually brought us here so we could congratulate you, yes?' She paused, one eyebrow raised. Then, to everyone's surprise, she said, 'Well done, Jarfin.'

A smile of delight spread across his face. 'Thanks, Marlah.' He looked expectantly at the others.

'Oh! Yes, that's great news,' added Clovis.

Montgomery nodded agreement. 'Yeah, congratulations on becoming an apprentice.'

'Sorry,' said Alcott. 'What's an apprentice?'

After finishing their Melladie and helping Jarfin to struggle into his new jerkin, it was almost time for Montgomery to head home. His mother had made it very clear that he was only allowed to Lundarien on school days if he was home by dinner time, so the children headed through the alleyways of the Vines towards the Town Hall and the road that would take him home.

'So come on then,' said Jarfin, nudging Montgomery as they crossed the stone bridge that spanned the Timbris, the fast-flowing river that fed the city's enormous lake. 'When are you going to take us up to Surface?'

'What?' Montgomery stopped dead. Behind him, Clovis dodged to the side with Hunter speed, leaving Alcott to walk straight into the back of him. Montgomery only just managed to stay on his feet. 'I never said *anything* about taking you to the Surface. I can't. Wyndham wouldn't allow-'

'I seem to recall,' interrupted Marlah, 'that Wyndham

banned you from Lundarien, back when you first came here. That didn't stop you then, did it?'

'Yeah, but-' He paused as a small man, dressed in the brown clothes of the Bardles, struggled past, dragging a cloth-filled basket, almost as wide as the bridge itself.

'That'd be amazing!' said Alcott, leaning backwards as the man struggled past. 'We could go and look at all those things you told me about: buses, toasters, Big Bens, tevelisions...'

'Wait, I didn't mean-'

'It'd be easy,' said Clovis, nodding enthusiastically. 'We could meet you by that lift thing and you could smuggle us straight up.'

'I'm not *smuggling* any-'

'We'd need some Sunner clothes, though,' added Jarfin. He tweaked the sleeve of Montgomery's school jumper. 'We could disguise ourselves as Londians.'

Montgomery yanked his sleeve back. 'It's *Londoners*. And like I said, I can't, even if I wanted to. Your dad would-'

'What's going on over there?' said Clovis. She was the tallest of the group, by at least half an inch, and had the superb eyesight of a Hunter, and she was peering over the others towards the Westerly Portal.

Montgomery turned to look and was surprised to see a crowd of people pouring in through the entrance to the city cavern.

'Let's go and have a look,' he said, glad of the distraction, and they set off up the hill towards them.

'They're not from Lundarien,' said Jarfin, hurrying along next to Marlah. 'Who do you think they are?'

'How should I know?' she said. 'They look in pretty bad shape, though.'

Sure enough, though most of the people wore brightly-coloured jerkins and bodices, they looked dirty, their clothes torn and stained. As he watched, several of the people, mostly young children and a few of the older men and women, collapsed onto the grass at the roadside. Almost all of them, were shielding their eyes from the diamond light, as though they'd spent days in darkness.

From the streets nearby, many of the Lundarien townsfolk had spotted the newcomers, dropped whatever they were doing and hurried towards the Westerly Portal.

'There is rather a lot of them,' said Alcott, his voice sounding a little nervous as they approached the crowd. 'How many people do you think there are?'

'One hundred and thirteen,' said Jarfin, seizing the opportunity to show off his Watching skills, his ability to "see" with magical clarity and detail, whether in memories or in real-time.

Alcott whistled. 'As many as that?'

'*Exactly* as many as that.'

Montgomery studied the faces in the crowd, but didn't recognise any of them. And down here in the Underworld, Montgomery could remember every face he had ever seen, even those of people he'd forgotten existed, like the old lady who used to run his nursery school when he was a toddler or the bearded man in Barnstaple, who had once sold him some chestnuts. This was all thanks to his own Watching skills; skills he'd only discovered he possessed three weeks ago, when he'd accidentally caused his apartment building's lift to drop into the Underworld.

'Er… Hello?' said a voice, and a short, bald man staggered through the press of bodies, almost tripping over a small girl as he pushed through to the front. He was dressed in the yellow, moth-emblemed jerkin of the Cealers, those who use magic to create illusions, and he was clearly concerned about something, wringing his hands together, as though washing them without water. 'Tell me, what place is this?'

'Don't tell him,' whispered Marlah.

'This is our city,' said a deep voice from nearby. Startled, the man span round to find the massive bulk of Jarfin's father, Wyndham, towering over him. The man let out a gasp and vanished.

'Whoa!' said Montgomery, both surprised and impressed at this display of magic. 'Did you see that? Where'd he go?'

Marlah shook her head. 'He didn't go *anywhere*, genius,' she said. 'He's just Cealed himself, that's all. He's still right here.' She stepped forwards, a hand out, feeling for the man, but the space was evidently unoccupied. 'Where did he go?' she said, waving a hand around in the empty air.

'That's what *I* just said.' Montgomery narrowed his eyes and peered around, and although he couldn't see the man, it was as though he could sense him, a bit like the feeling he got sometimes that he was being watched. 'I think he's over here.' He pointed and, with a sound like the hissing of a hundred snakes, the man reappeared, a metre or so in front of Montgomery's finger.

He looked down at himself. 'What? What happened? How did you do that?' He turned his nervous, gerbil-like eyes towards Montgomery. But as usual, he had no idea how he'd done it. Stupid magic!

'It's not even worth asking,' said Clovis.

'If you've all quite finished...?' said Wyndham. He turned and fixed the man with a stern gaze. 'So who are you lot? And what exactly are you doing in Lundarien?'

'Lundarien, you say?' The man sagged with evident relief. 'Oh, thank goodness. We were trying to make our way to the capital, but we've been wandering the Southern Tunnels for weeks, trying to find our way. I can't tell you how good it is to finally stumble upon somewhere... friendly.' He gave Wyndham a look that begged for confirmation.

Wyndham surveyed the crowd of newcomers. 'So who are you lot? And what exactly are you doing here?'

The man bowed his head towards Wyndham. 'Forgive me, Watchman.' He pulled his wringing hands apart and placed one on his chest. 'My name is Bressalan. And these are my people, all that remain of the town of Dursehaven, on the western border of Brytellian.' Montgomery hadn't heard of Dursehaven, but knew that Brytellian was the Underworld country that stretched beneath most of England and Wales, and a few bits of France and Ireland .

'Dursehaven?' said Wyndham, his eyebrows raised. 'But that's hundreds of miles away.'

Bressalan let out a sigh. 'It *was* hundreds of miles away.'

'What do you mean "was"? It can't have moved!'

'Dursehaven,' said Bressalan, his voice suddenly quiet and strained, 'is no more. It has been overthrown. Defeated. That is why we are here. We are heading east - as far east as we can. And I suggest you do the same.' He reached out a hand, gripping hold of Wyndham's dark-blue jerkin in one small, grubby fist. 'They're coming, Watchman. They're coming for us all.'

'What do you mean?' asked Wyndham, glancing down at the man's hand, but making no move to free it. 'Who's coming?'

Bressalan swallowed and looked round at the group of his companions. 'We are at war,' he said, his voice now barely a whisper, 'with Atlantis.'

3. "Everyone's Heard Of Atlantis"

'It still sounds ridiculous!' said Montgomery, his voice reflecting exactly how ridiculous he thought it sounded. Although Vala had been going on at him about the threat from Atlantis, he couldn't help thinking of it as some made up, ancient myth. It couldn't be an actual, real place.

'Of course it's an actual, real place,' said Marlah, leaning against one of the brass statues in front of the Town Hall. Across the cobbled square, the people of Dursehaven stood, sat and, in some cases, sprawled, while a growing crowd of Lundariens gathered around them. 'It's Atlantis. *Everyone's* heard of Atlantis. Even you, and you're a Sunner.'

'Well, what I heard,' he said, 'is that Atlantis was an island up on the Surface, and it got swallowed up by the sea hundreds of years ago.'

Marlah shook her head at him. 'Unsurprisingly, what you've heard is wrong.'

'It's pretty close, though,' added Jarfin, giving Montgomery an encouraging smile. 'What actually happened was that Atlantis tried to build the biggest cavern in the Underworld and mined too close to the Surface. They weren't swallowed by the sea. They let the sea in!'

'According to the stories,' said Alcott, clearly eager to show off his knowledge as well, 'the only survivors were a family of a Manser. Being able to see the future, they'd known what was going to happen, so they built themselves a huge boat and filled it up with food and animals. When the sea came in, they were washed out through the hole and went on to populate the Surface.'

'That's a joke, right?' said Montgomery, grinning at Jarfin. 'This Manser wasn't called Noah, by any chance, was he?'

'I believe it was a woman,' said Clovis. 'She was called Nora.'

Montgomery coughed to hide his amusement. 'O-kay. Let's pretend for a crazy moment that this is all true. If Atlantis got wiped out by this flood, how can they still be around today, attacking this lot?' He jabbed a thumb towards a nearby Dursehaven group.

'Oh, that was all hundreds, maybe thousands, of years ago,' said Jarfin. 'Atlantis was rebuilt and new people settled there.'

'But how did they get rid of all that water?'

'Magic, obviously!' said Marlah.

Montgomery rolled his eyes. 'Of course.'

Marlah opened her mouth, probably to say something sarcastic, but was interrupted by the Town Hall doors bursting open and slamming back against the stone walls as Wyndham strode out onto the steps.

'Bressalan!' he called, his voice booming out across the square

The Dursehaven leader inched out to meet him and said, in his far smaller voice, 'Yes, Watchman?'

'The Novaristee would like to discuss with you further about the attack on your people, and about your knowledge of this threat from the west. However, I am aware you have travelled a great distance and suffered much, so you may prefer, for now, to get some rest and something in your bellies.' Much nodding greeted this suggestion and Wyndham raised expansive arms to include all those hanging around the square. 'You can count on receiving a warm welcome from the people of Lundarien. Can't they?' This last was delivered in an even more booming voice, and was not a question that invited a negative response. He looked around at his fellow townsfolk, who straightened up and tried to look welcoming. 'If you are able, and I know few here who are not, please open your doors to our fellow countryfolk. Show the people of Dursehaven the full measure of Lundarien hospitality. Tomorrow, we shall gather here again at the fourth hour.'

As Wyndham's words died away, Bressalan bowed to him. 'Thank you, Watchman. This,' he gestured to a well-built boy of around sixteen, who, despite his yellow and green striped jerkin being spattered with dried mud, managed to look rather dashing and impressive, 'is my son, Kolter. We are indebted to you and your city.'

Wyndham nodded to Kolter. 'You'll both be my guests tonight. I'd like to hear more about these Atlantean invaders. Come on, Jarfin!' And without waiting for a response, he strode away, Bressalan and Kolter hurrying behind.

'So are you coming?' asked Jarfin, turning to Montgomery.

He frowned back at him. 'Coming where?'

'Here, of course. Tomorrow morning.'

'Oh right.' Montgomery looked unsure. 'I'm not sure,' he said. 'I've got school tomorrow and it's only my second week. But I'll ask my mum, anyway. If she knows Lundarien is in danger, she might be okay with me taking the day off.' He looked at his watch. He was already late for dinner. 'I'd better go. Keep me posted on anything your dad and Bressalan say about Atlantis.'

'And how's he going to do that, exactly?' asked Marlah. 'Write you a letter and leave it in the lift?'

'That's not such a bad idea,' said Jarfin. 'You could lend me one of your keycoins so I could call the lift, and sneak up to deliver it to you in person. You said you live on the third floor, yes? Whatever that means.'

But Montgomery was shaking his head. 'I can't lend you a keycoin for the lift. Payton stole my spare one, remember? And we've still not found it. Anyway, imagine if your dad found out you'd been to the Surface! You know how cross he gets.'

As if in response, Wyndham's voice bellowed from the other side of the Town Hall. 'Jarfin!'

'See you tomorrow,' said Jarfin, scurrying away across the square.

As he wandered through the maze of tunnels that led to the lift shaft, Montgomery thought about Atlantis. He wasn't surprised to find out that Vala had been right since, in addition to whatever other magic she had, she was a Manser, which meant she could see into the future, though he wasn't exactly sure how it worked. Maybe it was like flicking through a book to see what happens at the end. That wasn't the issue. *Atlantis* was. And the idea that it actually existed still seemed crazy; even more crazy than the fact that there was a magical world full of people living hundreds of metres below the Surface of the planet.

The lights in the Lift Tunnel were still dazzlingly bright from his magical meddling a few weeks, and seemingly forever, ago. He heaved open the panel in the floor and slid in his keycoin, one of fifty that had been left to him by his granddad. This particular one, which was engraved with a lion surrounded by four small stars, made the lift in his apartment building drop down into this tunnel, sometimes at a terrifying speed. He suspected the other keycoins accessed similar entrances, but he wasn't certain. He hadn't had the chance to try any out.

The lift door slid open with a "ping" that echoed off the tunnel walls and Montgomery stepped inside, pressing the button for the third floor and wrinkling his nose at the unpleasant, armpit-and-public-toilet smell of the lift.

'Mum?' he called, as he closed the apartment door behind him.

'In the kitchen!' came the reply. His mum, whose name was Philippa, but was known as Pepper, was standing in front of the oven. She was a tall woman with dark hair, and a permanently stern expression. She looked especially stern today, even wearing a pair of flowery oven gloves. She used them to pull back her sleeve so she could look at her watch. 'And why are you late, young man?'

Montgomery glanced over his shoulder into the living room, where his sister, Gabriella, was sitting on the floor in front of the sofa, engrossed in a game that involved toy ponies and various items from her dolls house. She was four and half. 'Where's dad?' he asked.

'He's in the bedroom having a lie down.' Pepper lowered her voice. 'He's had a tough day at the brewery.' She coughed, and continued in her normal voice. 'So *why* are you late?'

It was Montgomery's turn to lower his voice. 'It wasn't my fault. Something's happened. In Lundarien.' He pointed at the floor, in case there was any confusion where he was talking about, despite the fact his mum had grown up in the Underworld city. 'There's a meeting at nine o'clock tomorrow morning.' He paused, but Pepper, busy taking the chicken casserole out of the oven, made no response. 'It sounds like it's really important, mum. The city could actually be in danger. So... can I go along?'

Pepper set the steaming dish down on the cooker and turned to Montgomery. She was frowning. 'In Lundarien?'

He nodded. 'Can I go mum? Please?'

'You've got school tomorrow!'

'But it's important, mum,' said Montgomery, adding a slight whine to his lowered voice. 'It's about Atlantis.'

The frown increased. 'Atlantis?' She quickly lowered her voice again. 'What's Atlantis got to do with anything?'

'They've attacked some place called Dursehaven. The people who lived there had to run away and they turned up at Lundarien about an hour ago.'

Pepper pushed a sheet of hair from her face with the oven glove. 'Are you sure?' she said. 'So soon after all that business with my sister?'

'I'm sure. And Wyndham has called a meeting of the Novaristee tomorrow morning, and I really need to be there.'

'Did Wyndham ask you to be there?'

'Well… no,' he admitted. 'But it sounds really important. I don't want to miss it.'

'And *I* don't want you to miss school. You've not even been there for a whole week.' Montgomery opened his mouth to argue, but Pepper cut him off. 'I'm sure Lundarien will survive a few hours without you. You'll just have to find out what happened when you've got home from school. And done your homework.'

'But-'

'It's not open for debate, young man. You're lucky I'm even letting you go after school, since you failed to come back on time today. I don't mind you spending some of your free time with Jarfin and the others, and on your magic lessons with Vala, but not at the expense of our *real* lives here in London.' She raised her gloved hand to cut him off again. 'Dinner will be ready in five minutes, so you've got time to tidy up your room first. I don't know how you get it so messy.' And with that she turned back to the oven, the conversation closed.

Montgomery stomped down the corridor to his bedroom and slammed the door behind him. The room really was a mess, so he tackled it in the usual way, stuffing dirty clothes under his bed and sweeping everything on his desk into a handy drawer. Unfortunately most of the drawers were already filled with screwed up bits of paper, odd socks and sweet wrappers. All except one. But as Montgomery yanked it open, poised to sweep the desktop rubbish into it, he stopped.

There, in the bottom of the drawer, were some of the items given to him by his Granddad, Dalton Stroud: the deck of cards they used to play with, the leather pouch full of keycoins, and, nestling beneath them, the brown leather cover of the old notebook, its pages filled with random-looking scribbles. He had tried many times to decipher them, but he wasn't even sure the jagged lines and curving swirls were even writing - it looked like the 'art' Gabriella produced with her crayons, though not quite as colourful. For a moment, he almost pulled it out to have one more go at reading it, but instead he swept the stuff on his desk into the drawer and slammed it shut again. He could always show it to Vala sometime. After tomorrow's special meeting maybe. Because, no matter what his mum said, he was definitely going to Lundarien in the morning.

4. "That Doesn't Sound Like A Good Idea"

The narrow tunnel stretches away before him, filled with the hoards of men and woman crouching in the dim glow of the diamonds that hang from their necks. Not one of them makes a sound, they barely seem even to breathe as they strain to listen, waiting for the signal. He leans back against a rock, one of the many that line the cavern behind him, jutting up from the ground like the fossilised teeth of some vast Underworld monster.

'How long?' he asks, his voice a whisper as thunderous as a landslide in the darkness, yet barely audible over the rapid thundering of his heart. There is no reply. There is only the expectant silence of the waiting army.

He senses a movement, something shifts behind him, and he turns to look, to peer into the shadows beyond, but there is nothing there, only the rocks and the solid tunnel wall. Again, he feels the movement, a quiver from the rock he was leaning against, and he steps back in confusion, unable to make sense of what he is seeing. The rock is moving, coming to life, unfolding itself like a waking troll, human features melting into its surface. From somewhere fingers snatch at him, at his clothes, his arms, his face. He opens his mouth to cry out, to warn the others, but a hand clamps across it, stifling not only the words but his breath as well. From the red-lined face, barely an inch from his own, black eyes glare at him with undisguised malice.

'I have you!'

Montgomery sat up in bed, breathing hard, partly relieved that he *could* breathe, but mostly still overwhelmed by the sense of panic in his nightmare. Ever since he moved to London, only a couple of days before he stumbled across the Underworld, he had suffered vivid, often terrifying, dreams. And most of them had come true! It was a form of Mansing, or so Vala said, seeing visions of things to come. So far, though, he'd only realised these nightmares were coming true when they were already happening, when it was too late to do anything about them.

'Stupid magic!' he muttered to himself and, since his bedside clock informed him it was time to get up, he got up.

'Those are mine!' cried Gabriella from across the kitchen table. 'Mummy, tell him!'

Montgomery paused in the act of filling his bowl with Choco-Puffs. 'How can they be yours? You don't earn any money. They're *everyone's*.'

'They're mine, because they're my favouritest. And I chose them with mummy, so there!'

'That's enough arguing, you two,' said Pepper, without turning round from where she was busy making packed lunches. Gabriella took the opportunity to stick her tongue out at Montgomery.

He shook his head at her. 'Stop being babyish!'

'What did I just say?' said Pepper, looking over shoulder. 'For that, you can have cornflakes instead.'

'What?' Montgomery was outraged, while his sister grinned at him over the pink unicorn doll she had brought with her to breakfast. 'But-'

'No buts, young man. Cornflakes! And get a move on. You need to leave for school in five minutes.'

Ten minutes later, a still-disgruntled Montgomery dragged his feet across the pavement in front of the apartment building, pausing to look up at his mum, who was watching him from the lounge window as usual to make sure he was safely on his way. He carried on up the road, peering round occasionally until Pepper disappeared back into the apartment. Then, in a kind of running crouch, he scurried back, ducking behind the parked vehicles that lined the road to watch the apartment building door through one of the car's windows.

He didn't have to wait long as, barely a minute later, Pepper came striding out with Gabriella clutching her hand and skipping along next to her.

'What's you doing?' said a voice nearby, and Montgomery jerked round to see a scruffy-looking boy about Gabriella's age standing, hands in pockets, looking at him as though he'd spotted something strange and wondered if he should poke it with a stick. His nose was running.

Montgomery quickly glanced back at Pepper and his sister. They had joined the other mums and kids, and were heading in his direction. Realising they were going to pass right by his hiding place, he turned back to the boy.

'Nothing,' he whispered, flicking his fingers at the boy in an attempt to shoo him away. 'Go on, push off! Don't you know it's not safe to stand in the road?'

'You're standin' in the road,' protested the boy, wiping a sleeve across his nose. 'You hidin' or sumfing?'

'Please, just go away,' said Montgomery, a note of pleading entering his voice as his mother drew near to the car.

'Give us a quid, then.'

Montgomery turned to the boy, speaking in a loud whisper. 'What? I'm not giving you anything.'

'Alright,' said the boy, shrugging and wiping his nose again. 'Then I ain't going nowhere.'

Montgomery sighed and stuck a hand in his pocket,

drawing out a conker he'd found the day before, a chewy sweet he'd forgotten about that had fluff on it, some change and his keycoin to get into the Underworld. 'Look, I've only got ... forty-six pence. If you go now, you can have that.'

The boy nodded, holding out a grubby hand to receive the money. Once it was safely clutched in his fist, he kicked Montgomery in the shin and ran off. Montgomery covered his mouth to keep from crying out, because at that moment, Gabriella pulled her hand from Pepper's and stopped on the other side of the car. She was looking up at a bird that had just landed on the telephone cable directly above his head.

'I wish *I* could fly, mummy,' she said. Montgomery ducked down lower as Pepper came to a halt, and banged his ear on the wing mirror. Without meaning to, he let out a small grunt, causing his mum to look round. Ducking completely out of sight, Montgomery held his breath. He was sure his thundering heartbeat was going to give him away.

'Come on, Gabriella,' said Pepper at last, and her footsteps started up again. 'Stop daydreaming!'

As soon as they were both safely out of sight, Montgomery let out a long sigh of relief and scurried back into the apartment building, glancing at his watch on the way. It was twenty-five to nine - plenty of time.

'I reckon I'll be early for once!'

'You're late,' said Marlah, as Montgomery hurried round the side of the Town Hall into the square to join her, Jarfin and Clovis.

He rolled his eyes at her. 'You would not believe how busy that lift gets at this time of day.'

'What?' said Jarfin, his eyes wide. 'Who else has been going up to the Surface?'

For a moment, Montgomery thought this was supposed to be a joke, but Jarfin seemed genuinely alarmed at the idea that hoards of Underworld travellers were busy using the lift.

'The lift doesn't only come here,' he said. 'People who live in my apartment building use it to go up and down the building.' Jarfin's face turned to one of bewilderment. 'Forget it. Sorry I'm late. Did I miss anything?'

'Nothing much,' said Clovis. 'The Novaristee and that Bressalan guy went inside a few minutes ago and nothing's happened since.'

Montgomery glanced up at the Chronolith, Lundarien's version of a clock. It was only made from two circular stones, one larger than the other, but he still found it difficult to work out the time on it. As he looked, though, he noticed a small window, high up in the wall. He closed his eyes for a moment, using his Watching skills to recall the layout of the rooms inside the Town Hall.

'You see that window up there?' said Montgomery, opening his eyes and pointing to it. 'I reckon that opens straight into the room where the Novaristee meet.'

'It's called the Novaristee Meeting Room,' said Jarfin, proudly. Montgomery sighed.

'Marlah?' he said. 'Why don't you Move yourself up there and see what's going on?'

'You mean *fly?*' She looked at him as though he'd asked her if she could grow a second head. 'I'm a Mover, not a bird.'

'Oh!' Montgomery was surprised. 'I thought that might be a Mover kind of thing. Er, what about using a broomstick or something?'

'A broomstick?'

He shrugged. 'Isn't that how people fly with magic? On a broomstick?' Montgomery looked at Jarfin and

Clovis for support, but they stared back at him, their faces blank.

'Er, my mum's got an old broomstick somewhere, I think,' suggested Jarfin.

'Okay, forget the broomstick. What about...?' He stepped across to the wall and snatched up a short wooden plank that had been left leaning against it. 'What about if you stood on this plank? Could you Move it up to the window with you on it?'

Marlah glanced up at the window again. It was at least five times her height from the ground. 'Not a chance,' she said. 'Moving your own weight is very advanced Moving magic - you need Transak training first. I'd be surprised if I could even get the plank off the ground.' Montgomery slumped against the wall next to Jarfin. 'I might be able to Move *you*, though.'

'Good idea!' he said, alert again.

'That doesn't sound like a good idea to me,' said Jarfin. 'That window's really high.'

'And these cobblestones are very hard,' added Clovis. Montgomery looked down as she tapped them with her foot, then turned to Marlah.

She shrugged. 'I'm happy to give it a shot if you are.' She held out a hand, palm towards the plank, and it rose up next to Montgomery, so he could sit on it. With another quick glance at the window, which didn't look *that* high, he sat, and Marlah narrowed her eyes in concentration. At first nothing happened. Then a wave of nausea swept over Montgomery, as his stomach lurched and his sense of balance was jolted. He swallowed and looked down to see his toes still resting on the cobbles.

'I guess-' he began. Without warning, the ground dropped away beneath him as he rocketed into the air, slamming against the stone wall about half way up the Town Hall.

And then stopped.

He wasn't falling, but nor was he rising. Instead, the plank began to pivot, turning slowly onto its end, and Montgomery had to wrap his arms around it to stop himself being tipped off.

'What are you doing?' said Marlah, trying to shout through gritted teeth. 'Stop fighting me!'

Montgomery's bottom slid off the plank and he scrabbled to get the piece of wood under his arms, wishing it wasn't quite so splintery. He looked down at the scattered groups across the square, but no one seemed to have noticed what was going on by the corner of the Town Hall. He focused on Marlah.

'Fighting? I'm not fighting you. I'm not doing *anything* except trying to stop myself falling off.' Now dangling from the plank, he started to drift away from the Town Hall, rising even higher into the air. He scraped at the wall with the tips of his shoes, but there was nothing to catch hold of. The roof of the Hall drifted past and he looked up to see the lowest branches of the trees only a few metres away, from which a cluster of birds peered out at him through the foliage. He tried not to look down as he hovered even higher. Tried, and failed. The cobblestones and the people in the square below looked a long way down, and he wasn't sure he could hold on much longer.

5. "I Suggest You Run"

Montgomery snatched at the nearest branch. He almost slipped from the plank on his first attempt, coming away with a handful of unfamiliar-shaped leaves, but managed to get a proper hold on his second try. A shower of birds burst from the foliage and disappeared into another tree across the cavern. Breathing hard and using the branch to pull himself up, Montgomery kicked a foot over the plank, gripping it with his knees. It was like trying holding a float underwater between his legs, as the plank tried to force itself upwards but, with an effort, he pushed it down and got himself back into a sitting position.

Perching on the suddenly small-seeming length of wood, and gripping it with both hands, he looked back down to the sickeningly small figure of Marlah, her face, and those of his other friends, still turned up towards him.

'Come on, Marlah,' he thought, willing her to Move him back down out of the tree, and he glanced back at the small window. Ever so slowly, the plank began to inch its way back towards the Town Hall.

As, at last, he neared the window, he reached out a hand to steady himself against the wall, trying to make as little noise as possible. The last thing he wanted to do was attract the attention of those inside. The window was slightly ajar, so he teased it up a little higher and peered through at the gathering below.

He was already familiar with the Novaristee Meeting

Room, with its large table surrounded by nine chairs, each belonging to a representative of the magic circles, and coloured to match.

In the dark green chair sat Catrain, Clovis' mother, who was standing in as leader of the Huntsfolk since her husband, Rowan, had was still recovering from being badly injured in the battle against Payton's followers. Next to her, in the yellow chair of the Cealers, sat the large, round figure of Bryce and, next to him, in the green chair, was the tall, slim figure of Bancroft, head of the Movers.

Seraphina, the nervous-looking head of the Changers, sat in her orange seat, while the moustachioed Bardle chief, Berinon Lord Chapman, perched on the brown chair next to her, his black cane laid in front of him on the table. Montgomery didn't recognise the woman in the red chair, but guessed she must be the Manser leader, who had been kidnapped by Payton. Wyndham was standing by his dark-blue chair, while the light-blue one of the Healers was filled with the plump, motherly figure of Angmar Jarrody, who was easily the oldest person in the room. The purple chair of the Lectimentors sat empty as before and even from this height, as he peered past the hundreds of glowing diamonds hanging from the enormous chandelier, he could see it was still covered in dust. Apparently there hadn't been a Lectimentor on the Novaristee for many years.

'That is all well and good, Berinon,' boomed the voice of Wyndham, clearly audible from the small window, 'but it is best if we hear it from Bressalan, don't you think? After all, he was there. Your speculations and concerns can wait.' He gestured to the area directly below the window and, as Montgomery leaned forwards, he made out the figure of the Dursehaven leader, sitting in another, uncoloured, chair.

Bressalan stood up and cleared his throat. 'I wish to

thank you for the great kindness you and your people have shown to us,' he began, bowing to the Novaristee. 'You have made us feel most welcome. And, with our bellies full of good food and our weary bodies rested with soft beds, I dare say we could be fooled into thinking life may now go back to normal - that we have nothing to fear. And yet I bring terrible news of an invasion from the west.' He paused to look at the faces around the table, before continuing. 'For years, the town of Dursehaven has enjoyed good relations with Atlantis. We are not a large community, by any means, but we are, or rather *were*, the last keepers of the dreamsheep and used to trade their wool with the Atlantean merchants at the Western Post. All had been well for years. Then, about six months ago, that all changed.'

'What happened?' asked Seraphina, leaning forward in rapt attention.

'We never found out, my lady,' said Bressalan, with a shake of his head. 'Our Bardle traders reported that the Western Post was deserted - not a man, woman, child or beast anywhere to be found. And then, when a few of the traders decided to head further into Atlantean territory, to find out what was going on … they never returned.'

'They were killed?' said Berinon, though it sounded more of a statement than a question.

'Not according to the delegation from Atlantis that arrived a month or so later. They told us they had taken our people captive and would only return them to us if we agreed to join them.'

There was silence as everyone considered these words, before Berinon spoke up again. 'What do you mean, "join them"? Join them in what?'

'In their invasion of Brytellian, Lord Chapman,' said Bressalan.

'Their *invasion*?' echoed Seraphina.

'Oh, they didn't actually call it that, but an invasion is what it boiled down to. They claimed they were looking to unite the Underworld to prepare us all for the Great War to come. But their idea of uniting had little to do with unity and everything to do with forcing people to do their bidding. We refused, of course, and demanded that they return our people to us.'

'Why didn't you take the Atlantean delegation hostage in return?' asked Bryce. 'Play them at their own game?'

'You would not ask if you had seen them, sir. They would strike fear into any heart.' Bressalan lowered his voice as he recalled their appearance, and Montgomery had to strain to listen. 'Their fingernails and teeth were sharpened to points. Their faces were covered with a vein-work of glowing, red tattoos. And their bodies were shrouded in black as though their wore the darkness itself. But it was none of these things that made us want to get rid of them as soon as we could. It was their eyes. They were black. But not the shiny black of rat eyes. These were like holes cut into a void. Cruel, inhuman and pitiless.'

'How did you get rid of them?' asked Seraphina, leaning even further forwards than before.

He shrugged. 'Once they had delivered their message and told us their conditions, they simple turned and walked out the way they had come.' Bressalan rubbed at his eyes as though worn out by this talk of Atlantis, and when he continued, there was a quiver in his voice. 'Ten days later they returned, with an army at their side. Our city was sacked, hundreds of people, *my* people, were captured. We didn't stand a chance. This mere handful of our townsfolk,' he gestured towards the wall below Montgomery, 'is all that remains of our once-thriving community, driven from our homes. And so we are fleeing to the east, because you can be sure, my friends, that Atlantis is coming this way. They are coming to take us all.'

'This must have happened weeks, maybe months ago,' said Berinon, sounding annoyed. 'Why has it taken you so long to get here and warn us of this threat?'

'We sought refuge in the maze of caverns in south Brytellian. If you had ever ventured into them you would understand why it has taken us so long. For weeks we were lost, wandering and going in circles, before we found our way again. We would no doubt still be there, were it not for a small party from Ethenside, who had also fled there after Atlantis attacked *their* community. Together we made our way back towards the Great Tunnel.'

'And what of Salistra?' asked Berinon. It took Montgomery a moment of Watching to recall where he had heard this name before. Salistra was the another city somewhere in Brytellian. 'Why did they not send word to us after you told them of this threat?'

Bressalan shook his head. 'We never made it there, Lord Chapman. As I said, we lost our way in the Southern Tunnels and ended up here. We never found Salistra, and we have no intention of travelling west, heading back towards... *them.*'

'Any other questions?' asked Wyndham, turning to the others sitting at the table as Berinon slumped back in his chair.

Angmar raised a hand. 'I have one,' she said. 'Who is it that leads Atlantis now? When I was young, I remember hearing stories of Queen Maiara, who rebuilt much of the Golden City, and her son, Ujarak, Master of the Sceptred Circles, who reigned after her. But I've heard nothing of Atlantis for over twenty years.'

'Ujarak was succeeded by his nephew,' said Bressalan. 'His name is Kuruk. He came to the throne about fifteen years ago. He was barely a man then but, by all accounts, he ruled well. The Razor King, they called him, because of his wisdom and good judgement. Atlantis flourished under his rule, and it was he who improved the trade links with Brytellian and set up the Western Post.'

'He doesn't sound like the kind of leader who'd wage war against his neighbours,' said Bryce, spreading out his huge hand on the table. 'Has he been overthrown?'

Bressalan shook his head again. 'Oh, Kuruk's still the king, my lord. We believe something happened to him. Something terrible. His mind has become warped. And now it seems he is set on ruling the whole of the Underworld and will allow nothing to stand in his way.'

'Anything else?' said Wyndham, looking round at the Novaristee again. No one moved. 'Very well,' he said, getting to his feet and stepping towards the Dursehaven leader. 'Thank you for this warning, Bressalan. We are sorry for what has happened to you and your people. And we will give you whatever provisions you need for your journey east.'

'Thank you.' Bressalan bowed his head.

'And now, may I ask you to wait in the vestibule as we,' he gestured to the others around the table, 'discuss these matters further and consider what should be done.'

Bressalan headed to the door but, as he pulled it open, he turned and said, 'I suggest you run.'

'I say we take his advice!' said Berinon as the door clicked closed. 'We are no match for the people of Atlantis.'

Across the table, Wyndham sat down and even from his high vantage point, Montgomery could see the withering look he gave the Bardle leader. 'I knew we could count on *you* for a courageous response.'

'You forget, Wyndham, that *I* have been to the Western Post. I have traded with the Atlanteans, though it sounds like their appearance has changed somewhat. And I have seen the strength of their magic. Once I even visited the Golden City itself, many years ago.'

'We are not running!' said Bryce, thumping a massive fist on the table and causing Berinon's cane to roll off and clatter onto the floor. 'I say we stand and fight.'

Seraphina shook her head. 'If Dursehaven wasn't able to stand against Atlantis, what makes you think *we* have a chance against them?'

'What makes *you* think we would face them alone?' asked Catrain. 'Atlantis may be strong and their magic may be very powerful, but they are a mere handful of communities built around a single city. Brytellian has many cities. If we stand together-'

'Stand together?' Berinon threw up his arms as if warding off Catrain's stupidity. 'This is Brytellian we're talking about. A less "together" country you'd be hard pushed to find!'

'He's right,' said Bancroft, nodding sadly. 'Most of the Brytellian communities aren't even talking to each other. I've heard nothing from the North in… well, I can't remember *ever* hearing from most of the cities up there.'

'We've always had a good relationship with Salistra,' said Angmar in a quiet voice. 'And from what Bressalan has said, they may not even be aware of the threat Atlantis poses. I suggest we meet with *them* before making any kind of decision.'

'Agreed,' said Bryce. Beside him, Catrain nodded.

'Apart from running,' said Seraphina, 'I can't see we have any other option.'

Wyndham turned to the woman sitting in the red chair next to him. 'Yvaine?' he said. 'You've been very quiet. What do you have to say on this matter?'

Montgomery squinted down at the leader of the Mansers. She had a strange, glazed expression, as though she wasn't really paying attention to anything that was going on around her, and when she spoke, her voice was a dreamy monotone, as though reading the words from a script only she could see.

'There is one other whose counsel we must seek first,' she said, apparently talking to one of the stuffed animal heads mounted on the wall above Wyndham's head. 'One who has a bond with the people of Atlantis. We must speak with Payton!'

'Payton?' The word burst from Montgomery's mouth in surprise, and he quickly ducked back from the window. Unfortunately, he had been so engrossed in the debate that he had quite forgotten he was perched on an old plank high above the Town Square. He toppled backwards, just managing to catch hold of the wood with his knees, which left him dangling upside down. Then the plank began to twist slowly towards him and he knew he was going to fall.

He caught sight of Marlah, far below, her hands still raised, though she wasn't looking at him. She was talking to a boy in a green and yellow jerkin, though Montgomery couldn't quite make out who he was. Nor was he that interested.

'Help!' he cried, but it was too late. The plank flipped over, pitching him off and there was nothing to catch hold of, only empty air. The last thing he saw, as he plummeted towards the hard cobblestones at a bone-shattering speed, was Marlah's startled face turned up towards him. He screwed his eyes tight shut and braced himself for the impact. But it never came. Instead, he plunged into ice cold water. He had been screaming, but quickly closed his mouth, saving what little breath he still had in his lungs, and opened his eyes.

The underwater world was hazy and indistinct, but he could just make out the looming shapes of columns and towers covered in long tendrils of seaweed. In the distance there was what might have been the mouth of a large cave, but he wasn't that interested in his surroundings. What he wanted to know was how to get out.

Montgomery had heard about people falling into water and not being able to tell the difference between up and down. He always thought it sounded like nonsense, but now, as he thrashed frantically around in the water, he realised it was true. He had no idea which way would take him up to where there was air.

Air!

He *really* needed air. And the more he thought about it, the more his lungs felt like they were burning. He tried desperately to stop himself trying to breathe, but the desire was overwhelming. He *had* to take a breath, even if it was a breath of cold water. How typical of his luck, to avoid splatting on the ground by drowning instead!

Without warning, something from below him wrapped itself around his foot and it began to tug at him, pulling him down, down into the vastness of the water beneath him. He tried to shake himself free, kicking out at the creature with his other foot, but its grip was far too strong. It felt like a long, powerful tentacle and it was dragging him into the darkness of the deep.

6. "They've Let Payton Out Of Prison!"

Struggling against the creature's grip, Montgomery peered down, trying to make out what it was, but everything was so indistinct and blurred. And light! Through the pain in his chest, Montgomery was surprised. Why was it light in the depths below him, while above, the shoals of fish and weed-covered ruins faded into darkness? Unless…

He burst from the water, dragging air into his lungs with a sound like a sheep trying to neigh. Air! How wonderful it felt to be able to breathe! If only he had more lungs.

'How did you get in there?' said a voice. A voice which, despite the thumping in his ears and his frantic gasping, Montgomery recognised. Blinking the water out of his eyes, the world came slowly into focus and Montgomery found he was hanging, upside down, by his foot, his head against the wooden edge of a boat. It wasn't a tentacle that had pulled him out. It was Alcott.

'Alcott?' he said, between breaths. With barely any discernible effort, his Bardle friend yanked him into the boat, leaving him sitting and dripping in amazement. 'It *is* you, Alcott! I *knew* it was you. You …' He gazed around, getting his bearings. He was still in Lundarien. Above him were the trees he'd been stuck in only a short while before, and away to his left was the crowded square, the Town Hall looming above it. And beneath him were the deep waters of Lake Altis from which he had just been rescued. He leaned over the side, gazing into the dark-blue waves, and shivered. 'You saved my life!' he said.

'Well, I don't know about that.' Alcott looked down at the bottom of the boat and started fiddling with the oars to cover his embarrassment. 'How did you get in there, anyway?'

'I wish I knew!' said Montgomery. 'One moment I was falling from the Town Hall, the next I was underwater. Obviously it was magic of some sort, but I'm pretty sure it wasn't me.'

He turned at the faint sound of someone shouting his name.

An oar jabbed past him, pointing towards four small figures on the distant shore. 'Looks like Marlah and the others,' said Alcott. 'Want me to row you back?'

'Would someone care to explain exactly what just happened?' said Montgomery as he trudged, dripping, back towards the square. Jarfin, Marlah and Clovis were waiting for him, together with another boy, whom Montgomery recognised as Bressalan's son, Kolter. 'Anyone?'

'Kolter just saved your life,' said Clovis, gesturing to the newcomer.

'I think you'll find it was Alcott who saved my life, actually.' He narrowed his eyes at Kolter. 'Hold on. Did you do that? Did you magic me off into the lake somehow?'

'Sure,' said Kolter, as though he'd done nothing more impressive than open a cupboard door. He pushed the mop of blonde hair out of his face, revealing an evidently well-practised heroic look. He'd cleaned up well since yesterday, and had the glistening white teeth and powerful shoulders to go with the look. 'I went over to introduce myself to this lot and next thing I know, you're dropping like a stone. I just acted on impulse. Teleported you to the softest place I could think of.'

'Well, *almost* the softest,' said Marlah. 'You could have dropped him onto Alcott.'

'I heard that!' called Alcott from where he was pulling his boat onto the shore. Marlah grinned but didn't look back.

Montgomery was still frowning at Kolter, while trying to wring some of the water out of his school clothes. 'So, which of the Magic Circles includes teleporting? Moving? Hunting?'

'Oh, it's not just *one*,' said Kolter, flashing his teeth at him again. 'I'm a Multifex. You met my dad earlier, right?' Montgomery nodded. 'Well he's a Cealer. And my mother's a Mover. As for me,' he jerked a thumb at his chest, where the yellow and green striped jerkin gleamed in the diamond light, 'I happen to be *both*, which means I can teleport things. And people, of course.' He gestured to Montgomery, to emphasise the point.

'Okay, that is pretty amazing!' said Montgomery, forgetting his crossness in the face of this revelation. 'Er… Thank you.'

'No problem.' Kolter slapped Montgomery on his damp shoulder. 'Best get back though, eh?' And he turned away to join the rest of his townsfolk, still waiting in the square.

'So, is that normal?' asked Montgomery, when he was out of earshot. 'Can all Multifexes do special types of magic?'

'Of course!' said Marlah, as though he'd asked whether they all wore clothes. 'Every different combination of normal magic creates an extra, special form of magic. They're called Conjurings. *Everyone* knows that.' Montgomery gave her a withering look. 'Are you ill?' she asked. 'Only you *look* ill.'

He gave up. 'What other sorts of things are there, then, apart from teleporting?'

'Oh, loads of things,' said Jarfin. 'Talking with animals, breathing underwater, flying, stopping other people's magic - though that's really something only an Omnifex can do - creating fire and so on. But Multifexes are quite rare, even those who have only two types of magic, like Kolter.'

'They're not so rare in your family, though,' said Clovis, 'what with you mum, your granddad and Vala. And Payton.'

Montgomery gasped. 'Payton!' he said, already hurrying towards the Town Hall.

'What's the problem?' asked Jarfin, running to keep up. 'What's happened?'

Montgomery increased his pace. 'It's Payton. The woman who leads the Mansers said the Novaristee needed to talk to her.'

'But she's locked up in the cells,' said Clovis, who was keeping up with no discernible effort. 'You don't think...?' She left the question hanging, but was evidently thinking the same thing as Montgomery. But surely the Novaristee wouldn't let her out of the cells. As he had found out when freeing the kidnapped Hunter children, it was impossible to perform magic in the Lundarien prison. But if they let her out...

He took the Town Hall steps two at a time and heaved the doors open. As he barged into the vestibule, he noticed Bressalan's face turned towards him, looking startled, then he skidded to a stop, almost slipping to the stone floor in shock. There, striding serenely along the left hand corridor, a Lundarien Watcher on each side of her, was Payton.

The last time Montgomery had seen his aunt, she was lying in a crumpled heap amid the ruins of the Town Hall steps. She had tried to seize control of city, kidnapping men, women and even children. In the end, there had been a battle between the people of Lundarien and Payton's army, and even Montgomery's mum, Payton's sister, had been involved. Pepper had been overpowered, but before Payton could hurt her further, Montgomery came between them, his powerful magic leaving Payton in that crumpled heap. But although he had defeated her, her sudden presence still came as a shock.

Montgomery opened his mouth to speak, but couldn't come up with any words to fill it, so he closed it again, settling instead for glaring angrily at his aunt. She was tall and slim, with the same dark hair as his mother. The same hair Montgomery had, though his was much shorter. It was strange to see her in a plain, brown robe, instead of the black one she had worn on the few occasions he had seen her before. It was not *this* that caught his eye, though, but what she was wearing on her hands. He had expected handcuffs or preferably manacles, but instead there was just a strange glowing sphere, about the size of a tennis ball, dangling from a chain that snaked around her wrists.

As Payton drew alongside him on her way to the Novaristee Meeting Room, Montgomery looked up at her and was surprised to see her smiling back. He frowned, his eyes fixed on her face and, as she stepped into the room beyond, she winked at him. Then the door closed behind her, and Montgomery turned back towards the square, and ran.

'Enjoy your swim, did you?' asked Vala, not looking up from whatever she was poking around in her cauldron as it steamed away over the fire.

Montgomery leaned against the door, trying to recover from sprinting all the way from the Town Square.

Vala's cottage, which looked from the outside more like a jumbled mess of rocks and straw, and much the same from the inside, was out on the otherwise deserted marshland in the southern corner of the cavern. 'I... What? How did you know about that?'

'Apart from the fact you're dripping all over my nice, clean floor?'

Montgomery looked down at the large, flat stones beneath his feet. They were filthy, with bits of hair, mud and twigs, and even a few lumps of old food wallowing in the thick dust and dirt that formed a horrid carpet across the flour.

He pulled a face and began picking his way across the room. 'I just saw my aunt,' he said, still breathing heavily. 'She was in the Town Hall.' He looked expectantly at Vala, but she was still staring into the cauldron, apparently unconcerned by this news. 'The Novaristee have brought her up out of the cells. She's with them right now, *inside* the Town Hall!' Still, Vala made no move to show she'd even heard him. He stopped, on the opposite side of the cauldron and glared at her. 'Did you hear me? They've let Payton out of prison! Which means she can do magic again! Are you even listening to me?'

Vala's eyes snapped up to glare back at him through the steam. 'I'm trying not to,' she growled. 'I'm busy.'

'Busy?' He felt like kicking the stupid cauldron over. What could possibly be more important than Payton being out of prison? What was she making in there? Some sort of magic potion?

'A "magic potion"?' she said, though he hadn't spoken the words out loud.

'How..?' Montgomery began, forgetting his anger in his momentary surprise, and then remembered Vala was a Lectimentor - she could hear people's thoughts. 'Stop reading my mind!' he said, his anger resurfacing. 'So what is it?' He jabbed a finger at the cauldron. 'Is it a magic potion?'

'You mean like a serum for making your enemies turn into frogs? Or a love potion?' Montgomery pulled a disgusted face at the idea of Vala bewitching people to fall in love with her. Yuck! Without warning a glass jar shot past his ear and stopped, hovering in front of Vala. The lid unscrewed itself and, from somewhere, she produced her pipe and jabbed it into the jar, spearing out what looked like a dead scorpion. Her eyes were still fixed on Montgomery. 'Where do you get all this nonsense, boy? Magic comes from in here,' she tapped her pipe against the side of her head, and the scorpions lifeless tail flopped against her cheek, 'not from outside.'

'You mean there's no such thing as a magic potion?' Montgomery felt somewhat disappointed by this. He liked the idea of magic potions. 'So what *are* you making?'

Vala flicked the scorpion into the cauldron and, with a gloop, it was swallowed up with a burst of steam. 'Come here and see for yourself.'

He inched around the fire and peered in. The not-a-magic-potion was completely still; not a bubble or ripple disturbed the dark, glassy surface, and the things on strings that dangled from the beams were perfectly reflected in it. 'Well?' he said.

Vala tutted. 'Just breathe it in, boy. And focus.'

'But-'

'And stop your incessant waffling nonsense.'

Montgomery pulled a cross face, but said nothing. He sniffed at the steam rising up from the cauldron and was surprised to find it wasn't actually disgusting; odour of bins and marsh gas is what he'd been expecting, but instead it smelled of... He wasn't sure. He couldn't place it. But it brought to his mind the fields in Steepleford, the village he'd grown up in, where he'd spent hours playing hide and seek in the maize fields, and trying to dam the river with fallen tree branches and rocks. He could almost feel the swift, cool water flowing between his toes and the summer sun warming his back, the echoed shouts and green leaves, freshly-picked apples and evening shadows that stretched ever-longer towards dusk. He sighed as he breathed in more of the steam, but it was a contented sigh, full of the memory of laughter and happy voices, and he was surprised to find he could hear them too. Voices as faint as distant whispers. And they were getting louder.

They seemed to be coming from the cauldron, and he leant forward to listen. But it wasn't children he could hear. These were the voice of adults, or rather one adult.

'Wyndham?' Montgomery blinked in surprise and focused on the stuff in the cauldron. It was still calm and ripple free, but as he looked, the dangling objects it reflected shifted and warped, like ink dropped into water, and shapes, new shapes, formed on the dark surface. Colours and faces danced and swam, until, at last, he found himself looking into, 'The Novaristee Meeting Room?' He turned to look at Vala, who was also staring into the cauldron. 'You've been… *spying?*'

Vala grunted. 'You're a fine one to talk!' She waved a hand over the surface and the images melted and swam apart to form a new picture, showing Montgomery perched on the floating plank, peering in through the high window. 'That's some impressive Moving the young Vandar girl did.' She waved her hand again and the meeting room reappeared, showing Payton smiling serenely at the Novaristee.

'So you already knew about Payton then?' said Montgomery.

'Shh!' growled Vala. 'I'm trying to listen.'

7. "Why Were You Spying?"

Montgomery breathed in the relaxing steam and, as he did so, the voices became clear.

'...don't understand what this has to do with *her*.' That was Berinon's voice and, as Montgomery peered into the cauldron, looking around the Novaristee Meeting room, he caught sight of the leader of the Bardles, no longer sitting in his brown-covered chair, but standing against the back wall, as far from Payton as he could get. His walking cane lay forgotten on the floor nearby.

'Don't tell me you've forgotten about our little voyage?' Payton's voice was calm and clear, but had lost the hard edge it had had when she was trying to take over the city. 'The Seven Wonders of the Underworld, you promised me. Remember?'

Berinon shuddered, his pale cheeks flushing with colour. 'As if I could ever forget! But that was years ago. What bearing could that possibly have on our present situation?' He turned to look at Yvaine. 'Well?'

'She knows,' said the Manser leader, in her far away voice. 'She has tasted the power that now lies at the heart, and in the hearts, of Atlantis.'

Berinon threw up his hands. 'What does that even mean?'

'It means,' said Payton, 'that I know what you are facing. I know what is coming for you from the West. It is hunger and fury, it is lust and pride. It is all that is dark in the heart of humanity. It cannot be beaten with weapons or stopped with words. And I cannot help you.' She raised her hands and Montgomery saw again the glowing ball that hung from her wrists. 'At least, not like *this!*'

'You needn't think that's coming off any time soon,' said Wyndham, leaning forward in his chair.

'I have told you,' said Payton, her voice edged with desperation. 'Whatever it was that my nephew did to me, it has freed me from that darkness. I am not who I was, Wyndham. I can help you. Trust me.'

'Trust *you*?' Berinon let out harsh bark of laughter.

'Forgive us for not trusting you again a mere few minutes after you kidnapped a load of our children,' said Wyndham, unfolding himself and stepping towards her, 'but unless you have any light to shed on this Atlantis business, there's a nice, cosy cell that's missing its villain. Men!' This last word caused the two Watchers standing behind Payton to take hold of her shoulders and begin turning her towards the open doorway, the ball swinging below her hands.

'I am no villain!' she said. 'Not anymore. The darkness has gone, I tell you. I am free!' And then the door closed behind her and she was gone.

'Thankfully, not *that* free!' said Catrain, as Berinon crept back round the table and bent to pick up his cane.

Vala's hand swept across the surface of the cauldron again and the image began to swirl and blur, the sounds fading away into the hiss of steam.

'Fat lot of good that did!' she said, hobbling across to her table and slumping onto the bench. 'She knows something that girl, but she ain't saying what. Least, not exactly.'

Montgomery peered one last time into the cauldron, but all he could see were the reflections of his surroundings; the Novaristee Meeting Room was gone.

'How come Payton didn't try to escape?' he asked, joining Vala at the table and perching on a stool. 'I thought she'd at least try to get away. She's got powerful magic.'

'Not wearing that Heliorb, she hasn't.'

'That what?'

'The Heliorb. You must've seen it. The glowing sphere tied to her hands.'

Montgomery frowned at her. 'But what's-'

'It stops the wearer from performing magic,' interrupted Vala, in tones that suggested this was obvious. 'With that thing on her she'd be no more dangerous than any other young whippersnapper. She'd certainly be no match for Wyndham and his Watchers.'

Montgomery was stunned by this revelation. He hadn't even imagined such a thing existed. 'So, this Heliorb thing. Does it work on anyone who wears it?'

'Anyone who's even *near* it. It's got a sphere of anti-magic, like the Sun does on the Surface, only the Herliorb's is only three or four oars wide.'

'Oars?'

'Yes, oars.' Montgomery shook his head at her. '*Oars, boy!* Don't they teach you nothing in that wretched school of yours? An oar is about the length of this table.' She gestured to it with her pipe. 'Two breeches and one cob, to be precise.'

'Oh, I see,' said Montgomery, who had heard Jarfin talking about breeches. 'It's a unit of measurement. About,' he sized up the table, 'two metres?'

'What's a metre supposed to be?'

Montgomery glanced back at the cauldron. 'Why were you spying on the Novaristee? Why didn't you just go along to the meeting?'

Vala said nothing for a while, acting as though she hadn't heard him. She Moved one of the hanging bunches of herbs onto the table and started shredding it between her bony fingers, before stuffing it into her pipe.

Then, just as he was about to risk repeating the question, she said, 'Ain't part of the Novaristee, am I?'

'But, you should be!' he said. 'They need you, Vala. You heard them - they're worried about what's going on with Atlantis in the west.'

Vala humphed. 'No business of mine.'

'Of course it is!' Montgomery almost shouted at her. 'Did you hear what that Bressalan guy said earlier? The Atlanteans are heading *this way*. You could use your Mansing skills to see what Atlantis are going to do next - find out when they're going to attack.'

But Vala just shook her head. 'The future ain't like some book you can just flick through to see what happens at the end. It's suggestions, echoes of possibilities and occasional flashes of detail. No good would come of me meddling in all that politics stuff.'

'You would be helping!'

'Huh!' Vala carried on her shredding and pipe stuffing. 'That's what your grandfather told me when he convinced me join the Novaristee thirty years ago. Ten years I sat on that council, and what good did that do the city? I couldn't stop the rebellion or that poor lad from getting killed. *Help?* She growled out the word between her few teeth. 'Great help I was, with my own brother and his daughters exiled from the city.'

'Wait,' said Montgomery, pausing as he tried to take this all in. 'Are you saying you were part of the Novaristee? Back when Payton rebelled... the first time?'

'Course I was,' she said. 'And the old purple chair's been gathering dust ever since. Literally.'

'But you can't blame yourself for what Payton did!'

'Telling me what I can and can't do now, is it?' Vala scowled at him and took a few puffs on her pipe, before lighting it with a snap of her fingers. Montgomery, distracted again by this effortless display of magic, asked if creating fire was another of the Conjurings his friends had mentioned. 'Why you asking? Going to tell me I shouldn't use magic to light my old pipe now, are you?'

'I just wondered. Only, Kolter - one of the Dursehaven people - teleported me into the lake. Which is why...' He held up his sleeves, still heavy with water. 'Anyway, he said he could teleport because he's a Cealer *and* a Mover.' Vala waved a hand and a portal opened up beneath Montgomery's stool. It dropped through another across the room, leaving him sprawling in a damp heap on the floor.

'Sounds about right,' said Vala, looking a little less grumpy as Montgomery picked himself up off the floor and dragged the stool back to the table.

'Your granddad was the one for Conjurings. It was a pastime of his, finding out different combinations of magic.'

'Really?' Montgomery leant forwards, intrigued. 'How many are there?'

Vala creaked to her feet and hobbled back over to the cauldron. 'I don't know. Hundreds, maybe? I wasn't the one scribbling it all down in those precious notebooks of his. Now are you going to hang around here all day pestering me about doing my duty, or are you going to get to school?'

Montgomery looked down at his sodden school uniform. 'I don't suppose you know how to magically dry clothes, do you?'

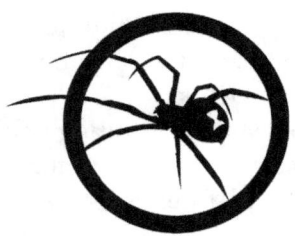

8. "You'd Better Watch Your Back"

Mike Jeffers, known as Jeff to his friends, was easily the worst thing about Montgomery's new school, St Kevin's Comprehensive. They had disliked each other from the first time they met and had even come to blows at the local sports centre just before the start of term, leaving Montgomery with a bruised forehead and Jeff with a bleeding nose. And a nasty grudge. By the time the new school year began, word had got around the Year Nine pupils that anyone who tried to make friends with Montgomery, or even talk to him, would answer to Jeff and his gang. So it was an unpleasant surprise when Montgomery, now perfectly dry though smelling disturbingly of Vala's cottage, ducked into the alleyway down the side of school and found himself face-to-face with Jeff and seven of his mates.

'What happened to you, Twinkles?' said Jeff, grinning at him from where he leant against the school wall. He had nicknamed Montgomery "Twinkles" the first day they'd met, knowing it annoyed him. 'We thought you was ill. We missed you, didn't we?' There was a mixed response from his friends, a 'Yes' or two and an 'Of course, we did!', but mostly jeers and head shaking.

'I've been busy,' said Montgomery, coming to a halt as Jeff pushed himself from the wall, blocking his path. 'Not that it's any of *your* business.' This provoked a few more jeers.

'Such hostility, bruv,' said Jeff, clearly enjoying himself. 'We could be friends, you and me.'

'I've got friends, thanks.'

Jeff made a big show of peering behind Montgomery. 'Is that them imaginary friends again? And how is they gonna have your back? Friends like *us*,' he gestured to the group around him, who were now standing in a sort of horseshoe shape, with Montgomery in the middle, 'looks out for each other. We could look out for you too, Twinkles.'

'Stop calling me that, *Michael!*' said Montgomery, angry more at himself for rising to Jeff's bait than at the boy himself. 'Just get out of my way.' He strode forwards to push Jeff out of the way, but one of the other boys tripped him as he did so, causing him to barge into Jeff, almost knocking him into the wall.

'You ain't gonna let that slide, is you?' said the nose-picking boy Montgomery remembered from the sports centre.

'Yeah,' said another, a skinny, rat-like boy that Montgomery hadn't seen before. 'Teach him some respect, Cuz!'

Jeff, who had recovered his balance, brushed down the front of his puffer jacket with both hands and shook his head. 'Not yet,' he said, squaring up to Montgomery so their faces were inches apart. 'Not here, with teachers and that around. But soon, Twinkles. And then you is gonna wish you'd accepted our generous offer.'

'Can I go now, Michael?' said Montgomery, sounding as casual as possible while trying desperately not to swallow or show any sign he was actually quite nervous. Not for the first time, he wished he could do magic on the Surface - then he'd show them!

Jeff stood to one side, bowing low as he did so. 'Please, be on your way.' Montgomery stepped out through the gap and headed up the alley. 'You'd better watch your back,' said Jeff. 'Coz no one else will, Twinkles!'

Montgomery walked away as quickly as possible without actually running, and resisted the urge to look back, though he felt the gang's eyes on him all the way across the weed-strewn playground.

His fists were clenched in angry frustration, as he wished there was some way he could get back at Jeff. But what could he do? Everyone at this school loved Jeff for some reason, and wherever he went he was surrounded by a group of followers, some of whom were quite big and intimidating. Montgomery, on the other hand, had no friends here - not even one after a whole week, thanks to Jeff.

He barged through the door into the school corridors, which smelled exactly the same as the ones in his old school - maybe there was a special spray all caretakers used, flavoured with disinfectant, cheese and vomit. He sighed. The fact that none of the other pupils would talk to him was annoying, but it didn't bother him as much as might be expected, since he wasn't that interested in school life. Or even London life. What he really cared about was life in Lundarien and, as he thought back to the adventures he'd had with his Underworld friends, and the ones that were yet to come, Montgomery was surprised to find he was smiling.

His thoughts were interrupted by the school bell, which rang slightly louder and longer than seemed necessary, calling his year to assembly.

The school hall echoed with the sound of pupils slouching into rows next to their form teachers. The teachers all had chairs to sit on and, while they were the uncomfortable plastic things that infest all schools, they were still a luxury compared to the dusty, hard floor of the hall.

'Settle down, settle down,' called a voice over the noisy chatter of the gathering pupils. Standing on tiptoes, Montgomery peered over the heads of those in front to see the headmaster, Mr Pemberton-Drake, waving his hands for everyone to sit and be quiet. All around him, children dropped to the floor, and Montgomery joined them, assuming that least-comfortable of all positions: sitting down cross-legged. 'Right,' Mr Pemberton-Drake continued. 'If I could have your attention.'

On the stage behind the headmaster, sat the twelve staff heads. Montgomery recognised a few of them already; Mr Vickers, the head of P.E., dressed in a dark-blue tracksuit and slicked-back hair, Miss Vega, the head of art, with her shaved head and face full of piercings, and Mr Gregor, the ancient head of the maths department. This last teacher was also the deputy head, a position which he was rumoured to have held since schools were invented, no doubt looking much the same as he did now: white haired, with huge dog-like eyebrows, small wire spectacles and hands that never seemed to settle. Every one of the teachers looked exactly as bored and uninterested as Montgomery felt himself.

When finally the hall was silent, Mr Pemberton-Drake raised his arms and boomed, 'Welcome back, Year Seven!' He paused, beaming at the assembled pupils. Behind him Mr Gregor leaned forwards in his chair and tugged at the headmaster's jacket. They had a brief, whispered conversation before Mr Pemberton-Drake turned back, arms raised once again. 'Welcome back, Year *Nine!*' he cried. 'This is an important year for you, as you are no doubt aware…' The headmaster turned again to look at Mr Gregor, a confused frown creasing his forehead. 'Er, why is it important exactly?'

'GCSEs, sir.' said the maths master, those impressive

eyebrows dancing. 'They're choosing their options this year.'

'Are they, by Jove?' Mr Pemberton-Drake ran his fingers across his chin as though stroking an imaginary beard, and turned back to the front. 'Well, it really *is* an important year for you. No doubt all of you have some idea of what you want to be doing, when you eventually emerge from school, yes?' He looked around the room, his gaze causing a kind of inverted Mexican wave as heads ducked down out of sight. Montgomery, who had not been in one of the headmaster's assemblies before, failed to copy them and caught the teacher's eye. 'You, boy!' he said, jabbing a finger towards Montgomery.

'Me?' said Montgomery, in a voice that begged for a negative answer.

'Yes, of course you.' All eyes turned towards Montgomery. 'Stand up, then, boy. What's your name.'

Wishing the ground would swallow him up, preferably straight down into the Underworld, Montgomery got slowly to his feet, his backside already numb from the hard hall floor. 'I'm Montgomery.'

'Montgomery, eh?' said Mr Pemberton-Drake. 'Like the general.'

Montgomery raised his eyebrows, reminded of his granddad, who used to call him "the General". 'I guess so,' he said.

'Excellent. And what do you want to be when you grow up?'

Montgomery shrugged. It wasn't really something he'd ever thought about. 'It's not really something I've ever thought about, sir.'

'Come, come!' said the headmaster with a dismissive wave of his hand, as if to flap away Montgomery's unimaginative response. 'All boys have dreams of what they want to be. I, for example, wanted to be one of those genies that live in lamps and get to grant wishes to people who summon them. Hah! Wonderful times. And Mr Gregor here wanted to be a librarian.' He chuckled to himself and gave a little shake of his head. 'Ridiculous, really. As if old Mr Gregor had any chance of being a librarian!' He paused and stared into space so long that Montgomery half-started to sit down again. 'Well, Montgomery?' bellowed the headmaster, his eyes fixed on him again. 'What do you want to be when you grow up?'

'When I was younger…' he began and had to pause to swallow. His face felt hot and he caught sight of Jeff, a short distance away, smirking at him. Montgomery focussed on the headmaster. 'When I was younger,' he repeated, 'I thought I'd quite like to be a vet.'

The headmaster looked unimpressed by this choice of career. 'Chopping up animals and stuff, eh? Bit grim for my tastes, all that blood and guts. I'd still much rather be a genie, leaping out of bottles with a puff of smoke. Marvellous! Each to their own, though, I suppose.' He gestured for Montgomery to sit down, which he did at a remarkable speed. 'So…' Mr Pemberton-Drake looked around as though surprised to find himself standing on a stage addressing a crowd of children. He opened and closed his mouth, but no words came out.

'Options, sir,' said Mr Gregor, leaning forwards again.

'Yes, that's it! Options.' The headmaster beamed at everyone. 'The key is to make good choices. Don't just go for rubbish subjects, like Music or French, simply because you're good at them. Think about the jobs you really want, and choose your subjects to match. Otherwise you'll end up as a teacher like poor old Mr Gregor, here.'

9. "Was He A Magician?"

Having promised his form tutor that he would bring in a note from his mother, which he'd have to write himself, Montgomery slumped his way through an afternoon of art. Instead of the usual attempts at creating bits of artwork, the class was subjected to one of Miss Vega's endlessly dull lectures. Today's topic was a medieval inventor called Leonard Da Vinci.

Like the other pupils, Montgomery spent the time daydreaming, though he was probably the only one thinking about the kind of revenge he'd have on Jeff and his gang if magic worked on the Surface - thoughts which mostly involved Moving them onto the stage during assembly, minus their clothes. He was just imagining joining in with all the pointing and laughing, when something Miss Vega said caught his attention.

'What did you say, Miss?' he said, raising a hand.

The art teacher's eyebrows, with their sparkly piercings, shot up in surprise; she was clearly not used to being interrupted, or having anyone actually listen to her. In fact, she looked as though she hadn't really been paying attention herself.

'Er, about Leonardo being from Tuscany?' she asked. 'In Italy?'

Montgomery shook his head. 'No, before that.'

Miss Vega consulted her notes. 'He was born in the third hour of the night?' she suggested.

Montgomery dropped his hand. He had never heard anyone talk about "hours of the night" before, except in the Underworld, where time was divided into twelve hours of the day and twelve hours of the night.

Without stopping to consider whether it was a sensible question, he asked, 'Was he a magician, Miss?'

Somewhere near the back of the class a couple of girls giggled.

'Well, he was certainly a remarkable man,' said Miss Vega, scratching her head with a long paintbrush. 'Leonardo was an inventor, a mathematician, a painter, a writer and even a sculptor. Some people say he was the most talented genius who ever lived. Did you know he wrote hundreds of pages of notebooks, all with the writing back-to-front to prevent other people from reading it?' She didn't wait for an answer, but flicked through the book on her desk. 'Have a look on page two hundred and seventy-two in *The History of Art*. It's quite fascinating. You see…'

As Miss Vega droned on, Montgomery flicked through the heavy book to the page in question. Among the blocks of text were a few black and white photographs. The first two were of the Mona Lisa and the village of Vinci. The third was labelled, "An excerpt from one of Leonardo Da Vinci's notebooks". He stared at the mess of illegible scribbles interspersed with strange pictures of circles and lines. Part of the apparently backwards writing had been printed in mirror-image, but as far as Montgomery could see, the words were still unreadable. He leafed through the rest of the chapter, the pages filled with paintings and diagrams of peculiar inventions, even a flying machine with wings that would have flapped like a bird's, something he could have done with that morning at the Lundarien Town Hall. Montgomery wondered if people at the time would have thought of a man flying through the air as magical. Maybe his question hadn't been quite so stupid after all?

Montgomery slammed the door, kicked off his shoes and hurried to the kitchen, but instead of the empty apartment he'd been expecting, as Pepper would still be picking Gabriella up from school, he skidded to a stop in front of the dining table. His dad, Victor, was sitting there, chin cupped in his hand as he stared at a point on the wall, somewhere beyond the dresser.

Montgomery was momentarily lost for words. What was his dad doing home at this time of the day? Had his morning's absence from school been reported? 'Er... Hi, dad,' he said at last, his mouth suddenly dry. 'Why... What are you doing home?'

Victor jerked as though he hadn't noticed Montgomery bursting into the room. 'Yes,' he said, which didn't quite answer Montgomery's question. 'No,' which didn't either. Victor shook himself, his eyes refocusing on his son. 'I had a half day,' he said in a flat, far away voice. 'Work's a bit, you know... slack at the moment.' He cleared his throat and smiled at last. 'How was your day? How was school?'

'Usual,' said Montgomery, deciding he was probably in the clear and heading for the fridge. 'Art and stuff.' He yanked it open and stared in at the densely packed shelves, trying to work out what he fancied. After a couple of minutes debating with himself, he grabbed a bunch of yoghurts and closed the door. 'We learned about Leonardo Da Vinci,' he said, peering in the bread bin and pulling out half a sliced loaf. 'He invented helicopters.'

'Did he?' said Victor, in that far away voice. 'Good for him.'

Montgomery couldn't think of anything else to say; it was normally his dad that did all the talking. So, stuffing an entire slice of bread into his mouth, he headed for his bedroom, leaving his dad still slumped at the table.

Sitting at his desk, Montgomery tore the flimsy lid from one of the yoghurts, before realising he had failed to bring a spoon. Recalling he'd seen one in a desk drawer a day or two ago, he yanked them open, rummaging around among the rubbish and stationery, despite the fact it would have been much quicker to go back to the kitchen.

At last he found one, tucked underneath the pouch of keycoins, and, as he dug into the yoghurt - toffee, his favourite - he poured the coins out across the desk and started turning them face down, diamond side up, the way he and his granddad used to. The rules were simple. After all, he'd only been seven when Dalton had taught them to him.

'Sit yourself down, young General,' his granddad had said, waving Montgomery towards the chairs he'd set up on the pavement in front of his house. He lived in Steepleford's old post office, aptly named "The Old Post Office", which had long ago stopped delivering people's mail and had, instead, become a home: the cottage with a postbox in the wall. Montgomery did so, catching sight of the coins lined up on the chessboard-topped table, the sun glittering off their shiny, silver surfaces.

'What are they, granddad?' he asked. 'Is it another magic trick?'

Dalton chuckled. 'Not today, my lad. This is a game. A *memory* game. Have a look at these coins and tell me what you notice.'

Montgomery subjected them to some careful scrutiny. 'They've all got different patterns on them.'

'Have they?' said Dalton, in the voice that suggested that wasn't exactly true. 'That's not exactly true, is it? Look again.'

This time he gave them a full ten second's scrutiny.

'These two are the same!' he said, excited at this discovery and jabbing a finger at the coins in question. 'And these!'

His granddad chuckled again. 'That they are. In fact, all the coins have another one with the same pattern.' He pointed out a few more. 'There's twenty-five pairs in all. Give 'em a good, look, young General.' He waited while Montgomery ran his eyes across the coins. 'Right. Now what we need to do next is turn them all over.' They did so, revealing the single diamond that inlaid the reverse of each coin. 'There we go. That's all the patterns hidden.'

Montgomery nodded, then frowned. 'Is that the game, granddad?' he asked.

'Do you think I'd waste our special time together on a game of turning coins over?' He shook his head as the idea. 'Afternoon, Mrs Farley,' he added, as one of the ladies from the village hurried past, an "I'm very busy" look on her face.

'Mr Stroud,' she said, giving him a curt nod, while not slowing her pace. Montgomery watched until she turned left into the Village Store, leaving the road quiet and empty again, lazing in the June sunshine.

'Where was I?' said Dalton, looking confused.

'You said we weren't just going to turn the coins over.'

'Ah yes. Quite right. What we do, is take turns turning over the coins.' Montgomery made an unimpressed sound. 'Wait for it!' Dalton turned over one of the coins nearest him. It had a pattern of a crescent with a small circle between it's claw-like points. 'We take turns turning over *two* coins only. And if they match,' he turned over another coin at the far side of the table. It bore the same crescent and circle pattern, 'you add them to your pile. Otherwise, you turn them back over.'

Montgomery stared in amazement at the two identical coins. 'How did you do that?'

Dalton beamed at him, the wrinkles around his eyes creasing with smiles. He tapped the side of his head. 'Memory, young General. It's all about memory.'

And now memories was all he had. Montgomery sighed, still sitting at his desk, the keycoins untouched in front of him. It had been almost nine months since his granddad's heart had failed and taken him away, and Montgomery's own heart still ached as much as the day his mother had told him. He sighed again, glancing at the open drawer by his elbow, where Dalton's notebook stared up at him.

At a sudden urge, he pulled it out, scattering bits of screwed up rubbish onto the floor, and opened it up on the first page. The scribbled mess stared back at him. And yet it seemed to him, today, to be slightly less of a mess than before, as though it might possibly be more than a bunch of random doodles. It looked, at least a bit, like the backwards scrawl of that Leonardo Da Vinci picture in his art book.

Could it really be something that simple?

He picked up the book and, getting to his feet, turned it outwards so it faced the long mirror behind his door. Unconsciously holding his breath, he squinted at the reflected pages, expecting to see words he could actually read. Words written by his granddad especially for him.

But it made little difference. If anything, the writing - if it even *was* writing - looked even more like a load of haphazard markings than before. He sagged, letting out his breath in a long, low sigh.

'Typical,' he said, stuffing the notebook back into the drawer. 'I guess it was nothing after all.'

10. "I'm Going To Be A Squire"

'I guess it was nothing after all,' said Marlah, shaking her head at the small, red dot staring, unblinking, from the cobbles. She'd offered to help Montgomery with his Moving, since there was no sign of Vala at her cottage, but it wasn't going well. He almost wished he hadn't bothered coming down here. If Pepper had had her way, he wouldn't have. She wanted him to stay at home and have "family time". Thankfully, Victor had nodded vacantly when Montgomery asked if he could go out and play, so here he was, crouching on the shore of Lake Altis, having to put up Marlah's sarcasm about his inability to Move a button. 'It's only a button!' she said. 'It's not like you're trying to magic up a forcefield or something. It's only tiny. This is *supposed* to be easy.'

'Well it isn't!' he said, cross more with himself than her comments. 'It's alright for you. You learned to do this stuff when you were little. I had times tables instead.'

'What's a times table? Is it like the Chronolith?'

Montgomery glanced up at the Chronolith on the Town Hall tower. It was just before the twelfth hour of the day - five pm in normal, o'clock hours. He shook his head. 'Not really. Right,' his eyes dropped back to the ground. 'I'm going to give it another go.'

'Remember,' said Marlah, as she also bent forward to watch, 'you have to *want* it to Move.'

'Of course I want it to Move! That's why I'm here.'

He gritted his teeth, and glared at the button. It glared back, unmoving. He narrowed his eyes, commanding the button to Move with his mind. As in his previous lessons, nothing happened. 'Come on,' he growled. 'Move. Moooooove!'

For a sliver of an instant, he thought he noticed a slight shift in the button's position, a mere shadow of movement. He blinked, wondering if he had imagined it. 'Did it...' He gave Marlah a pleading look. 'Did it Move?'

'Move?' said a delighted voice. 'Are you doing some magic?' Marlah groaned, more loudly than was necessary, and Montgomery turned to see Alcott pulling his boat up onto the shore, his netful of fish dangling over the side. Alcott leaned forward and squinted at the ground. 'What is that? What are you Moving?'

'*Nothing*, so far,' said Marlah. 'But he's *supposed* to be Moving this button.' She pointed at the small dot. Alcott heaved his boat up onto the dark sand and stepped in for a closer look.

'A button? Is that it? But it's only tiny.'

'It might be tiny,' said Montgomery, giving him an irritated frown, 'but it's actually proving quite hard to Move. Maybe *you'd* care to give it a try?' Alcott tapped a finger on the bee emblem that was stitched to the front of his tunic: the mark of the Bardles. Montgomery sighed, feeling bad. 'Sorry,' he said.

'Have you thought of trying something a bit smaller?' suggested Alcott. 'Like, I dunno, maybe some sand? That'd be easy to Move, I reckon.'

'What are you lot up to?' The three children turned to see Jarfin hurrying across the square towards them, his dark-blue jerkin gleaming as though he'd spent all day polishing it - which Montgomery thought he probably had.

'Montgomery's trying to Move this titchy, little

button,' said Alcott, pointing at the item in question.

'What?' said Jarfin, non-plussed. 'He's Moving a *button*?'

'Er, no actually,' said Marlah. 'So far, he's Moved nothing.'

'Oh. Well, why not try Moving something smaller, if you're struggling? A grain of sand, perhaps.'

Montgomery's jaw tightened as he tried to control his irritation. 'Thank you so much for your helpful advice,' he said, in the voice that means the opposite, 'but why don't you all just-'

'It don't understand,' interrupted Alcott. 'I've seen you Move *much* bigger things than a button!'

'We all have,' said Marlah.

'Remember how you made that forcefield?' said Jarfin. 'The one that stopped that alboar stampede?'

'And now he can't even move a button.' That was Marlah's voice, but they were now talking over each other, as Montgomery got to his feet, his fists clenched, his irritation bubbling into real anger.

'I don't understand what the problem is...'

'It's only a button.'

'Remember what he did to Payton?'

'... you'd think he should be able to Move *anything*!'

'Maybe a grain of sand would-'

The three voices faltered as a whining, whirring sound came from the ground near their feet. They looked down to see the cobblestone beneath the button glowing faintly. It started out as a dull purple, but brightened to a deep red as the sound grew in pitch and volume.

As one, the children stepped backwards as the stone began to pulse, turning a bright, blood red, as the whirring grew so loud it hurt. Alcott clamped his hands over his ears, and still the noise increased as the cobble turned orange. Then yellow. Then white.

Montgomery's fists shook slightly at his sides.

Suddenly, as the whirring shifted up into a shrill whine, and the children had taken another cautious step back, there was a sound like a hammer punching through thick glass, and a shaft of light burst from the ground. The beam illuminated the tree that hung above them, as though someone had switched on a powerful searchlight.

'Wow!' said Jarfin, his voice an awe-filled whisper. He nudged Montgomery, whose anger had drained away, leaving him, like the others, dazed, staring at the brightly-lit branches above. 'You just *made* a diamond... out of a cobblestone!'

Behind them, the Town Hall doors slammed open and the four children span round, clustering together in front of the light beam, trying to block the glowing cobblestone from view. They looked guilty. To Montgomery's surprise, it was Vala who came hobbling out, her staff tapping on the stone steps. She had just reached the expanse of cobbles, when she stopped and cocked her head to one side, peering up at the cavern roof.

'She's noticed,' whispered Jarfin through the corner of his mouth.

Montgomery cleared his throat. 'Hi, Vala,' he called, trying to sound as though nothing was going on.

She turned slowly to fix him with one of her suspicious stares, jabbing towards the spotlit branches with her staff. 'What's going on?'

'I was just, you know, practising... some magic... er, stuff.' He faltered weakly under her gaze and stepped aside to reveal the source of the light. 'I might have accidentally...' he paused uncertain exactly what sort of magic he had done to transform the stone into a diamond, 'done that.'

Vala shook her head at him. 'I take it you weren't

deliberately trying to blind the paratillos?'

'Para-what-os?'

She jabbed upwards with her staff again. 'Them birds!'

'Oh. Er, no.' He scratched the side of his head, embarrassed. 'I was trying to Move a button. I went up to your cottage,' he added, trying to change the subject, 'but you weren't there.'

'Well, aren't you a fount of information!' She hobbled towards them. 'I weren't there, because some pesky brat keeps hassling me to *do my duty*, as if the brat in question knows anything about such matters. I had a meeting with young Farle.'

'My dad?' said Jarfin. Vala ignored him.

'You mean, you're going to help Lundarien?' asked Montgomery, realising what she meant. 'You're going to join the Novaristee?'

'No I ain't! Least not the Novaristee bit. But I *am* going to help. And you needn't look so pleased,' she added, glaring at his triumphant grin. 'Wyndham's just agreed to make you my squire.'

Montgomery blinked in surprise, stunned at this unexpected news. 'Wh-' he began, but then all the air was knocked out of him as Alcott slapped him on the back. It felt like he'd been hit with an oar.

'Did you hear that?' said Alcott. 'Congratulations!

Jarfin thumped him on the arm, far more gently. 'That's fantastic news!' Even Marlah looked impressed. Montgomery, struggling to breathe, said nothing.

'Well, we'll see just how fantastic you think it is next Forsday, when we head off to Salistra.'

'Salistra?' said Marlah, sounding every bit as surprised as Montgomery felt. 'You're going to Salistra? What for? What's going on?'

'Questions, questions,' said Vala, scowling at her.

'You'll find out soon enough, young girl. Now, have you lot finished with that light?' She nodded at the ground behind them, then, without waiting for an answer, struck her staff on the cobbles and the light winked out. Then she turned and hobbled away towards the marsh, leaving Montgomery, still slightly winded, staring after her.

He turned to the others. 'I'm…' he took a few more deep breaths and tried again. 'I'm going to be a squire!'

North of the city's main cavern was the Agra, Lundarien's three farming caverns, the first of which was a paradise of colourful plants, through which the Timbris meandered lazily, while birds called to each other from the hanging fruit trees and vine-covered walls. The second was something altogether different, filled with all the manure-related smells and animal noises you would expect to find in a pig farm. The alboars, however, were no ordinary little piggies. Their bristle-covered bodies were massive, the size of large bulls, and they snorted and grunted at the five children as they emerged from one of the connecting tunnels.

In celebration of Montgomery's squireship, they had come to watch a group of Movers and Changers rebuilding one of the farm-buildings. It had apparently been knocked down by an alboar that hadn't wanted to go to market.

The enormous creatures wallowed around in their high-fenced pens, nudging and sniffing the mud as though convinced there was food hiding in there somewhere. After his run-in with a stampeding herd of them on his way back from a hunt three weeks before, Montgomery kept his distance from the alboar pens, just in case they felt like trying it again.

'They make it look so easy,' he said, watching one of the workers Move five large stones into the air at once and slot them neatly into the barn wall as a Changer turned the old, hardened mortar back to the soft stuff Montgomery had seen his dad use to build the barbecue at their old home.

Marlah made a tutting sound. 'That's because *they* practice, rather than hoping they just happen to fluke it whenever their magic is required.'

'Still finding it difficult?' asked Clovis, who had joined them on their way here. 'I remember when I first started Hunting. I had to practice for hours every day, starting with slow movements and working my way up, so that I wouldn't injure myself. As for moving without making a noise? That was the worst.'

'But you did it, though,' said Montgomery, still transfixed by the repair work - it was like watching the barn being demolished, but in reverse slow motion. 'You mastered all that Hunting stuff.'

Clovis laughed. 'I wouldn't say "mastered". I'm still trying to develop my Hunter sight and hearing. But it takes-'

'Practice! Yeah, so I hear.' He turned to look at her, the tall Huntress with her long blonde hair and her dark green bodice with its cat emblem. She even *looked* magical. 'I just wish I was making some kind of progress instead of scowling at buttons and blowing things up.'

'What did you blow up?' said Alcott, who was standing behind them, patting an alboar as if it was nothing more dangerous than a small puppy.

'Doesn't matter,' said Montgomery and gestured towards the Movers and Changers. 'I just wish I could perform this sort of magic.'

'Look out!' shouted Marlah. Montgomery turned to see one of the large, stone tiles slip off the roof and spin down, heading straight for Alcott. Without even realising what he was doing, without even thinking, his hand shot out towards it and the tile jammed to a halt, inches from Alcott's surprised-looking face. 'That's it,' said Marlah, talking gently as though she'd just found a small child playing with a machete. 'Careful. Just hold it there.' The tile remained in front of Alcott's face, his eyes crossing as he tried to focus on it. 'Now, gently Move it towards you. That's right.' Montgomery, uncertain how he was doing it, watched as the tile hovered through the air and stopped just in front of his face. 'Good,' said Marlah. 'Now, see if you can make it float down to the floor.'

The tile moved so fast Montgomery could hardly make it out - it went from hovering in front of him to smashing across the ground at his feet as though rocket-propelled.

He stared at the shattered mess. 'Yes!' he said. 'I did it!' He turned to the others. 'Did you see? I actually just use Moving magic. Properly.' He glanced back down at the scattered shards that had once been the stone tile. 'Well, sort of anyway.'

Marlah placed a hand on his shoulder. 'Just remind me never to ask you to pass me anything by magic,' she said.

Alcott, who hadn't moved since the tile was hurtling towards his face, turned to Montgomery. 'You saved my life,' he said.

Montgomery grinned. 'Consider it payback for rescuing me from the lake yesterday.'

'Don't be an idiot,' said Marlah. 'I wouldn't have actually let it hit you, Alcott. Well, probably not. Maybe.'

'Hold on,' said Jarfin. 'Was that you? Did you make that tile fall down on purpose?'

Marlah produced one of her more infuriating smiles, the one that suggests she's been very clever. 'Of course I did.'

'Hey!' said Alcott. 'You nearly killed me!'

'If you lot are quite finished,' said a voice and they span round to see a woman dressed in a bodice that was divided into quarters, two of orange and two of yellow. Montgomery hadn't seen her before, but there was something familiar about her light purple eyes and the streak of white in her long brown hair. 'I'll have that back now, please.' On the ground the bits of tiles scraped across the ground, like a swarm of stone flies honing in on something unpleasant. And then there was the tile, complete and undamaged, lying on the ground as though it had never shattered. 'Thanks,' said the woman, as the tile span up into her hand, and she Frisbeed it up towards the roof, where it slipped neatly back into position.

'That,' said Montgomery, 'was amazing!'

The lady smiled at him, then headed back to the barn, ruffling his hair on the way.

'That's Emony Ellendrie,' said Jarfin in a whisper.

'Don't tell me. She's the sister of Seraphina, the head of the Changers, right?'

'Lucky guess!' said Marlah. 'Emony's a Multifex, though - a Mover as well as a Changer.'

Montgomery pushed his fringe out of his face, where Emony had left it. 'A Multifex? So she can do those Conjuring things like whatever-his-name-was?'

'You mean Kolter?' said Clovis, smiling and staring off into the distance.

'Hey!' said Montgomery, struck by a sudden thought. 'How come he didn't just teleport everyone out of Dursehaven? Wouldn't that have been easier than wandering around all that time?'

Jarfin shook his head. 'It's line of sight only. You can't open a teleport to somewhere you can't see.'

'Unlike Summoning,' said Marlah, 'which is what Emony can do.' She nodded to where the purple-eyed woman had rejoined the others in front of the barn.

'Summoning is like Moving really, only you don't have to be able to see the object - you can just call it from wherever you are.'

'Enough about her,' interrupted Jarfin. 'I want to see *Montgomery* Move something again. Go on!'

Montgomery looked around for something suitable to practice on and found Marlah standing with her hand out, her fist clenched shut. She opened it slowly to reveal a small, red button.

'Will this do?' she asked.

It was with a definite spring in his step that Montgomery headed back to the lift a short while later. He had managed, at last, to perform Moving magic with at least a little control. Admittedly, he had sent the button whirring off into the alboar pens, but he then stacked three of Alcott's coins almost on top of each other, and pulled off Jarfin's boots. He hadn't actually meant to pull them off, he was trying to untie his laces, but at least something happened.

That night, despite the fact he was in trouble with Pepper for going out, he went to bed smiling, so pleased with himself that it took forever to fall asleep.

11. "Teach Him A Lesson!"

The creature is so close he can almost reach out and touch it. Even the cavern itself seems dwarfed by the monster as it towers over him, its head shrouded in the dark clouds above, its armour-plated back even more like a mountain than the walls themselves, its tail trailing away across the floor into the distance, ending in a cluster of spikes like some medieval weapon. Despite the brightness, it is somehow more terrifying in the light than it would be in the dark. To see this monster is to fear it.

He stumbles back in alarm as a sounds like a series of lightning strikes explode above him, so loud, the cavern itself could be collapsing. And, as he stares up in terror, straining his eyes to see through the haze of dust that billows towards him, it looks as though it is. Nearby, someone shouts, but he can't tear his gaze away. He can't move. He can only stand and stare as the avalanche of rocks begins to fall, tumbling towards him in a shower of crushing death that is only seconds... moments... a mere instant away.

'Are you paying attention, Mr Vane?'

Montgomery's elbow slipped off the edge of his desk and he jerked awake.

'Wassasay?' he mumbled, blinking in an effort to get the weariness out of his eyes. He looked around to see faces staring at him from every side. Somewhere behind him a girl giggled. He was in Physics class, and their teacher, Mr Spears, did not look at all impressed. 'Er, yes, sir?' he said in a half-yawn.

The teacher perched on the edge of his desk, his arms folded. 'Is the Electromagnetic Spectrum not *fascinating* enough for you, Mr Vane? Not gripping your attention?'

'Electromagnetic…?' Montgomery tried to make sense of the word, but it meant nothing to him.

'Or perhaps you are so well acquainted with it,' continued Mr Spears, 'that you do not feel the need to listen, or indeed even to stay awake, during my class. Would that be correct?'

'No, sir. Sorry, sir.'

'If you know *so* much about the Electromagnetic Spectrum, perhaps you'd like to come up and teach the class instead of me?'

Montgomery was wide away now. 'No, I really don't, sir. I don't know anything about the … the spectrum thing. Honest.'

'Well, in that case, I suggest you spend a little more time listening and a little less time mumbling away in your sleep!' With a shake of his head, Mr Spears stood up and returned to the whiteboard, leaving Montgomery to sag with a mixture of relief and embarrassment.

He turned to the girl sitting at the desk next to him. 'I wasn't mumbling, was I?' he asked, but the girl turned away without responding. Montgomery was relieved when, fifteen minutes later, the bell went and everyone piled out to lunch.

By the time break was over, however, it seemed news of his brief doze had spread throughout the school, and the kids who passed him in the corridors either smirked at him or called him rubbish names like 'School Zombie' and 'Snoozer Loser'. Montgomery ignored them all.

Well, *nearly* all of them.

'Alright, Sleepy-head,' said Jeff, yawning dramatically at him as he made his way along the Languages corridor where Montgomery was waiting for class. His large, nose-picking friend was with him, also yawning, while stretching hugely.

'Did you think that up all by yourself, Michael? asked Montgomery, trying out his withering look on him.

Jeff frowned. 'Is you feeling sick? Only you looks kinda ill, bruv.' Montgomery gave up. 'Maybe you should have a lie down.' He jabbed a thumb at the classroom door. 'I believe the desks in French class is proper cosy, yeah?'

'Nice one!' said the nose-picking boy, whose name Montgomery still didn't know.

Jeff grinned. 'Thank you, Steve.'

'Yes, well done,' said Montgomery, in his most sarcastic voice. 'Did you make that up all on your own? You'll be needing a lie down yourself.'

The boy behind him let out a snort of laughter and Montgomery peered round to see Julian Poore, the shortest boy in his class, grinning. He was wearing clothes that were *almost* the standard St Kevin's uniform, but not quite. His trousers were a slightly-too-light shade of grey, with a hole in one knee, and his navy blue jumper had clearly been knitted for him by someone who expected him to "grow into it". Julian's smile vanished as Jeff stepped threateningly towards him.

'Something funny, *Poore Kid*?' he growled, pinning the boy against the wall with one hand.

Montgomery shoved Jeff in the shoulder, turning him away from Julian. 'Leave him alone,' he said. 'Why don't you just take your pet gorilla,' he jabbed a thumb towards Steve, 'and get lost.'

Jeff pushed him back while, in the background, Steve looked as though he was trying to work out a sum in his head or maybe spell his own name. Montgomery went to push Jeff again, but the boy knocked his hand away and gripped hold of the front his jumper .

'Hey,' said Steve, realisation lighting up his face. 'Was you talking about me?'

Montgomery gripped Jeff's jumper in return and, in unison, the boys raised their non-jumper-holding fists, poised to attack.

'I say, what on *Earth's* going on here?'

Jeff quickly let go of Montgomery's jumper and they stepped apart, faces angry, knuckles white. Montgomery turned to see Mr Pemberton-Drake striding along the corridor towards them. 'What is the meaning of all this hullaballoo?' he said, towering over the boys, his eyes flicking from one to the other.

'He called me a gorilla,' said Steve, pointing at Montgomery.

'Don't be preposterous,' said the headmaster. 'Gorillas are huge, great things, all hairy and whatnot.' He peered at Steve over his glasses, making the boy's face light up with embarrassment. 'You're far too weedy to be a gorilla. A lad like you wouldn't last a day out in the wilds of the Congo.' He turned to Jeff. 'Well, boy?'

'Sir?'

'I asked what's going on here? Why are you and...' He narrowed his eyes at Montgomery, searching his face for something he recognised. 'You're the lad who wanted to be a vet, aren't you? Montague?'

'Montgomery, sir.'

'Yes, that's it. Like the General. Well done! So then, Michael, what's all this grabbing and pushing nonsense all about?'

'Nothing, sir,' mumbled Jeff.

'Nothing was it? Well, I expected better from the son of a school governor than to find you going around fighting over *nothing*. What would your dear mother say? Perhaps a spell in detention after school on Wednesday would give you some time to think about it, yes?' He turned to Montgomery, leaving Jeff to glare at them both. 'The same goes for you, young Montgomery. I'll see you in my office on Wednesday after school. And in future,' he added, holding up a finger to forestall any arguments, 'I suggest you leave the fighting until there something worth fighting about!' And with that, and a swift waggle of the upheld finger at them both, he stalked away, muttering to himself about gorillas.

'Come on, Steve,' said Jeff, still glowering at Montgomery. 'Let's leave Twinkles to rest in peace.'

As on every other day, Montgomery walked home from school alone, his bag slung over one shoulder, his head down, eyes on the few metres of path ahead. The quickest route back to his apartment building took him across the edge of Battersea park, an oasis of grass, trees and even a boating lake amid the jungle of buildings and rivers of tarmac that made up most of London. It was a place where joggers jogged, earphones jammed into their ears, where mums pushed pushchairs and where students did anything that didn't involve actual studying.

He was halfway across the park when he noticed a boy step onto the path ahead. Glancing up at him, Montgomery recognised the boy as a member of Jeff's gang, who had been hanging out in the school alleyway the other day. As he looked, another boy turned through a nearby gate to join him and, to Montgomery's right, a third stepped out from behind a large sycamore tree from which seed helicopters spun down in the breeze.

The boys just stood there, blocking the footpath and did not look like they were here to play football. Montgomery stopped and looked over his shoulder to see three more boys approaching along the path behind him. The boy at the front was Jeff.

He marched towards Montgomery, an accusing finger

leading the way. 'You just couldn't be nice, could you?' he demanded. 'Well, now it's *my* turn not to be nice. Remember I told you your time would come? Well, guess what.' He stopped a couple of feet away and gestured to himself with both hands. 'Here it is!'

Suddenly feeling very vulnerable, Montgomery stepped backwards, accidentally treading on the foot of one of the boys who had come up behind him. It was Steve. And he was picking his nose. With his free hand, he shoved Montgomery in the back.

'Go on, Jeff,' he said. 'Teach him a lesson!'

Montgomery looked around for an escape route, but he was surrounded. Apart from jumping into the lake, which did not look at all inviting, there was no way out. He turned to face Jeff again.

'Look...' he began.

'No, *you* look!' said Jeff, pushing him backwards into Steve, who gripped hold of his arms. Montgomery was surprised at how strong the boy was; maybe "gorilla" hadn't been such a bad description after all. 'I don't like you, country boy. Nobody likes you. In fact you *are* a nobody. And it's about time you learned your place.' Jeff raised a fist and Montgomery tried to pull free of Steve's grip, but his arms were firmly pinned. He closed his eyes, waiting for the impact... but it never came.

'You can't be all that tough,' said a voice, 'if it takes six of you to beat up one kid.'

Cautiously, Montgomery opened his eyes so he could peer at the speaker. There, standing behind Jeff's shoulder, Jeff's punching arm clamped in one of his hands, was a tall teenager about four years older than them. He was wearing a black leather jacket, a tatty pair of jeans and an expression that suggested he was enjoying himself. But it wasn't how he looked or what he was doing that caused Montgomery to stare in amazement. It was the fact that

Montgomery knew who he was. The guy winked at him. 'I, however,' he continued, '*am* tough. So I suggest you walk away… No, make that *run away*, before I give you a hiding you won't soon forget.'

Finding his wrist suddenly free, Jeff scurried out of reach. 'You can't hit us,' he said. 'My dad'll get the police on you!'

'They'll have to find me first. And it won't make any difference to how long you have to spend in hospital.' He stepped forwards suddenly and the boys all flinched backwards.

'Let's go, boys,' said Jeff, his voice higher than usual. 'It's rubbish here, anyway.' He started to back away. The others followed and, when he was safely out of range, Jeff jabbed an angry finger at Montgomery. 'You'll get yours, Twinkles. Your *boyfriend* won't always be around to protect you!' And then they were gone, slipping through the hedge and out of the park.

'Did you hear that?' said the leather jacket wearer. 'He called me your boyfriend. Is he always that hilarious?'

Montgomery, who hadn't moved since opening his eyes, shook his head, trying to clear it and make sense of what he was seeing. 'Merek?' he said. 'What are *you* doing here?'

12. "She Mind-Controlled Me"

'Saving your backside, of course,' said Merek. He held up his hands, defensively. 'No, no. Please, don't thank me. It's all part of the service.'

'I meant, what are you doing in London?' said Montgomery, still stunned by the presence on the Surface of someone he'd only ever seen in the Underworld. How could Merek be *here*? The last time he had seen him, Merek had been guarding the entrance to Lundarien. On Payton's orders!

'Well, I'm stuck here, aren't I?' said Merek, waving a hand at the Surface in general. 'After the battle and you doing what you did to Payton - nice work, by the way - her magical hold on me broke. So I legged it.'

'But how did you get here?' asked Montgomery. 'How did you get up to the Surface?'

'Oh, that was easy.' Merek stuck a hand in his pocket, pulled something out and held it between a grubby forefinger and thumb. 'I used one of your keycoins. Payton had entrusted it to my keeping, see, so I nipped off back to that super-bright tunnel of yours and came up in the lift. I've been hiding out in the parks and stuff ever since - just another vagrant, living in the shadows.'

Montgomery frowned, trying to make sense what he was hearing. 'What was that about Payton's magical hold on you?'

'Well, it's obvious, isn't it?' Merek flashed

Montgomery his best smile. 'She mind-controlled me, didn't she? Used her dirty Lectimenting skills to force me to do her bidding. Why else would I have done the things I did?'

Montgomery didn't know what to think. There was something about Merek that he liked, his cocky over-confidence in himself, his easy-going nature, but the guy had tried to kidnap Marlah. Plus he'd been one of Payton's most important henchmen, entrusted with leading the Novaristee into Payton's lair in the heart of the Labyrinth. Could he really have been under her spell all that time?

'Are you saying you were only working for her because she bewitched you? Surely she couldn't have had control over you *all* the time. I mean, what about when she was asleep or... on the toilet? She couldn't have controlled you from there!'

'Course she could! If you're a powerful enough Lectimentor, you can "bewitch" someone - nice word that, by the way, good choice - and they'll pretty much stay bewitched until you or someone else breaks it.'

'Which is what *I* did?' said Montgomery uncertainly.

'Which is what *you* did.' Merek slapped him on the shoulder. 'Exactly! And thanks for that by the way. I didn't see it myself, of course, what with being on the other side of the cavern, but I heard about it. Impressive stuff! Much more impressive than me scaring off that bunch of school kids.' He paused, his face suddenly serious, and when he spoke, there was the slightest quiver of emotion in his voice. 'Look,' he said. 'I really am sorry for all the stuff I did, for trying to kidnap your friend and all that. Even though I was under Payton's spell, it was still wrong of me.' He smiled suddenly. 'At least I got you through that awful Labyrinth without getting you all killed, though.'

'I guess so,' he said, half-smiling as he remembered Merek's eagerness to demonstrate his Moving skills to him. 'Show off!' Though he wasn't entirely won over, Montgomery found it hard to be angry with Merek. 'Did you hear about Atlantis?' he asked, changing the subject.

'Atlantis?' Merek frowned. 'What about it?'

'Apparently they're invading Brytellian.'

The frown deepened. 'Invading? Are you sure?'

'By the sound of it, they've already started. They sacked some place call Dursehaven. Have you heard of it?'

'Yeah,' said Merek, 'but I've never been there. I haven't really been anywhere in the Underworld except Lundarien and the Labyrinth, but my parents taught me all about Brytellian and its history.'

'Your parents?' Montgomery was intrigued. 'Are they still around?'

A shadow passed across Merek's face, but he smiled quickly. 'That's not important. Look, I've got to shoot off. Got a bit of sofa surfing to arrange. But why don't you and me meet up again later in the week? Let me prove to you I'm not the evil guy you think I am.'

Montgomery hesitated, recalling how he'd found Marlah bleeding and unconscious in the mouth of the Labyrinth the day Merek tried to kidnap her. But that wasn't entirely Merek's doing. Marlah had caused that injury herself, using her Moving to knock Merek out with a rock and accidentally hitting herself in the process. And it was true about Payton being a Lectimentor, so maybe she *had* used her magic to control him. Maybe Merek wouldn't have done any of those things without her bewitching him.

'Okay,' he said, with a nod. 'My school's just up the road. St Kevin's Comprehensive. It's a big, ugly building.'

'All brown squares and concrete?'

'That's the one. I'm usually out by half three.'

'Ace,' said Merek, holding out a hand to Montgomery which, after a brief pause, he shook. Then, zipping up his leather jacket, Merek turned and strode back along the path. Montgomery watched him go, and was about to head home, when he remembered Merek still had his spare keycoin.

'Hey!' he called, but he was already out of earshot

Montgomery woke late on Saturday morning and was surprised to find his dad had gone to work. He hadn't worked at the weekends since one of the huge copper vats at his old brewery had been pierced when a colleague drove a fork-lift truck into it, losing a whole week's worth of beer. It was good news for Montgomery, though, as this meant he was free to spend as long as he liked in Lundarien, practising magic and hanging out with his friends.

Or so he thought.

Pepper, however, had other ideas.

'You've been rushing off enough this week,' she explained, busying herself in the kitchen and ignoring the pleading look his was giving her. 'I need you home this weekend.'

'But why? There's only you and Gabriella here.'

'Your dad will be home after lunch and I want us all here together. As a family.'

'What do you mean?' he asked, confused. 'We're *already* a family!'

'And it would be good if you remembered that!' Pepper gave him a meaningful look, which was entirely lost on him. 'Now, why don't we make sure the apartment's looking nice for when dad gets home?'

Montgomery turned and surveyed the room. It was a single space, with the lounge area by the window, marked out by the sofa, armchair and television, the kitchen area off to one side, where the carpet gave way to lino, and the dining area, which took up the rest of the space, complete with table and chairs, the sideboard and a bookcase, in the corner. As far as Montgomery could see, the place looked spotless, everything in its place, clean and tidy. He knew from experience, though, that his mum saw it completely differently. Seemingly from nowhere, she would discover dust and dirt, things that needed putting away or throwing away, and areas of previously undetectable mess.

He opened his mouth to argue, or at least *attempt* to argue, his way out of it, when an idea came to him.

'Okay, mum,' he said, making his voice sound, if not eager, at least not moody. 'What should I do first?'

The reaction was much as he had expected. Pepper's face took on a mixture of surprise and pleasure, and should looked around at the living room. 'You can make a start on the dresser. It's filthy!"

Montgomery's plan was to show willing, helping to tidy up and staying around until dad got home, in the hope that, as a reward, he would be allowed out that afternoon. After all, it had worked before, when he'd wanted to go swimming in the river with his friends in Steepleford when he was grounded. It *had* to work now!

But it didn't.

And when Victor got home, he barely glanced at the room that Montgomery and Pepper had spent the morning getting ready. He just slumped on the sofa and flicked through the channels, and Montgomery noticed his dad wasn't even looking at the screen; he was just staring out of the window, frowning. A shadow seemed to settle over the apartment, and Montgomery wanted more than ever to get out, but Pepper was insistent.

Sunday was much the same, and on Monday, Montgomery had so much homework to do, much of which he'd put off over the weekend, that it was after nine by the time he had finished.

Tuesday was no better, since his parents went out for dinner at the house of someone from Victor's work at the brewery, leaving Montgomery to babysit Gabriella. She spent the first half of the evening asking him for help with her Maths sheet, containing twelve addition sums below the title "Adding Up To Ten". Montgomery pointed this title out to her, with the helpful prompt, 'So, if it's about adding up to ten, the answer must be...?' Gabriella still managed to get all the sums wrong.

The rest of the evening was spent watching a children's television channel, while he sat on the sofa, trying to learn French vocabulary. All he actually managed to do was get frustrated about inanimate objects having to be male or female. And about not going to Lundarien to practise more Moving with his friends.

His *friends*!

He sighed as he considered his friendless life at St Kevin's. If anything, school was even worse since his run in with Jeff in the park. Not only would no one in his year speak to him, but they wouldn't even stand near him and would even walk away if he approached them. At the same time, Jeff's gang members sought out opportunities to pick on him, barging into him in the corridors and calling him various infantile names. Montgomery began to wish he had at least one friend at the school. That would make going there slightly more bearable and less lonely.

And so it was with a surprising stab of excitement that he caught sight of Merek hanging around on the pavement as he wandered out of the school gate after detention on Wednesday afternoon.

Merek spotted him and ambled over. 'Three-thirty, you told me. I've been waiting here for hours.'

'It's only quarter past four,' said Montgomery. 'The headmaster kept me in after school. Did you bring my keycoin?' Merek patted his pockets and shrugged. 'I guess that's a "No" then.'

'Sorry,' said Merek. 'I stashed all my stuff at a mate's house. Next time, though, I promise. Fancy grabbing a coke up at Kelly's café?' He waved a hand in the vague direction of the High Street.

Montgomery looked at his watch. 'I would,' he said, 'but I've got to get back. Don't want to get into trouble or I won't be allowed to go to Lundarien this evening.'

'I'll walk with you,' said Merek, and together they headed up the road. 'It must be great being able to come and go between here and the Underworld. Don't your parents mind you nipping off there all the time?'

'My dad doesn't actually know. He's not from the Underworld.'

'So, where does he think you go off to all the time? Playing Bingo with the grannies?'

'Just out with friends,' said Montgomery, hoping Merek wouldn't ask if he actually *had* any friends in London, 'which is kind of true. But he's too caught up with work stuff anyway, so he doesn't really notice.'

Merek laughed. 'So you're going down to Lundarien tonight? Do you reckon you'll find out anything else about Atlantis and that?'

'Dunno.' Montgomery shrugged, causing his school bag to slip off his shoulder, and hook awkwardly around his elbow. He yanked it back up again. 'I hope so. I'm supposed to be going to some Underworld city called Salistra, wherever that is.'

'Salistra?' Merek halted by the entrance to the park and gave Montgomery a disbelieving look. 'City of the Seven Caverns? You're going all the way to Salistra?'

'What do you mean?' asked Montgomery, worried. 'Where is it?'

Merek blew out his cheeks as if trying to work out

how to break bad news. 'Have you heard of a place called Salisbury?' Montgomery nodded, recalling the signposts to Salisbury when he'd visited Stonehenge a few years ago. 'Salistra's around there someplace. It must be seventy or eighty miles from Lundarien.'

Montgomery was stunned. For some reason, he'd imagined it would be nearby, maybe in another part of London. He'd never even considered it might be *that* far away. How were they going to get all the way there? Would they ride on alboars or something? After all, they didn't have any cars or underground trains. Or did they?

'Do they have underground trains?' he asked, pointing at the path as they wandered past the boating lake.

'Well, yeah,' said Merek. 'Of course. There are loads of them.'

Montgomery was astonished. 'Really?'

'Sure. London's famous for its underground trains. How do you not know that?'

'I meant trains in the Underworld, of course!'

'Oh right,' said Merek, grinning at him. 'No. No actual trains. You'll probably have to go there on the Transak. It's not as fast as a train, but it's a heck of a lot quicker than walking.'

'Transak?'

Merek laughed. 'You haven't heard of that either?'

'What do you mean, "either"?' said Montgomery, trying to sound cross, but actually quite enjoying having someone to talk to who didn't just call him names or ignore him. 'I *have* heard of the London Underground.'

'Sure you have.'

They passed beneath the sycamore, though there were no seed helicopters whirring down today. Nor was there any sign of Jeff and his gang. In the far corner, a man in a suit sat on a wooden bench, feeding something to a cluster of pigeons, which scratched around in front of him, bobbing their heads about as if to some music only they could hear. The man looked up as they walked past and Montgomery noticed the thin briefcase on the bench next to him.

'I wish I could do that,' said Merek, drawing Montgomery's attention away from the man.

'What?'

'Just nip down to the Underworld in that lift whenever you want.'

'I can't go *whenever* I want,' said Montgomery, feeling a bit sorry for Merek, who was undoubtedly banned from Lundarien after his involvement in Payton's attempt to seize control of the city.

'Yeah, but you can at least go there.' He sighed, and the two of them walked together in silence for a while, along the quiet back roads towards Montgomery's apartment. 'Oh, by the way,' said Merek, his voice back to its usual good-humoured self, 'I remembered something Payton had said about Atlantis when we were busy setting up all those traps and stuff in the Labyrinth.'

'Yes?' said Montgomery, eager to hear what she'd said.

'It's kind of odd, really. Doesn't make much sense. But she said the darkness in Atlantis will fill the whole world. Creepy, eh?'

Montgomery paused at the pavement, waiting for a couple of cars to pass before stepping into the road. 'The darkness? What does that mean?'

'No idea,' said Merek, holding up his empty hands to emphasise his no-idea-ness. 'But she was pretty insistent about it. Is this your place?' he asked, coming to a stop as they turned the corner into Montgomery's road.

'Yeah,' he said and pointed along the street. 'It's that big, ugly block of flats there.'

'Block of flats?' said Merek. 'Don't they call them apartment buildings, so people think they're not quite so grim?'

'Something like that. Want to have a look?'

Merek shook his head. 'Best not. We don't want your mum to see me!'

13. "Only For One Night"

The apartment was empty when Montgomery got in so he dumped his school bag by the front door, flopped onto the sofa and flicked on the TV.

'About time too!' said Vala. Her face burst onto the screen, causing Montgomery to shrink backwards into the sofa cushions. 'I thought that school thing, or whatever it is, finished ages ago.'

'Er...' said Montgomery, trying to gather his thoughts. 'Yeah. But the headmaster put me in detention. I had to stay behind after school.'

'Ha! No surprises there. He sounds like a sensible man, got his head screwed on right. Go get your mother in here. I need to talk to her about this wretched visit to Salistra.'

'She's not here,' said Montgomery, relieved this was the case. He still hadn't spoken with Pepper about him spending the whole of Thursday in the Underworld, mainly because he was sure she wouldn't let him. 'I can pass on a message though.'

'Huh!' Vala snorted. 'We'll see about that! Let's see if you can manage to tell her you'll not be back until late Feivday. That's Fri-'

'Friday,' Montgomery interrupted. 'Yes, I know.'

'It's about *all* you know, you cheeky swine. Just make sure you're here by the third hour tomorrow morning. I take it you know when that is! We'll be leaving then, with or without you.'

Montgomery nodded slowly, trying to take this all in. 'Wait,' he said. 'Do you mean we need to stay in Salistra overnight?'

'Wyndham doesn't seem to think so, but then he ain't no Manser. From what I've managed to discern,' she tapped the side of her head with a bony finger, 'we'll not be returning until Feivday. Don't ask me why.'

Montgomery couldn't help himself. 'But why?'

'No idea!' Vala's face flickered and vanished from the screen, and a news programme about a volcanic eruption appeared in its place. Montgomery changed the channel and, in an attempt to drown his growing unease at how he was going to tell his parents he wouldn't be home tomorrow night, he began his usual routine of flicking through the channels at high speed, watching just enough to note what was on, but moving on before the sound caught up. He eventually settled on a programme about people buying bits of old rubbish at a car boot sale and trying to get more money for them at an auction. One couple made almost twenty pounds.

Just after five o'clock, the front door flew open and Gabriella raced in, closely followed by Pepper and finally Victor, carrying a box so large that he could only just peer over it.

'This is boring!' said Gabriella. She snatched up the remote from the arm of the sofa and began the channel hopping all over again.

'Where have you lot been?' asked Montgomery, swivelling round to face his parents. 'And what's that?'

'This,' said Victor, placing the box carefully on the table, 'is a *surprise*.'

'A surprise?'

'It's a lizard,' said Gabriella, not turning away from her sprint through the channels. 'Me and mummy went to pick it up from daddy's work.'

Montgomery laughed at her. 'Don't be stupid. Of course it's not a lizard. It's not, is it?' He looked back at Victor to see him lifting something out of the now open box. It looked like a fish tank, but instead of being full of water and little swimming things, all it contained was a bit of sand, a couple of rocks and a log, on which sat. 'A lizard?' Montgomery pulled a face. 'But… why would you buy a lizard?'

'We didn't buy it,' said Pepper, heading off to the kitchen to get dinner ready. 'It was left behind by one of dad's workmates, who was sadly laid off by the brewery yesterday.'

'She's called Lizzy,' said Victor, bending down to peer in at the creature. 'I think it's short for Elizabeth. Come on, Lizzy. Come on.' He tapped on the glass. 'That's right, Lizzy. There's a good girl.'

Montgomery peered at the lizard. It was so bright a green, it looked like it had been painted, though its throat and back were covered with a line of dark spines. Its creepily long fingers were wrapped around the sides of the log, while its green and black striped tail lolled across the sandy bottom of its tank. It was completely motionless. Not even its eyes moved.

'Is it alive?' he asked.

'If you could put her somewhere other than on the table?' said Pepper, as she tried to lay out the knives and forks. Victor heaved up the tank, cleared a space for it on the dresser with his elbow and set it down. He then knelt down on the floor trying to get the plug into the socket that was handily hidden behind the bookcase. Montgomery shook his head at him, but was pleased his dad was a little more like himself today. 'So how was your day, Montgomery?' asked Pepper, working her way around the table.

He shrugged. 'Okay.'

'Learn anything exciting today?'

'Stuff,' he said, then, swallowing nervously, he decided to broach the subject of tomorrow night. 'Er, mum?' he said, getting up from the sofa and sidling across to the kitchen. 'Would it be okay if I stay over round a friend's house tomorrow?'

'Stay over?' said Pepper, rummaging in the fridge. Montgomery was reassured by the only-half-listening tone of her voice.

'Only for one night,' he said, as though it was a mere nothing.

There was silence for a moment, before Pepper's head popped out from behind the fridge door. She was giving him her full attention. 'Who is this friend?'

'Just one of the boys in my class.' He coughed, his throat suddenly feeling very dry.

'And what's this boy's name?'

'Er…' He realised, too late, that he should have thought of this already. He tried to concentrate on who was in his class, but his brain kept presenting him with an image of Jeff instead, and there was no way he was going to suggest *him*, even if he wasn't really going to stay at *anyone's* house. 'Julian Poore,' he croaked at last, the short boy's face popping into his head.

'You haven't mentioned him before,' said Victor, getting up from the floor and brushing a cobweb from his moustache.

'Haven't I?' Montgomery's voice, which had been breaking for the past few months, sounded about an octave higher than usual.

'So where does this Julian Poore live?' asked Pepper, still standing in the open fridge door.

Again, Montgomery realised he was not properly prepared for this conversation. 'I'm not sure,' he said. 'On the other side of St Kevin's, I think. His mum said it'd be okay,' he lied.

Pepper narrowed her eyes, and Montgomery had the uncomfortable feeling that she was reading his mind. He tried not to think about his plans to go to Salistra, just in case it showed on his face. The eyes continued to stare and the silence dragged on, while around him the world seemed to freeze. Even the sound of the kids' programme Gabriella had found, became muffled. The room seemed to bulge, the space between him and his mother stretching out. He felt sick, he needed to confess, to explain, to tell her why he had lied. He opened his mouth...

'There we go!' said Victor, as the light in the tank flickered on. Montgomery blinked and the room snapped back to normal, the television blaring back to life.

Pepper closed the fridge door. 'Fine,' she said, tearing a piece of paper from the pad that was stuck to a cupboard door. She rested it on the table and snatched up a pen from the worktop. 'But I want you to give my mobile number to this Julian boy's mother, okay?'

Montgomery started breathing again. 'Thanks, mum.'

She held out the piece of paper to him but, as he went to take it, she drew it back out of his reach. 'You needn't think you're nipping off out tonight, though,' she said.

'But I was-'

'Not tonight.' She was using the voice that was not going to be argued with, so Montgomery gave up. He didn't want to push it and end up not being able to go tomorrow. 'And you can give me a hand getting dinner ready.'

He sighed. 'Fine. What do you want me to do?'

'For starters, you could rustle us up some garlic bread,' said Victor, and looked round expectantly at his children. 'Do you get it? Garlic bread? For starters?'

Montgomery rolled his eyes. He'd preferred it when his dad was miserable.

14. "It's A Flying Boat!"

Montgomery dragged his feet across the tunnel floor, wishing he'd left his school bag, full of heavy text books, behind. Not at home, of course, as he'd had to go through the trouble of pretending to leave for school then hide behind the parked cars again, but he could at least have ditched it at the Lundarien Town Hall before they left.

The group heading to Salistra was fairly small. From the Novaristee, only Wyndham and Catrain had come. Stepping in for Bancroft was another Mover, Marlah's dad, Favian. Vala was there too, of course. Jarfin had tagged along in his new role as Wyndham's squire, but Montgomery was delighted and surprised to find the other adults were also bringing their squires.

'I didn't know you two were squires,' he said, hefting his bag up onto his shoulder again.

'You never asked,' said Marlah. 'I happen to have been my dad's squire for four months now, ever since my fourteenth birthday.'

'So have I,' said Clovis.

'Yeah, but I've been one longer than you.'

Clovis bristled. 'What, by three days?'

'So… you agree with me, then?'

'Well, I'm glad you're both here,' interrupted Montgomery. 'It's just a pity Alcott's not allowed to come with us.'

Marlah gave him a sideways look. 'You're joking,

aren't you? Alcott? Why would we want *him* with us?'

'Because he's our friend,' said Jarfin, who had lagged back from his dad to join the others.

'Possibly,' conceded Marlah, 'but he's just a Bardle. What actual use would he be?'

'He could give me a hand with this bag for starters.' Montgomery shifted it onto his other shoulder, but it made little difference.

'So…' Clovis glanced over her shoulder to where her mother and Vala were walking along together. 'How is going being Vala's squire?'

'Dunno' said Montgomery. 'I've not been around much since I became her squire. Hopefully it won't be too awful!'

'What do you mean, awful'

As one, the four children span round, startled to find Vala right behind them and, although her eyes were permanently set in a disapproving glare, the look she was giving them seemed even more displeased than usual.

'How did you do that?' said Clovis. 'Are you a Hunter as well as a… whatever else you are?'

Vala grinned her few teeth at them and Montgomery was disgusted to notice she had what looked like a bit of meat stuck between two of them. 'You, young girl, need to be careful how loudly you're thinking. The Lectimentors probably heard you all the way off in Salistra.'

'Which is a long way,' said Wyndham, who was striding along ahead of them. 'So, let's pick up the pace. It's another few brides before we reach the Great Tunnel.'

'Brides?' Montgomery whispered to Jarfin. 'What is he talking about?'

'A bride is seven hundred and forty-five oars,' said Jarfin, as though these measurements were obvious to everyone.

Montgomery hefted his bag higher up on his shoulder

and continued trudging. They were still in what he'd always called the Lift Tunnel, heading in the direction you would go if you walked out of the lift and just kept going, but apparently it was actually, not-quite-so-catchily named the Vena Caverna Delta, the main route from Lundarien to the Great Tunnel.

'What's so *great* about it, anyway?' asked Montgomery, after what felt like another hour of walking. He'd had quite enough of tunnels for one day, and he was finding it hard to talk while drawing in enough air to keep his body going at this pace. 'It's just a tunnel, isn't it?'

'There are tunnels,' said Jarfin, in a voice he clearly thought was mysterious, 'and then there are *tunnels*.' He wiggled his fingers to add to the mystery.

Marlah slapped them away. 'Ignore that idiot. It's called the Great Tunnel because of its size. It's massive.'

'I've heard it stretches from the Steppengrads all the way to Pacifactris, right through the Shifts,' said Clovis.

Montgomery looked at her blankly. 'Is that a long way?' he asked.

'Oh yes,' said Jarfin. 'Thousands and thousands of miles.'

'Feels like *this* tunnel's about that long too.'

Instead of telling him he was stupid, Marlah just laughed at him, but the effect was much the same. '*This* little wormhole?' she said, gesturing to the rock walls around them. 'It's nothing more than a crack in the rock compared to the Great Tunnel. As you'll find out.'

'If we ever get there that is,' said Montgomery.

'We're here,' came a shout from up ahead, and he dragged his gaze up from the floor to where Wyndham was standing in what appeared to be a dead end.

'*Where* are we?' he asked as the group gathered in front of the solid rock wall. 'We've run out of tunnel.'

'Haven't you learned nothing about the Underworld,

yet?' said Vala, hobbling up the to the wall, her staff scraping across the dusty floor. 'Magic, remember?' She placed the palm of one hand on the wall, her crooked fingers stretched almost straight.

There was a long silence

'Try "Open sesame",' Montgomery suggested.

'The day I need magic lessons from you, I'll let you know,' said Vala, hand still against the rock. 'In writing. It'll say, "Kill me now". Aha! I've got it.' She slid her hand up the wall, sweeping it first to the right, then to the left, before bringing her hand back and slapping it hard against the wall.

The rocky surface didn't exactly collapse or break apart, but nor did it just disappear. Instead, as Montgomery watched in fascination, it seemed to fold in on itself, like origami in stone, the rock tumbling away to reveal a tall and ornate archway, with a passageway that led through the wall to whatever lay beyond.

'Now that,' he said, 'is a pretty cool trick.'

Vala, not waiting for the others, hobbled off through the archway. 'It's not a trick,' she said, her voice echoing around them. 'A trick is where you pretend something's happened when it hasn't. This,' she struck the top of the passage with her staff, 'is called magic!'

As impressive as it was to see the archway appear in the solid rock wall, it was dwarfed by the sight that met them as they stepped out through the other end. It wasn't that the Great Tunnel was especially high or wide, though it was at least four times the diameter of the Lift Tunnel, but the way it stretched into the distance gave Montgomery a dizzying feeling of being somewhere immense, a limitless void reaching away in both directions, the ends disappearing in a distant haze. The triple spine of bright, white diamonds that ran along the roof bathed the tunnel like the midday sun, lighting up the dusty stone floor, the walls from which grew something that looked like the hedgerows back in his old village, the short, blossom-covered trees that grew from the roof, and the occasional stalls that sold everything from pottery and strange-looking tools to brightly-coloured plants and steaming cauldrons full of who-knew-what. There was a busyness to the place, with people hanging around the makeshift stalls, wandering along in groups and there were some who appeared to be gliding up and down the tunnel. He understood now why they call it the *Great* Tunnel.

'Wow!' he whispered.

A rumbling, scraping sound made him look back at the passageway they had come through, to see the archway on this side unfolding, the rocks billowing out towards each other like solid, grey smoke. Within moments Montgomery could no longer make out even the slightest crack to reveal where the break had been. They shouldn't have any problem in working out which piece of wall would lead them back to Lundarien though, as, carved into the face of the rock, was a circle, about three metres across. And in the circle was an image Montgomery knew well: the picture of a lion, surrounded by four stars.

'Lundarien,' he said, dumping his bag on the ground and running his fingers across the lion's perfectly etched muzzle and mane. 'This is the symbol of Lundarien, isn't it?'

'Of course it is!' said Vala. 'The Lion and the Four.'

'All the exits along the Great Tunnel are marked,' said Favian, pointing away to their left, 'and we're headed for the seven-fingered hand of Salistra.' Montgomery stood on tiptoes to look at the tunnel as it swept away into the distance.

'Is that far?' he asked,

'Oh, eighty miles or so,' said Wyndham, stepping out further out into the tunnel. 'But don't worry, we won't be walking. We're taking the Transak.'

Montgomery nodded as though this made perfect sense. But, although Merek had mentioned the word, he had no idea what it was. 'What's the Transak that exactly?'

'That!' said Wyndham, nodding to the right.

One of the groups of people Montgomery had seen, who appeared to be gliding along the tunnel, were much closer than before, and he could now see that they were indeed gliding, travelling along on some sort of floating thing.

'Are they floating?' he asked. 'I mean, actually floating? Like on a magical flying carpet?' He turned his look of wonder towards the others. They returned it with looks of something like pity.

'You are *such* a Sunner!' said Marlah.

The group settled themselves against the wall to wait for their ride and Montgomery took the opportunity to lighten his bag by eating the peanut butter sandwiches from his lunchbox. He was slightly put off by Vala squatting down next to him and producing a small pot, from which she picked bits of what looked like raw mince and stuffed them into her mouth.

'Is that raw mince?' he asked, shuffling away a few inches.

She smiled, giving him a view that didn't improve matters. 'Best there is!' she said. 'I ground it myself a few weeks ago.'

'A few *weeks*?' Montgomery shuffled further away, nudging up against Marlah, who jabbed him in the ribs with her elbow. Vala ignored him and carried on fingering lumps of mince into her mouth, chewing on it with a horrible, sticky noise, like a pig with its trotters stuck in mud.

It was with both relief and a thrill of excitement that

he joined the others, climbing to their feet, as a vehicle slewed across the tunnel and pulled up in front of them.

'Good day, Watchman,' called an old man from the front of the floating object. 'What brings you out to the Great Tunnel, then?'

'None of your business, Lockley, you nosey old git!' Wyndham called back. Montgomery was relieved to see he was smiling; the two men evidently knew each other well.

'Hah,' called Lockley. 'But I suppose you'll be wanting *my* business, eh? Where are you headed to, if I might be so bold as to enquire?' He produced a mock bow.

Wyndham laughed. 'Up to Salistra,' he said. 'Business with the Aristane… if you *must* know.'

'It's a boat!' said Montgomery, pointing at the object that was hovering in front of them. And it definitely was a boat, like a Viking longship. It had no oars or sails, but there was a carved goat's head sticking up from the front. 'It's a flying boat!'

'Course it is,' said Lockley, as it lowered to the ground in front of the group. 'The Trago is the best in the business.' He leant forwards to pat the goat's head affectionately. 'Belonged to my great-grandfather's great-grandfather. And then some. As long as there's been the Transak, the Lockleys have had the Trago. Of course, there are the "Johnny-come-lately"s who use any old bit of scrap and call themselves part of the Transak - even a red double-decker bus from up on the Surface, if you'd credit such a thing! - but I don't hold with that sort of nonsense.'

Wyndham rolled his eyes at Montgomery and gave him the look that says, *You had to ask!*

'Are you going to bore us to death all day,' said Vala, smacking the side of the boat with her staff, 'or can we get on your old wreck now?'

Lockley gave her what he clearly assumed was a winning smile, but looked more like he was sneering. 'Oh, I can do both, my lovely. Hurry up then, you lot. I'm waiting on you now. Permission to come aboard!'

One by one, they clambered onto the boat and sat down on the benches that were set up at intervals along the inside. Montgomery nodded to the only other passenger, who was sitting, hunched over, at the rear of the boat. The person nodded back, but the face was so concealed by the shadow of its hood, Montgomery couldn't tell if it was a man or a woman.

'Sitting comfortably?' asked Lockley, from his platform at the front. The old man didn't wait for a reply, but placed the palm of his hand on the carved goat's head, and the boat rose into the air and began to glide forwards. Jarfin, who was still inching his way towards the space on the other side of Montgomery, was knocked off balance and sent sprawling towards Clovis. Moving in a blur, Clovis slid along the bench, leaving Jarfin tumbling towards Marlah instead, and he had to grab hold of her to stop his fall.

'Sorry,' he said, as Marlah shoved him off, and he promptly stepped on her foot

Marlah shook her head. 'This is going to be a long journey!' she said.

15. "The Darkness Will Rise"

The boat cut smoothly through the air, its keel a foot or so from the tunnel floor, and settled into a brisk enough pace that Montgomery felt a little concerned about the lack of a seatbelt.

'So, is this a magical flying boat, then?' he whispered to Jarfin, so Marlah wouldn't hear.

'Where are you getting this from?' asked Marlah, whose hearing was clearly better than he'd realised.

Montgomery sighed. 'Well, it's a boat. It's flying. And I guess it's flying by magic. So doesn't that make it a magical flying boat?'

'I'm sorry to disappoint you,' said Marlah, as though talking to a child, 'but there's no such thing as a magical flying… anything.'

'*He's* flying it,' said Jarfin, nodding towards Lockley.

Montgomery looked at the old man, who was still standing in the bow, his hand on the figurehead, and whistling happily to himself. 'But, I thought you said that Moving your own weight is very advanced magic, let alone Moving a boat full of people.'

'The Transak *are* advanced. They're some of the most powerful Movers in the Underworld.'

Montgomery watched as Lockley scratched his backside with his free hand. 'Really?' he said. 'This guy? But he's so… old.'

'You mean, *experienced?*' said Vala, jabbing her staff at

him from two seats in front. 'Doesn't matter how gifted you are, lad. Without practice and hard work, you'll never control your magic.'

Montgomery lapsed into an irritated silence.

Clovis turned to look at the hooded figure sitting at the back. 'Are you going to Salistra too?' she asked. For a moment, the person didn't move, as if they had no idea what to do when someone spoke to them.

'No,' he said at last, in a deep voice, and even though it was only a single word, Montgomery could tell he had a thick accent.

'Have you come far?' asked Clovis.

Again the man froze before, eventually, speaking again. 'Yes. I come here from many of miles.'

Encouraged by this almost chattiness, Clovis ploughed on. 'I'd love to travel one day, and visit some of the Underworld's famous sites, like the caverns of the Silver Deci-Bells, the Hollow Mountains and the Hanging Gardens of Amarantine. Have you see many sights on your travels?'

The hood shook slightly. 'No. They don't told me of these places.'

It took Clovis a moment to work out what he meant. 'Oh. Well, maybe they're not *that* amazing. So, whereabouts are you headed? Is it far?'

There was another long pause as the figure looked out from deep inside his hood, and Montgomery could just make out his eyes glinting in the diamond light. 'No.'

Clovis gave up and turned back to look at the tunnel ahead.

Now and again, they passed other Transak heading in the opposite direction, each one with a different mode of transport. There were a few other boats, which earned waves from Lockley and a friendly greeting, but the rest he either scorned or ignored entirely as they drifted past. One was nothing more than a log, with a couple of ragged branches dragging along beneath it. Another looked like a sheet of rusty corrugated tin. And as they headed past another emblem, this one of a flaming bow and arrow, which apparently meant they were about half way to Salistra, a cluster of children sped past on what was definitely a rug.

'It's a magical flying carpet!' said Montgomery, pointing excitedly while nudging Marlah with the other hand.

'Is there something actually wrong with you?' she said, slyly tying his shoelaces together with her Moving magic.

'Rest stop, everyone!' called Lockley from the front of the boat, as he steered it gently to the side of the tunnel. 'We might as well break here for lunch. I've got a couple of passengers to pick up from the mines.'

'Mines?' said Montgomery. Lockley jerked a thumb at the far wall and Montgomery turned to see a two crossed hammers and a diamond carved into the rock. He reached into his school bag to pull out his pouch of keycoins to see if any of them matched, but changed his mind. It would be much easier to use Watching to look at them instead of getting them all out, so he closed his eyes and focused his mind on the memory of when he'd first seen them.

Almost immediately, the Watching kicked in, and the Steepleford street burst into his vision, complete with blue skies, birdsong, the cottage with the postbox in the wall, and the table with the keycoins laid out, pattern side up. It was so vivid, he felt like he was actually there, as though transported through time and space back to that sunny afternoon, when his granddad was still alive.

He opened his eyes and the Trago snapped back, the

Great Tunnel stretching away beyond it. At the other end of the boat, Vala and Wyndham were looking at him, talking to each other quietly, as though sharing secrets.

He closed his eyes again, and was back in Steepleford. Turning to his left, he found Dalton smiling at him, gesturing to the keycoins. When his granddad spoke, his voice was muffled slightly, as though it was a recording played in another room.

'Give 'em a good, look, young General.'

Montgomery turned back to the coins, running his eyes across the patterns. There were so many of them, and yet they were all there in perfect detail, the images stored away in the depths of his memories. There were the two coins with the pattern of a lion with the four stars - he must remember to get the second one back from Merek - and there were the ones with the crescent and the circle, the first his granddad had shown him. But, although he inspected them all twice, the pattern of the crossed hammers and diamond was not there.

'The darkness will rise, young General.' Montgomery blinked in the surprised and turned to look at Dalton.

'What?' he said. He glanced up at the sky, which only a moment before had been clear blue, but was now thick with dark, rolling clouds. A chill wind whipped up along the deserted street, tossing leaves and litter in his wake. What was happening? This wasn't part of his memory. 'What?' he said again. 'What do you mean?'

Dalton reached out a hand and gripped Montgomery's arm as he gazed into his eyes. 'The Great War is coming, my boy. It's coming and you need to be prepared. The darkness *will* rise.'

Montgomery shook his head. 'I don't understand, granddad.'

'Are you coming or what?' Montgomery's eyes flicked open, to find Jarfin's face inches from his own. He jerked backwards. Jarfin grinned. 'Come on. We're going to have a look in the mines.'

Puzzled by what his granddad had said in his vision, Montgomery peered across the tunnel to see the rest of the Lundarien party heading towards the carving in the rock.

'Er... okay,' he said, getting to his feet.

'Wait!' said Jarfin, holding up a hand. He pointed down to Montgomery's shoelaces. 'You'll want to untie them first.'

He did so, muttering under his breath, then zipped up his school bag and shoved it under the seat. 'Can I leave my bag here?' he asked.

'Course you can,' said Lockley, leaning against the carved goat's head and chewing on what looked like an old stick. 'I'll be staying aboard. I've always got Mr Chatty back there to keep me company.' He gestured to the hooded figure in the stern. The hood nodded, ever so slightly.

By the time he and Jarfin had reached the far wall, Vala had already performed whatever magic was required to open the entrance, revealing a long tunnel beyond, lit by far more diamonds than was really necessary.

She glanced back and nodded to Montgomery. 'Keep your wits about you, lad,' she said. 'The mines may come as something of a surprise.'

'What do you...?' But she was already hobbling away along the tunnel, her staff ringing out each step.

The tunnel was about fifty metres long, and Montgomery was busy trying to work out how many "oars" this might be, when he emerged into the cavern beyond, and all thought of Underworld measurements were scattered from his mind. It wasn't the vastness of the place that struck him, though it could easily have contained the whole of Lundarien twice over as it swept away to the right and left, above and below. It wasn't the brightness of the light either, which was almost painful, a dazzling, desert-bright glare that burst from the rocks in all directions, shining out of every crack and fissure, every nook and cranny. Nor was it the thick dust that hung in the air, forming a dark fog that obscured the depths and distances in its shadowy folds. It was none of these things that sent Montgomery stumbling backwards into the tunnel, tripping over his feet to leave him half-sitting half-lying in the thick dust.

It was the dinosaurs.

16. "That Could Have Been Messy"

'Dinosaurs!'

The word struggled out as though Montgomery was being strangled, his mouth opening and closing as he gazed, wide-eyed, at the massive creatures. Though he had not yet visited the Natural History Museum, due to Victor's strange mood of late, he had done a project on dinosaurs back when he was in year four. The main things he could recall, through his terrified panic, were images of skeletons with teeth the size of his arm, creatures whose length was measured in buses and, most importantly of all, the fact they were supposed to all have died out millions of years ago. And now, as he cowered in the tunnel entrance, his brain couldn't quite accept the presence of these actual, real-life, very-non-extinct lizards. Lizards that really could be measured in buses!

Long, scaled tails snaked across the cavern floor, leading up to broad and armoured bodies, like tanks propped up on vast tree trunks. Some had plates growing from their spines, from others sprouted vicious-looking spikes. Necks of all lengths and girths stretched up to where the creatures' heads were half-hidden, apparently burrowing into the roof and the walls. The sounds they made were almost as scary as the monsters themselves. Deep bellows rumbled across cavern from all directions, punctuated by occasional screeches and roars, and behind these was the constant cracking and crashing of rocks. A booming echoed from the right, and Montgomery turned to see one of the beasts close by, its squat body covered with jagged horns. Montgomery recognised it as an Ankylosaurus, and was busy swinging its hammer-headed tail against the rock wall.

With an effort, he tore his gaze from the dinosaurs and looked around to see where his friends were. To his horror, they were already quite a distance away, heading past the towering form of what he recalled from the school project to be a Diplodocus. Or maybe a Brontosaurus. What did the name matter? Diplodocus or Brontosaurus, it was still a monster! And the others were ambling past it as though a cavernful of dinosaurs was a normal, everyday phenomenon.

'Dinosaurs!' he said again, his words swallowed up almost before they were out of his mouth.

The small figure of Jarfin broke away from the others and headed back towards him. Montgomery squinted through the bright, dusty air, worried his friend was in danger, fleeing back towards the safety of the tunnel, and was astounded to see him smiling.

'What's up?' Jarfin called over the din of the cavern. 'Are you hurt?'

Montgomery's mouth opened and closed, and he ducked back as a dinosaur, walking upright on its back legs mere metres away, shifted closer. His eyes were almost perfect circles as he stared at his friend, but all he managed to say was, 'Dinosaurs.'

'Yes, I know. Aren't they amazing? Even better than the alboars, eh?' He gave Montgomery a playful thump on the arm. 'Come and see.'

Montgomery's eyes swivelled back to the nearest dinosaur and he ducked further into the tunnel. 'Can't,' he said, his voice still a croak. He swallowed and said again, 'Dinosaurs.'

Jarfin grinned. 'Don't tell me you're afraid of them! They're perfectly safe.' He turned and pointed up towards the creature's head. 'Look!'

Montgomery inched forwards a little, craning his neck to see what he was pointing at. The dinosaur was barely ten metres away, and was easily as tall as his old cottage in Steepleford. It had strange, horn-like thumbs, which it used to dig into the wall, while its head tilted back, its nosing rubbing against the rock. And there, clearly visible now he was really looking, Montgomery made out the figure of someone perched on the creature's left shoulder.

'Who's that?' he said, stepping a little further into the cavern to look and noticed the person was sitting on some kind of saddle, his hands gripping a thick leather strap that must be attached to the dinosaur somewhere. 'It... It looks like he's riding it!'

'That's because he is. See his jerkin?' Jarfin pointed up again. The jerkin in question was striped in alternate bands of dark green and purple. 'He's a Hunter *and* a Lectimentor, see? Which means he can control the dinosaur. Well, *guide* it, anyway.'

Montgomery nodded, his fear of the terrible lizards subsiding slightly, at least for the moment, as his curiosity was roused. 'So, that's another Conjuring skill, is it? Like teleporting?'

'Exactly.' Jarfin gestured across the cavern. 'All the riders are Multifexes. They come from all over Brytellian and beyond to work in these diamond mines. My dad says the pay is amazing. Well, actually, he said it was outrageous, but he probably *meant* amazing.'

Montgomery squinted through the dusty haze and the dazzling light, focussing on the creatures' heads and necks. Sure enough, each one had its own rider, sitting on various types of saddle that were clearly designed to suit each individual type of dinosaur.

Turning back to the closest one, he pointed, suddenly excited. 'It's an Iguanodon!'

Jarfin frowned. 'A what? Don't tell me you have dinosaurs on the Surface?'

'No. Or at least, not any *alive* ones. But I recognise it from a drawing I had to do at school.'

The frown remained. 'A drawing?' Jarfin took a few paces towards the Iguanodon, stopping just next to its thick, scaly tail. 'We call this type a Sniffer, on account of it being so good at finding where the diamonds are. They're not my favourite, though. I'll show you where that is.' He turned away from the dinosaur and started back across the cavern. After a few paces, he stopped and glanced back at Montgomery, who was still poised in the entrance. 'Come on,' he said, beckoning. 'It's all perfectly safe.'

Not entirely confident of his friend's assurance, Montgomery began to pick his way across the cavern behind Jarfin, giving the Iguanodon a wide berth. As he did so, he gazed, open-mouthed, at the number and variety of the dinosaurs. A handful of them he recognised, and, in addition to the Ankylosaurus, Iguanodon and whatever the long one was, he spotted a group of Triceratops on a ledge, industriously carving out an enormous diamond with their large horns, and a Stegosaurus, its tiny head turned towards Montgomery as it chiselled into the floor with its spiked tail. A flash of Watching assured him that they were all plant eaters, and as he scanned the cavern his fear of these prehistoric monsters was slightly eased by the lack of Velociraptors and the dreaded Tyrannosaurus Rex. But only slightly.

Up ahead Jarfin disappeared behind a wide outcrop of rock, which jutted up from the floor and reached almost all the way to the roof. Finding himself suddenly alone, Montgomery hurried to follow, but as he rounded the outcrop, he skidded to a stop, the gritty floor scraping beneath his school shoes.

'Ta dah!' Jarfin gestured theatrically to the dinosaur, a delighted grin on his face. 'This one's called the Hammer. He's the only one of his kind in these mines. My dad's only brought me here a couple of times, but I reckon I've seen all the different types of dinosaur, and *this* one is the best. Just look at him!'

Montgomery could do nothing else. The creature was immense, its long reptile body stretching up the wall like a scaly tree, its feet gripping to the rock with long, powerful claws. High above, so high Montgomery's neck hurt to look, its club-like head turned slowly, its forked tongue flicking out to touch and taste. Despite all this, what struck him most of all was how much it was like Lizzy, the lizard his dad had brought home, both in shape and in colour, the scales along its body so green it almost glowed.

'Not bad, eh?' called Jarfin, who had walked round to the other side of the dinosaur. The creature let out a deep booming sound, its throat swelling and shrinking again. 'Here we go!' he said, pointing up to where the tiny rider perched, half-shrouded by the dust-filled air. 'You're about to see why it's called the Hammer.'

Montgomery swallowed and edged nervously along the rocky outcrop to get a better look. The creature was so close he could almost reach out and touch it. At this distance, the vastness of the cavern itself seemed dwarfed by the monster as it towered over him, its head shrouded in the dust clouds above, its armour-plated back even more like a mountain than the walls themselves, its tail trailing away across the floor into the distance, ending in a cluster of spikes like some medieval weapon. Despite the brightness, it was somehow more terrifying in the light than it would have been in the dark. To see this monster was to fear it.

Montgomery stumbled back in alarm as a sound like a series of lightning strikes exploded above him, so loud, the cavern itself could have been collapsing. And, as he stared in terror, straining his eyes to see through the haze of dust that billowed towards him, it looked as though it was. Nearby, someone shouted, but he couldn't tear his gaze away. He couldn't move. He could only stand and stare as the avalanche of rocks began to fall, tumbling towards him in a shower of crushing death that was only seconds... moments... a mere instant away.

Something slammed into him, knocking the breath out of his lungs. He slewed across the cavern floor, away from the tumbling rocks, and everything went dark.

Montgomery braced himself for the expected crash as the rocks smashed to the ground. But the seconds passed and still he lay there in the darkness. Whatever was pinning him down began to move, to draw back, and light emerged on the edge of his vision, a light full of dark swirls and shadows. Montgomery blinked and tried to see what had knocked him down, expecting to see the dinosaur's spiky tail nailing him to the spot, but all he could make out were what looked like dark folds of cloth. The weight shifted again and withdrew, allowing him to move. Although he was a little winded and his arm ached where he'd landed on it, he appeared to be unhurt. The air was full of dust, thick and clinging, making him cough, his nose tingling with the sharp edges of a sneeze. A hand gripped his free arm and heaved him, effortlessly to his feet.

'Well, that could have been messy!' said the owner of the hand, and Montgomery started at the sound of the voice. It was one he recognised. He waved his now free arm in front of his face in an attempt to clear the air, but the dust was too thick.

'Vala?' called another voice, unmistakably that of

Wyndham. 'Can you do something about this wretched mess? I can't see a thing!'

It was as though someone switched on an enormous fan. One moment the air was so clouded with dust it was impossible to make out anything but vague shapes, and the next it was completely clear, leaving Montgomery trying to blink away a few stray bits of grit. With his good eye, he caught sight of Vala, who was still waving a hand in magic, Jarfin, Wyndham and the cloaked figure of the other passenger on the Trago.

'Merek?' he said, certain he'd recognised the voice correctly. 'Is that you?' The cloaked figure reached up long-sleeved arms and pulled back the hood. Montgomery stared at him in one-eyed surprised. 'What are you doing here?'

'Saving your backside again,' said Merek, though his voice was edged with what sounded like concern.

'Merek!' Wyndham moved with Hunter-like speed, gripping Merek's shoulder in one huge fist. 'Fancy meeting you here, you little rat.' Wyndham grinned, but not in a very friendly way. When he spoke again it was through clenched teeth. He didn't *sound* friend either. 'Give me one good reason why I shouldn't feed you to this lizard here.'

Merek's eyes swivelled up towards the dinosaur's head, which had paused in its hammering while its rider peered down at the scene below. 'Um. It's a herbivore, isn't it?' he said.

Wyndham narrowed his eyes as his grip on Merek's shoulder tightened. 'Not good enough.'

'But he just saved my life!' said Montgomery. 'Those rocks would have landed right on me if it weren't for Merek.' He gestured to the ground at where he expected to find the rubble of the fallen rocks, but instead there was only dust.

'He didn't save your life,' said Vala, hobbling

forwards. She held out her hand and a lump of stone split away from the wall and landed with a smack in her palm. With a casual flick of her wrist, she tossed it up into the air. About three metres from the ground it burst apart, nothing more than a cloud of dust. 'Field of protection, see? Some health and safety nonsense they had magicked up about twenty years back. *That* was what saved your life. Not this good-for-nothing rascal.' She jabbed her staff at Merek.

'Well, *I* didn't know that,' said Merek. 'I was just trying to look out for my friend.'

'*Your friend?*' said Jarfin, cleared confused. He looked from Montgomery to Merek and back again. 'What does he mean, "your friend"? How can you be friends? You're not, are you?' There was pleading in Jarfin's voice.

'I don't know about *friend* exactly,' said Montgomery, trying not to make eye contact with Merek. 'It's just... we kind of hung out a couple of times recently. Up on the Surface.'

'What?' Jarfin mouth sagged open. So did everyone else's, except for Wyndham's, whose mouth was tightly closed, his lips almost white.

'You remember I was telling you how I don't really have any friends up in London?' Eyes stared back at him, but no one responded. Montgomery swallowed, blinked the last of the dust from his eye, and carried on. 'Well, there's this guy, Jeff, who really doesn't like me, and he's got this gang, see? Anyway, they tried to attack me after school last week and, well, Merek,' he pointed at him, to emphasise the point, 'stepped in and got rid of them. He saved me getting beaten up. And now,' he gestured to the rocks above, 'he saved me getting crushed to death. Or at least, he *thought* he was saving me. Which is a good thing, yes?' He examined their faces for any signs of support, but Vala and Wyndham's faces were unreadable, while Jarfin's looked horrified. There was a long pause.

'Right, Merek.' Wyndham's sudden, booming voice made Montgomery jump. 'You're coming to Salistra with us.'

Jarfin's head jerked round to face his father. 'What?' he said, even more confused than before. 'But, Dad-'

'But nothing. I want this wretch exactly where I can see him.' He jabbed one huge finger at Merek, fixing him with a gaze that would have made Montgomery shrivel into a heap. 'We've got important business to be getting on with. But when this is all over, I'll be taking you back to Lundarien and the Novaristee can decide what to do with you.'

'Lock him up in the cells, I say,' said Favian, who had ambled over with the rest of the party. He had been kidnapped by Payton and spent several weeks trapped in her lair at the heart of the Labyrinth and he did not look happy to see Merek. Nor did Marlah, who had been kidnapped by him, though she'd managed to escape.

'We should tie him up or something,' she said. 'Really, really tight.'

'Preferably around his neck,' added Catrain.

'Come on, guys!' said Montgomery, positioning himself next to Merek. 'It's not his fault what happened. Payton bewitched him into working for her. He told me all about it. Honestly.' Across the group, disbelieving eyebrows were raised. 'Plus, he saved me from being crushed to death just now. Sort of. Hasn't he proved that we can trust him?'

Wyndham, still gripping Merek by the shoulder, half-led, half-dragged him back across the cavern. 'I certainly don't trust you, lad. And I don't much like you either. But as I don't have time to deal with you right now, I'll hold off on my judgement. You'll come with us to Salistra and when we get back to Lundarien we'll see what's to be done with you. And don't forget,' he added, the words a whisper like the drawing of a sword, 'I'm Watching you!'

17. "We Are The Aristane"

There was a lot of activity in the Great Tunnel as the Trago approached Salistra, and it wasn't just the random hustle and bustle of people going about their own business, but the deliberate movement of people working with a single purpose.

'Drop us here if you would, Lockley,' said Wyndham, studying the scene ahead. 'I'd like to approach that lot on foot so I can assess the situation properly.'

The boat began to slow, drifting towards an outcrop of fruiting vines on the left side of the tunnel. 'Whatever you want, Watchman,' said Lockley, 'but it's still going to cost you the same. Fifty-seven schillings in all.'

'A rip off as always,' said Wyndham, pulling out his leather purse. 'I should have gone with Scolland or the Bainards instead.'

'Not if you'd actually wanted to get here!' Lockley Moved the coins from Wyndham's grasp and tucked them into a leather pouch. 'Off you get then. Go on, I've got other people what need my professional service, you know.'

Once back on the solid tunnel floor, Wyndham strode with a purposeful gait towards the crowd. They had gathered around the open archway that Montgomery guessed must lead to Salistra. Some of those ahead noticed and pointed out the approaching group to others. As the Lundariens drew near, the crowd parted and an important-looking man stepped through to meet them.

'Look out,' whispered Merek, next to Montgomery. 'It's the police.'

Montgomery gave a derisive laugh. 'Even *I* know they don't have police in the Underworld.'

'It's the police,' said Wyndham over his shoulder. 'Keep quiet and let me do the talking. Good day, sir,' he added as the man drew up in front of him.

He was tall, dressed in dark grey, and on the chest of his jerkin were two emblems, one showing the octopus of the Watchers and the other a sword. He held up a hand that could have either been in greeting or to stop them coming any further. 'Welcome, Watchman.' The man's eyes scanned the group. 'May I enquire as to your business here?'

Wyndham nodded. 'We've come from Lundarien to see the Aristane. Please could you take us to them? We bring grave news, I'm afraid.'

'*More* grave news?' His already weary face sank a little further and he shook his head. 'As if there wasn't enough of that already, what with Atlantis scything through our western cities.'

'So, you know about Atlantis?' said Catrain, stepping forwards. 'Who told you?'

In response, the policeman gestured to the busy crowd behind him. 'Who *didn't* tell us? The Atlanteans might as well have marched up to the city portals and announced the invasion themselves. But...' he frowned at Wyndham, 'how is it that *you* know about Atlantis? Don't tell me they've broken through to Lundarien!'

'No, no,' Wyndham assured him. 'Nothing like that. We were told about the invasion by the people of Dursehaven, who fled east through our city.'

'Enough of this idle chatter,' interrupted Vala, hobbling forwards and jabbing her staff at the policeman.

'Take us to the Aristane, boy.'

To Montgomery surprise, or maybe because she used her Lectimenting magic on him, the man turned immediately and beckoned them to follow as he headed through the archway.

Shifting his school bag onto his left shoulder, Montgomery leaned towards Jarfin. 'What's an Aristane?' he whispered.

'You've never heard of the Aristane?' Marlah's mocking voice echoed along the tunnel.

'I haven't either,' said Merek, looking back over his shoulder at her.

Marlah glared at him. 'I wasn't talking to you!' Merek winked at her and she quickly looked away.

Montgomery sighed. 'So come on, then. What is it?'

'The Aristane are the leaders of Salistra,' said Jarfin, before Marlah respond. 'In fact, in a sense, the three Aristers oversee affairs across the whole of Brytellian, though most cities, like Lundarien, have got their own group of leaders. We only bring issues to the capital if it's *really* important.'

'The capital? Salistra's the capital city of Brytellian?'

'Are you serious?' said Marlah, in the same mocking tones. 'How do you not know that?'

Merek grinned at her. 'I actually did know that.'

'Shut up, Merek.'

'I thought *Lundarien* was the capital city,' said Montgomery, ignoring the interruptions. 'After all, it is pretty massive. And it's right under London, which is the capital city of England.'

'I knew that one, as well!' said Merek. Marlah growled under her breath.

'Lundarien? The capital of Brytellian?' Jarfin shook his head at this clearly absurd idea, his messy, black hair bouncing as he did so. 'Our city's certainly very impressive, and very important as well. But you just wait till you see Salistra!'

'Not very big, is it?' said Montgomery as the group emerged from the end of the tunnel into the cavern beyond. He peered about at the handful of trees that grew around the roof's single diamond, the clusters of building in the standard "Underworld" style, including a single tall tower in the centre, and the cobblestone path that ran downhill all the way to another entrance in the far wall. 'This place is barely *half* the size of Lundarien.'

'This *cavern*, yes,' said Jarfin. 'But Salistra isn't called the City of Seven Caverns for nothing, isn't it?'

Montgomery held up his hands in frustration. 'Well, how would I know that? They don't teach Underworld Geography at my school. You could have told me.'

'I just did.'

They followed the others down the slope towards the tower, and had almost reached it when three people, two men and a woman, all dressed in clothes of brightly coloured stripes, strode through the doorway heading straight towards them.

'These people request an audience,' called the policeman, as the group made to pass them without looking. 'They've come all the way from Lundarien to talk with you.' They slowed, turning harassed looks towards him.

'Lundarien?' said one of the men. Short and almost spherical, with only a thin crop of white hair sprouting just above his ears, he looked almost as old as Vala. 'What trouble could there be in Lundarien compared with Atlantis?'

'They come with *news* of Atlantis, my Lord Arister.'

'Surely not!' said the women, tall and stick-thin, and of a similar age to the man who had spoken. 'Lundarien has fallen to Atlantis as well? How has our enemy flanked us without us knowing?'

Wyndham held up his hands. 'It's nothing like that,' he said. 'We only came to bring news of the threat in the east. But I see you are already well aware.'

The other man, much younger than his fellows, stepped forwards. His dark hair was just a little too long, and was greasy enough that flecks of dandruff clung to it, while his eyes, that were clearly sizing up the Lundariens over his large, pointy nose, were just a little too small. Montgomery couldn't put his finger on exactly what it was about the man, but Montgomery didn't like him.

'Since you are here,' said the Arister, his voice harsh and nasal, 'you can join us and help to work out how we are going to stop Atlantis pushing any further east.' He set off again towards the entrance Montgomery and the others had come through. 'We can talk on the way.'

Back in the Great Tunnel, the crowd was looking a little less frantic. This appeared to be mostly to do with the fact that someone was dishing out food to everyone. Montgomery watched as bowls of some sort of stew Moved over people's heads to land in the outstretched hands of others. Many of the people had settled themselves against the tunnel wall and were chatting together in groups while they ate. A few children were kicking stones around further into the tunnel, and the policeman tutted loudly, then headed off to sort them out.

To the right, a smaller group of around thirty men and women stood in an untidy line, not talking to each other, but looking as though they were all waiting for something. To Montgomery they looked exactly like the people who stood at the bus stop at the end of his road in London. Apart from their clothes of course.

'The Transak should be here shortly,' said the older Arister.

'So where are we heading?' asked Favian.

The younger Arister looked him up and down. 'And what's your name, Mover?'

There was a brief flicker of dislike on Favian's face, but he swapped it quickly for a smile. 'Favian Vandar.' He held out his hand. 'And you are?'

'I am Garrick Vospen. Together with Anselm and Emlyn,' he indicated first the other man, then the woman, 'we are the Aristane.' He looked down at Favian's outstretched hand, but made no move to shake it. 'You would do well to remember this.'

Favian withdrew his hand and wiped it on his sleeve, as though he'd touched something slimy. 'I only asked where we were going, Garrick.' But the Arister just turned away without answering.

'Please,' said Anselm, looking slightly embarrassed, 'excuse my companion. These are troubling time, you know. It puts great strain on us all. And with so many strangers seeking refuge, it can be hard to know whom to trust.'

'But we came here to offer our help!' said Catrain. 'If you don't want it, just say the word and we'll-'

Wyndham laid a hand on her shoulder. 'As you say, Anselm, these are troubling times.'

'And it looks like our transport's arrived,' said Vala.

Montgomery looked back up the Great Tunnel and couldn't quite believe what he was seeing. It was a bus. A big, red double-decker bus, just like the ones that polluted the streets far above them, except that this one wasn't doing any polluting. Its engine, if it even had one, wasn't running, and it was floating along a foot or so above the tunnel floor without a sound, except the rustling of plants that brushed beneath its wheels. According to the display on the front, this was the number 27 to Shaftesbury. As it drifted to the ground, its rear door opened in front of the queue, and they started to file on board.

'It's a bus!' said Montgomery, pointing to the massive red object in question. 'From the Surface.'

'It is indeed,' said Emlyn, offering him a slight smile. 'We're not actually going to Shaftesbury, though, if such a place even exists. We're headed west, to Yarnock.'

'Why Yarnock?' asked Catrain.

'It's the place Atlantis has threatened to attack next.'

18. "You Brought A Sunner Here?"

The bus drifted slowly down the Great Tunnel under the control of two Movers, known as the Bainard twins. Montgomery watched them as they worked together, one in the driver's seat at the front, the other standing by the rear door, one hand gripping the upright bar. Having already performed some fairly powerful Moving himself, such as stopping the alboars and smashing Payton into a wall, he wondered if he would be able fly something like this one day. He didn't dare try now, though. What if he caused the bus to crash and all these people were injured? He looked around at his fellow passengers. Who were they all, anyway?

'They're mostly leaders from the colonies in west Brytellian,' said Vala.

Montgomery gave her an accusing look. 'Will you stay out of my head?' he said.

'Will you stop thinking so hard? It's making my old brain hurt.'

'So what's at this Yarnock place exactly?' asked Montgomery, turning to the others.

'It's the latest city to receive a "visit" from Atlantis,' said Anselm.

Wyndham looked shocked. 'Yarnock's a long way from Dursehaven. What about the colonies in between?'

'All gone, I'm afraid. Ethenside, Cloister, Munn, Blayston-Braddock, even Honeytown… all gone.' The old man looked down at his hands with a sigh.

'But it wasn't that long ago that they invaded Dursehaven,' said Catrain. 'How can so many colonies have fallen since then?'

'Atlantis is a powerful adversary,' said Garrick. 'Our towns and cities are no match for such a formidable nation. At least, not individually. But together,' he swung out an arm expansively at the passengers, almost smacking a young woman in the head, 'we just might stand a chance.'

'If we can ambush them,' added Emlyn. 'That's why we're heading to Yarnock.'

'What?' A cold shiver ran through Montgomery. 'We're going to ambush Atlantis today?'

Garrick produced something like a grin, though his eyes remained cold. 'Don't worry, *boy*. Atlantis will not attack Yarnock today. Their emissaries delivered their message of "Join us or else!" yesterday. They will return for their answer in nine days' time. According to our scouts the Atlantean army have settled in Honeytown. For now.' He looked at Montgomery for a moment, as though trying to work him out, the grin fading into a frown. 'Who *are* you, anyway?' he asked. 'Why are you dressed like… like a Sunner?'

'Because he *is* a Sunner,' said Marlah, packing all her usual scorn into that single word.

Garrick's frown deepened into a scowl, which he directed at Wyndham. 'You brought a Sunner here? To Salistra? What were you thinking, Watchman?'

'I was thinking sense, Garrick. A Sunner he may be-'

'He is!' interrupted Marlah, which earned her a warning glare from Wyndham.

'-but I reckon Montgomery here has more magic in him than all of us put together. He is the grandson of Dalton Stroud.'

The background hum of conversation stilled at the mention of Montgomery's granddad, and he noticed many of the faces had turned to look at him. He wasn't sure if it made him feel special or just awkward, but he was pleased to see his granddad was clearly a legend.

'The Last Omnifex,' said Anselm in an awed whisper. 'Why, it must be twenty years since I last saw Dalton. A more powerful magician I have never had the fortune to know, nor probably will either. And this boy is his grandson, you say?'

'That's correct.' Wyndham placed one massive hand on Montgomery's shoulder.

Anselm looked at him for a moment, then nodded. 'I believe you.'

Garrick, however, did not look impressed. 'And where is the great Omnifex now, when his people need him most? Hiding away up on the Surface, where he's nothing more than... than a useless old man.'

'How dare you speak like that about my granddad!' shouted Montgomery, leaping to his feet in anger as the bus veered suddenly across the tunnel. 'He was the kindest, cleverest, most amazing man who ever lived.' He stumbled slightly as, beneath them, the floor began to lurch and shudder. 'If he was still alive, he would be here, saving all of you. The only reason he isn't is because he's dead!'

The bus came to a juddering stop, its wheels skidding on the tunnel floor, and the Bainard twin by the rear doors stepped into the aisle. He did not look pleased.

'Right, which of you lot is mucking around and knocking us off course?' He stood, hands on hips, looking around at the passengers, none of whom met his eye.

'Sit down!' said Merek, whispering loudly through gritted teeth, while tugging the back of Montgomery's school jumper. 'Sit down and don't say anything.'

'Or *do* anything,' added Marlah. 'Especially any magic!'

'Well?' said Bainard. 'Anyone going to own up?' He looked around again, but, as it was evident no one was about to confess, he resumed his position by the rear door. 'Let's have no more messing about,' he said, pointing around the bus. He looked for a moment as if he was going to say something else, issue a threat perhaps, but he just shook his head and gripped hold of the bar again. The bus pulled away from the tunnel floor and continued on its way, while, from the corner of his eye, Montgomery noticed Garrick watching him. He did not like the expression on the Arister's face one little bit.

Yarnock was deserted. It looked as though the people here had simply stopped whatever they'd been doing, dropped whatever they'd been holding, and run for it. Baskets of clothes lay discarded on the floor, food sat untouched in bowls, and tools were left scattered beside unfinished repairs and half-fashioned goods.

The various heads of the western towns and cities spread out across the cavern and into the two tunnels beyond, each one looking for something, for anything that might give them the advantage in the coming battle with Atlantis. Wyndham instructed Merek to wait in the Town Square, while he, Favian and Catrain set off in a clockwise direction, closely followed by their squires, leaving Montgomery to follow Vala's hobbling footsteps to the centre of the cavern.

It was roughly the same size and shape as Lundarien, with many similar features. The Yarnock Town Hall perched on a hill in the north of the cavern, its Town Square spread out below, surrounded by densely packed houses and alleyways, like those in the Vines. The southern half of the cavern was evidently their farming area, as Montgomery could make out various crops and fruiting plants growing from the floor, walls and even trailing from the roof above. Here and there bright red chickens scratched and pecked among the plants. Although there was no lake, the Yar, the broad and fast-flowing river that gave the city its name, cut through the middle of the city, and Vala's staff rang out on its bridge as she walked across it. She came to a stop in the middle and turned slowly on the spot, looking out across the cavern and up at the trees hanging above them.

'What are we looking for, exactly?' asked Montgomery, who felt like they were doing little more than admiring the view.

Vala kept turning, her eyes sweeping across the cavern. 'No idea,' she said, 'but I'll know it when I see it. Unless you keep distracting me with your nonsense.'

Montgomery leant over the side of the bridge to look at the water rushing below them. Maybe that was the answer. 'What about the river?' he said, excited. 'We could hide under the water, wait for the Atlanteans to arrive and then burst out and take them by surprise!'

Vala was silent for a moment, as though considering this proposal. 'Reckon you can hold your breath that long?'

'Well, no. But what about using magic? Aren't there people who can breathe underwater? Jarfin said-'

'Oh, sure,' interrupted Vala. 'There are a few who can, I have no doubt, but you'd be lucky to find any here. That's Multifex magic, breathing underwater. Conjurings. As I recall from my brother's research, you'd need to be a Manser, a Cealer, a Hunter and a Healer - all at the same time. That you is it, lad? Want to give it a little go?' Her head snapped round, her eyes fixing him with a stare that was almost a physical force, disturbing and unnerving. Montgomery shook his head. 'Good. Now, can I get back to my search?' Montgomery opened his mouth to answer, but she got their first. 'Without any more of your interruptions!'

Just over an hour later, everyone gathered back in the Town Square to present their findings.

'So,' said Anselm, when the leaders had spoken, 'it would appear our options amount to hiding in the houses, climbing into the trees, and disguising ourselves as rocks in the western tunnel.'

'Or a combination of all three,' added one of the leaders from Blayston-Braddock, a small mousy-looking woman, whose triple-coloured bodice declared her to be a Multifex with Moving, Healing and Watching magic.

'Or a combination of all three,' echoed Anselm. He paused to look at the assembled faces. 'Not a very inspiring list of options, is it? How did you keep this place protected in the past, Destrian?' He turned a expectant look towards one of the two Yarnock leaders, a tall, gaunt man with a sparse crop of long, straggly-looking hair.

'That's just the thing,' he said, shrugging his bony shoulders. 'We never had the need to defend our city before. At least, not against anything more than a few raiding parties from Honeytown.' He gestured to the Honeytown party standing opposite. They smiled, looking pleased with themselves. 'But they were easily thwarted. A mere nothing compared to Atlantis.' The smiles faded.

'And how exactly did you *easily thwart* them?' asked Garrick, his tone mocking.

'By cheating!' said one of the Honeytown women.

The Yarnock leader gave her a withering look, every bit as good as one of Marlah's, before turning back to Garrick. 'By narrowing the two portals,' he said, pointing to the entrances to the city, which yawned open on two sides of the cavern. They were both roughly the same size as the Westerly Portal in Lundarien, which would allow four men to stand side by side, and Montgomery noticed they had stacks of boulders piled nearby. 'We just moved those rocks into the tunnel so only one person could get through at a time. After than, a couple of old biddies like Mildred here could thwart them.' He pointed at his fellow leader.

'Who are you calling an old biddy!' she growled, though Montgomery had to admit she did look very old. Maybe even older than Vala! She jabbed a crooked finger back at him. 'Any more of that and I'll thwart *you*, boy.'

Anselm sighed. 'Perhaps we could get back to the matter in hand?'

Without warning, Montgomery was struck by the feeling that he had seen something. Something here, in Yarnock. Something he was sure was important, even though he had no idea what it was.

'I think I've seen something,' he whispered, nudging Jarfin who was standing on his right. 'Something important, but I'm not sure what it is.'

'Watch it!' Jarfin whispered back.

'Sorry,' said Montgomery. 'Did I nudge you a bit hard?'

'No. I mean *actually* Watch it. Use your Watching to work out what it is you've seen. Like that time you found Marlah and me by Lake Altis, remember?'

Montgomery, wishing he'd thought of that himself, closed his eyes and tried to concentrate, letting the conversation of the others wash over him. The image of the cavern formed in his mind, gradually, at first, but then quicker as every inch of the cavern crystallised into place, from the cobbles on the streets to the diamonds shining through the branches of the trees. The volume and detail of the memory was almost overwhelming. Where was he to begin? Up or down? The wall or the houses? The river or the trees? It was all very well being able to use Watching magic, but he might as well be standing back on the bridge with Vala for all the good it seemed to be doing.

He decided to start with the trees and, almost instantly, he knew that the *something* was not there. Nor was anywhere on the roof of the cavern. Not really knowing how he did it, he made the whole area of the cavern above the level of the houses fade from the memory and turned his attention to what was left.

The something wasn't in the river. Nor was it on the bridge. He wasn't certain about the floor, so let that remain as the river and bridge faded from view. So did all the buildings, as these too he discounted.

Then, with another flash of certainty, he knew what he was looking for was on the walls. Not only that, but he knew it was *two* somethings, as well. And so he was left staring at the ring of rock that remained in his vision, with its two portals - one to the north, through which they had entered, the other to the west.

He rotated the walls in his mind, focussing his attention to the south and east, but all he could see was rock. What was it about these areas of the wall that had forced themselves into his thoughts? He zoomed in, as he had done the first time he'd Watched, when being grilled by Wyndham about a kidnapping. Then, he had recalled an emblem on the chest of one of the attackers, even though he'd only glimpsed it for a moment in the dark, while hiding behind a pile of rubble five metres away. But that was simple compared to trying to pick out a couple of small indentations in a mile long length of craggy rock wall.

'Small indentations,' he murmured, knowing for certain that this was exactly what he was looking for, even though he had not been aware of it seconds before. And then he had one. A small indentation in the southern wall: a circle with a crescent moon, another smaller circle nestling between its points.

It was a pattern he had seen before.

19. "The Perfect Solution To Our Problem"

'Something to contribute, boy?'

Montgomery's eyes snapped open to find everyone looking at him. 'Sorry?'

'I thought you spoke,' said Garrick, glaring at him, 'and wondered if there was anything you wanted to add to the discussion? Or maybe you were just having a little snooze?'

'No,' said Montgomery, shaking his head. 'I was just... I realised I'd missed something important.'

'This whole conversation, perhaps?' Garrick smiled at what he evidently thought was a witty comment, but his eyes still looked cross. 'I'm terribly sorry if we, mere mortals, are boring you, only we're rather concerned about Atlantis destroying our-'

'Shh,' said Montgomery, holding up a hand, palm out towards Garrick, who actually fell silent, clearly stunned by this outrageous behaviour. But not for long.

'Now look h-'

'Be quiet!' said Montgomery, and turned away from him, peering intently towards the rock wall on the south side of the cavern. 'Just give me a moment.'

'Have you worked out what it is?' asked Jarfin eagerly. Montgomery nodded and started to head towards the wall.

'What *what* is?' Wyndham sounded intrigued as he,

and a number of the others, followed him across the cavern. Montgomery made no answer, but picked up the pace, homing in on the section where he knew he would find the indentation. Even Garrick followed, though not until he'd made a show of rolling his eyes and throwing up his hands in desperation.

'For goodness' sake!' he said.

'Shh,' said Montgomery.

As he got nearer to the wall, he quickened his footsteps until he was almost jogging. 'Someone get my bag!' he called, without looking round.

By the time he reached the wall, everyone was running in his wake, even though most of them had no idea why. About a metre from the wall Montgomery stopped dead. Jarfin ran into the back of him.

'Sorry,' he said, but Montgomery ignored him, raising a hand to the wall.

'It's here,' he said, pointing to the rock ahead.

'You found a wall!' said Garrick, with Marlah-like sarcasm. 'Well done.' But as Montgomery drew his hand away from the rocky surface, there was a gasp from those behind him. There, carved into the stone, was a circle, about an inch and a half across. Inside the circle was, as he had expected, a crescent moon, with a small circle nestling inside it.

'Where's my bag?' asked Montgomery, turning to look, but couldn't see due to everyone trying to squeeze in to look at the marking on the wall.

'Here!' came a shout from the back and, with frustrating slowness, the crowd parted to let Merek through, clutching Montgomery's school bag in one hand. 'What have you got in here? This thing weighs a ton!'

In response, Montgomery started pulling out all his text books out and handing them to Jarfin.

'What's Sock-eye-ology?' he asked.

'Sociology? said Montgomery, rummaging around in the bottom of his bag. 'It's boring, that's what it is. Aha!' He drew out the leather pouch his granddad had left him, containing the various Underworld keycoins. 'Hold out your hands, would you?' he said to Merek, then started pouring them out into his upturned palms, searching through them for the pattern that matched the indentation on the wall. A pattern he *knew* was here somewhere.

'Let *me*,' said Merek and tossed the keycoins up into the air. They didn't fall, however, but hung just in front of Montgomery, each one turning so its pattern side was facing him.

Montgomery smiled. 'Nice!' Merek grinned back.

Nearby he heard Marlah mutter 'Show off!' just loud enough for Merek to hear

A moment later, Montgomery snatched a couple of keycoins out of the air and tossed the leather pouch to Merek, who, with a swipe of his hand, Moved the keycoins into it and dropped it back into the bag. Turning to the wall, Montgomery held up the one of the keycoins, its crescent moon and circle pattern facing away from him, and slid it into the indentation.

The way the entrances opened up was quite different from the ones he'd seen in the Great tunnel. Where those had emerged gradually as the rocks folded themselves away, the two new portals in Yarnock, one in the south, where Montgomery and others were standing, the other in the east, materialised, or rather *de*-materialised, in an instant, with a sound not dissimilar to someone biting into a crunchy apple. One moment there was the solid stone of the cavern wall, the next there were two openings that looked as if they'd always been there. Stale air wafted out from the darkness beyond, smelling of damp cellars.

The crowd took a step backwards, peering inside.

'It's a tunnel!' said Clovis

'Well spotted,' said Marlah, in her usual tone, as she looked over her shoulder into the entrance. 'Where does it go?'

'Only one way to find out,' said Vala, who had appeared next to Montgomery as if by magic, and started hobbling off through the portal. The keycoin shot out of the indentation and struck him on the chin.

'Ow!'

He picked it up and followed Vala, surprised to find it was not dark inside. Not completely, anyway. A faint purple glow filled the tunnel, casting eerie shadows on the wall that stirred and swirled, like cream mixing into coffee. The path twisted away to the left, following the line of the Yarnock cavern wall. It broadened as it did so.

'What're *those* things?' someone asked, and Montgomery turned to see everyone else creeping through the tunnel behind him. Emlyn, the Arister, was pointing towards the rear wall, which was lined with a long row of what looked like stone teeth, each about the height of a grown man. They were either stalagmites or stalactites, but Montgomery could never remember which was which.

'Stalactites, aren't they?' suggested Favian.

Marlah's sigh echoed around the tunnel. 'I think you mean stalagmites, dad. They're the ones that grow up from the floor.'

'Never mind all that,' called Vala, who had reached the widest part of the tunnel and was leaning over the source of the strange, dark-purple light. 'Look at this!'

Montgomery and the others headed towards her.

'What is it?' asked someone, as they crowded round, their faces bathed by the light as it danced and swirled inside a small globe, a little bigger than a tennis ball. It sat in a shallow hollow carved into the top of a single, short stalagmite.

'Is it some sort of diamond?' suggested someone else.

Destrian, the tall Yarnock leader, leaned over those in front to get a better look. 'It's not like any diamond I've ever seen,' he said. 'It gives me the creeps.' He shook his head, his long, greasy hair dangling all over Vala. 'To think this has been here for… who knows how long? Hidden away in our city, in a tunnel we never even suspected existed.'

Vala swatted his hair away. 'Tell me, Destrian, did Dalton Stroud ever visit Yarnock?'

'The Omnifex?' He scratched his head in contemplation, creating a shower of dandruff. 'I can't recall…' He looked around the group until he spotted his fellow leader, the "old biddy", who had no doubt lived in Yarnock the longest out of those present. He gave her a questioning look.

'Oh yes,' she said. 'Look at me, why don't you. Make *me* feel old!'

'But… but you *are* old, Mildred.'

She glared at him, her eyes narrowing to wrinkly slits. And then she shrugged. 'Can't argue with that, I suppose. And yes, Dalton came here a few times actually, though that must be thirty years or more ago. Is this *his* doing?' She waved a hand around to indicate the tunnel.

'I reckon those portals probably had something to do with him,' said Vala. 'Though what their purpose is exactly, I couldn't say. Who knew what my brother was up to when he went gallivanting off around the Underworld? *This* however,' she pointed to the glowing sphere, 'looks very much like his sort of thing. Though I've not idea what it is or what it does.'

Everyone gazed at the ball, clearly lost in their own imaginings of what it might be. Montgomery reached a hand between the two people in front and touched the glowing surface. It was warm and smooth. It also vibrated, ever so slightly.

'Well, it shouldn't be left here,' said Garrick, suddenly, stepping forward and snatching it up. He held it close to his face, examining it. 'This is clearly an important magical artefact which should be given the appropriate study. It is my duty to take this back with me to Salistra.'

'How dutiful of you!' said Wyndham. 'But before you start helping yourself to the mystery glowing ball, Garrick, I should point out that, if this did belong to Dalton Stroud, it surely belongs to Lundarien.'

'And yet it was found in a concealed tunnel,' said Garrick, glaring at Wyndham, 'over a hundred miles from your city!'

'Quite,' added Destrian. 'By rights, that thing belongs in Yarnock.'

'Enough of this nonsense,' shouted a voice and Montgomery was surprised to see it was Anselm, his previously complacent look replaced with one of anger, his wiry, white eyebrows bunched together. From the light of the diamond that hung from his neck, he looked almost scary. 'If we start fighting among ourselves we have no hope of ever defending our lands from Atlantis. See here.' He reached into the dish-shaped indentation where the globe had been sitting and picked up a slip of paper. In the half-light, Montgomery could just make out the neat, clear marks of writing.

'What does it say?' asked Jarfin, pushing against Montgomery's shoulder as he tried to get a look.

Anselm scanned the paper, before clearing his throat and reading it aloud. 'It says, "This orb is called the Trypasphere. It is the only one in existence and it does not belong to you, Garrick Vospen."'

'What?' said Garrick, his voice high-pitched and strangled. The Trypasphere slipped from his fingers, and if it wasn't for Catrain's Hunter reflexes it would have fallen to the rock floor.

Anselm continued reading. "'The Great War is coming and unless you want to the darkness to overpower you, the Trypasphere is to be placed in the possession of my grandson, Montgomery. Be ready. Be Vigilant. The darkness will rise." It's signed Dalton Stroud.' He passed the slip of paper to Garrick, who read it in silence. Then, like a man picking up a dead rat, he took the Trypasphere from Catrain and turned to Montgomery. He did not look pleased.

'I believe *this*,' he spat the word out, 'belongs to you.'

Montgomery held out his hand to accept it, stunned not only at being given this strange, glowing ball, but by the idea his granddad left it here for him and had known exactly what would be happening when it was found. And what was all this about the Great War again and the darkness rising?

'Good,' said Anselm, his face its normal, kindly self. 'Now we've got *that* sorted, let us focus on the problem at hand. Or do I need to remind you all that, in a few days, Yarnock will be overrun with Atlanteans seeking to take over our lands?' There was a general chorus of head shaking. 'It is quite possible that our young friend here,' he pointed at Jarfin, then, squinting at him in the half-light, pointed instead at Montgomery, 'has stumbled across the answer. Shall we see where this tunnel leads?'

The path continued to curve away to the left but, instead of getting wider, the walls began to draw closer together. Soon the run of stalagmites came to an end and the way ahead became lighter.

'Just as I thought,' said Anselm, as they approach an opening back into the Yarnock cavern, 'it comes out in the other new entrance. They're connected to each other. The tunnel must be a sort of crescent shape.' He peered at the wall for a moment before ambling over to Montgomery and holding out his hand. 'Might I borrow one of those keycoins, young man?' he asked.

'Sure.' Montgomery handed one over, slipping the other into his back pocket. Anselm, went over to the wall by the entrance and pressed the keycoin against it. Immediately, with that same crunchy apple sound, the entrance became a solid wall of rock. Anselm turned to the others, smiling in the light from the diamond round his neck. 'I believe this Crescent Tunnel will provide the perfect solution to our problem, agreed?'

Behind him the keycoin shot out of the wall and smacked into the back of the old man's head.

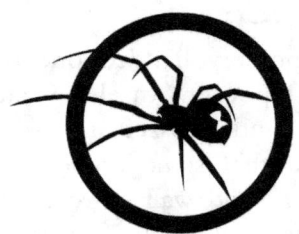

20. "What Use Would I Be In A Fight?"

By the time they had planned out how the ambush would take place, with much testing of opening and closing the secret entrances, using both the indentations in Yarnock's main cavern and those inside the Crescent Tunnel itself, Montgomery's watch said it was after nine o'clock in the evening. Around the Town Square, cooking fires had been lit and groups of people clustered around them, talking in hushed voices, both excited and fearful at the same time.

'We'll be staying here for the night,' said Wyndham, strolling across to where Montgomery and the others were sitting, eating the last of the vegetables Vala had gathered from the farming quarter. They looked something like a cross between melons and parsnips, but taste like lasagne.

Merek looked at the dusty rock floor without enthusiasm. 'Where exactly? I didn't bring a sleeping bag or anything.'

'A *sleeping bag*?' said Marlah, the scornful expression on her face flickering in the firelight. 'What's that supposed to be? Can you get "awake bags", too?'

'It's exactly what it sounds like,' said Merek. 'It's a bag that you climb inside to sleep in.' Montgomery pulled a face, realising for the first time how ridiculous that sounded. 'Imagine a blanket that zips up into a warm, snuggly sack.'

'You're as bad as him,' she said, thumbing in Montgomery's direction. 'A right couple of Sunners. I should have hit you a bit harder with that rock, Merek!'

Merek flashed her one of his smiles. 'Your hair looks especially beautiful in the firelight,' he said.

'We'll be sleeping in the houses,' said Wyndham loudly as Marlah's face flushed almost as red as her hair. 'The Yarnock folk aren't using them at the moment, since most of them are camping out in Salistra. Destrian said they wouldn't mind us sleeping in their beds. After all, we are here to help get their city back. Without our help, they mightn't have any beds!'

'Fair enough,' said Montgomery, snatching up his bag. 'Which house am I in? I'm shattered.'

Wyndham pointed behind them, where a cluster of small cottages were huddled together along on a steep slope. 'We've got those first three houses on the left there. Why don't you and Jarfin take the first? Favian and I will take the next, with Marlah and Merek, while Catrain-'

'Couldn't I share the house with Montgomery?' asked Merek, placing a hand on Montgomery's shoulder. 'Jarfin should be with you, Wyndham. He is your son and squire, after all.'

'And I don't want to sleep in the same building as... *him!*' Marlah jabbed a finger at Merek, her face still red from his comment about her hair.

Wyndham narrowed his eyes at Merek for a moment and, across the cavern, someone laughed loudly as if in response to Merek's request. 'Not a chance,' he said. 'You're staying right where I can see you.' He waved Montgomery and Jarfin away. 'Go on then. Get some sleep. We'll meet back here at the third hour and grab something to eat before we head back to Lundarien. And Montgomery?' he added, as the two boys got to their feet. 'You did well today, lad. To tell you the truth, I wasn't happy about bringing out along, but Vala insisted. She said you were our "secret weapon", and it turns out she was right.'

'You needn't sound so surprised!' growled Vala, through a mouthful of roasted vegetables.

Wyndham gave her a brief smile, and continued, 'I must thank your mother when we get back. It can't have been easy letting you come away with us, and overnight as well.'

Montgomery's breath caught in his throat. He'd forgotten about his parents. With a stab of panic, it suddenly seemed inevitable that they would find out about him coming here, about him lying to them and skipping school. What was he going to do? He couldn't keep his mum from talking with Wyndham and Vala forever. How would he-

'Are you coming?' Jarfin's voice shook Montgomery from his thoughts.

'Oh, er, yeah,' he said, his voice tight. 'Sure.' Well, there was nothing he could do about the problem tonight. Hopefully his secret would be safe and his mum and dad would never find out. 'Good night,' he said, then slouched off after Jarfin.

The door creaked open on what would be Montgomery's bedroom for the night, his first night in the Underworld, and he raised his diamond to get a good look at the place. It was surprisingly similar to his own room in London. There was a desk against the far wall covered with a mess of paper and books. The bed took up the opposite wall, complete with mattress, sheets and a bedside table. A large painting hung above the bed and behind the door was a wardrobe. But unlike Montgomery's, this wardrobe was filled with bodices and dresses. It was a *girl's* bedroom!

'Yes!' Jarfin's voice echoed from the next room. 'This bed is amazing. It must be ten times the size of my one back home.'

Montgomery went to have a look and the bed was indeed huge. So was the room, and it clearly belonged to a boy.

'Typical,' he said. 'I've ended up with a *girl's* bedroom.'

Jarfin grinned. 'Want to swap?'

'Can I? Really?'

'Nope,' said Jarfin, dropping backwards on the bed, his arms wide. As he sank into the covers, Montgomery perched on the edge of the bed and took the Trypasphere from his jacket pocket.

'So what do you make of all this?' he asked, holding it up. The purple glow cast the same eerie, swirling shadows around the room. 'Why did my granddad leave me this thing in a secret Underworld tunnel?'

Jarfin sighed, sinking deeper into the bed. 'No idea. But you can bet it was for something important. What was all that stuff he wrote on that bit of paper, about the Great War?'

'Bressalan mentioned it last week,' said Montgomery. And so did his granddad in that vision, but he felt uncomfortable about sharing that with Jarfin. 'He didn't say what it was, but it doesn't sound like a good thing, does it?' Raising the Trypasphere to his eyes, he tried to look into it, to see if there was anything inside, but all he could make out was swirly purple. He waved his hand on the other side, but couldn't see it through the globe. He sighed and slipped it back into his pocket.

'Do you think we're doing the right thing?' asked Jarfin. His voice sounded worried, and Montgomery pivoted to see that he'd raised himself up on his elbows, his hair even more scruffy and sticking-up than usual.

'What do you mean?'

'This plan to ambush Atlantis,' said Jarfin. 'It all sounds a bit... *dangerous.*'

'What other option do we have? If we don't stop them here, they'll just keep heading west, taking one city after another. Better to fight them here than in Lundarien, isn't it?'

'I suppose so,' said Jarfin, twiddling the bedcovers between his fingers. 'Only... to be honest, I'd rather not fight at all.'

Montgomery raised his eyebrows at this. 'You think we should take Atlantis up on their demands? You think we should *join* them?'

'What's the worst that could happen?'

Montgomery picked up the diamond from Jarfin's bedside table to look at his face, checking he was serious. 'Are you serious?' he said. '*What's the worst that could happen? Just use your imagination, Jarfin.*'

'You think they'd be bad allies?'

'I think they'd be terrible *masters*. Do you really think, from what you've heard about Atlantis, that they have any interest in being allies?' Jarfin slumped back onto his elbows in silence. 'We have to fight them,' Montgomery continued. 'I'm certain of it.'

'It's easy for you, though,' said Jarfin, at last. 'You've got real, proper magic. You can light up diamonds and smash people into walls, cast forcefields and even turn stones into diamond.'

'But I can't actually control any of those things. You saw how rubbish I was with that stupid button!'

Jarfin sat up again, still twisting the bedcovers in his left hand. 'But the point is that you *can* do it! And when you really need it, your magic is right there, ready to protect you and duff up all the baddies.'

'*Duff up?*' Montgomery laughed.

'Yes, duff up! *You* can duff up all the baddies, while all I can do is... remember stuff. Look at me,' he said, jumping to his feet and gesturing to himself. 'I'm not big and tough, like my dad, I'm not fast and good with weapons like Clovis, and I can't Move things around like Marlah. Even Alcott would be better than me in a fight. At least he's actually strong.' Montgomery opened his mouth to make a suggestion, but couldn't actually think of any suggestions to make, so he closed his mouth and grunted instead. 'What use would *I* be in a fight, except to use my Watching to remember who hit who?'

'Have you told your dad how you feel?'

'No way!' Jarfin looked shocked at the idea. 'I don't want to let him down. I've only been his squire for a few days.'

'Why do you think you'd be letting him down? Besides, he might decide to let you stay back home in Lundarien.' Even as he said it, Montgomery realised it was the wrong thing to say.

Jarfin's scowled at him. 'You see? Even *you* don't think I'm capable of defending myself, and you're supposed to be my friend.'

'Of course I'm your friend,' said Montgomery, getting to his feet in frustration.

'Not as good a friend as your new best pal, Merek, though, eh?'

'What's *that* supposed to mean?'

'Oh, forget it,' said Jarfin, folding his arms and turning away.

Montgomery clenched his fists, trying to control his anger and calm his nerves before he accidentally blew something up. Or deliberately *duffed* someone up! He couldn't work out what Jarfin's problem was. He was only trying to help.

'Look,' he said. 'It's late. Let's just get some sleep. Things'll look better in the morning, trust me.' It was the kind of thing his Mum said, but he thought it was worth a shot.

'Fine!' said Jarfin, with his back still turned to Montgomery. He didn't sound fine.

Montgomery sighed, which grew suddenly into an enormous yawn. 'Night, then,' he said, and headed for the door.

Back in the girl's bedroom, Montgomery undressed for bed, listening to Wyndham's deep voice rumbling away from the house next door. He couldn't make out any words, but he was pleased to hear that, whatever he had said, it made Merek laugh. Hopefully the two of them were getting on a bit better. Maybe, after a day together, Wyndham would see for himself that Merek was okay; that he really had been acting under Payton's spell. Maybe he'd even let him back into Lundarien.

Smiling at the thought, Montgomery pulled back the layers of blankets that covered the bed, and got in. Being used to his duvet, the sheets felt strange and annoyingly tight, and the mattress was nowhere near as comfortable as the one in his own bedroom. It was lumpy and smelled faintly of something sweet like peach or maybe mango. But no sooner had he turned out the light, by tucking the diamond under his feather-filled pillow, than he slipped off to sleep.

The last thing he heard was the sound of Merek laughing again.

The following morning, after a breakfast of more vegetables and a few sausages, or "Scarras" as everyone else kept calling them, which Favian had found, Montgomery and the others boarded the Transak bus that was still waiting in the Great Tunnel. It was a somewhat subdued party, as everyone spent most of the time gazing out at their surroundings in silence, caught up, no doubt, with thoughts about the ambush.

The journey took a lot longer than Montgomery had

expected, especially after stopping for an hour at Salistra while Wyndham spoke with the Aristane. The others waited in the Great Tunnel and bought lunch from one of the nearby stalls, selling meat and fruits.

Eventually Lockley's goat-headed boat arrived and they set off towards Lundarien. Jarfin barely said a word to Montgomery, though he did eventually apologise for having a go at him the night before. Clovis leaned against her mother, looking tired, and even Marlah seemed withdrawn and failed to seize opportunities to be sarcastic at people. Occasionally the adults would strike up a conversation about exactly when the soldiers of Atlantis might attack Yarnock, or about who should join the fight from Lundarien and who should stay behind to guard the city. This last item was Merek's suggestion, following Payton's overthrow of the city, while Lundarien's best fighters were all inside the Labyrinth.

According to Montgomery's watch, it was just after three o'clock by the time they arrived at the Lundarien symbol carved into the tunnel wall.

'Out you get then, you miserable bunch,' said Lockley, bringing the Trago to a halt.

After the long trudge along the Lift Tunnel, Merek turned a questioning look towards Wyndham.

'So what's the deal?' he asked. 'Are you going to arrest me?'

Wyndham shook his head. 'Not today,' he said. Then, at the delighted look on Merek's face, he continued, 'That doesn't mean you're off the hook, though.'

'Too right!' said Favian, scowling at him. 'All the chances you had to let me and the other hostages go, and you did nothing!'

'But I-'

'Leave it!' said Wyndham, holding up a hand. 'For now, you're free to return to the Surface, Merek. As you can see,' he gestured to Favian's continued scowl, 'not everyone is ready to welcome you into Lundarien with open arms. But I promise, I will speak to the Novaristee on your behalf.'

Merek nodded. 'Thank you, Wyndham. You've been very gracious. Please allow me to accompany you to Yarnock when you ambush Atlantis. Let me prove myself to you and the people of Lundarien.'

Favian stepped forward, his mouth already open in protest, but Wyndham cut him off.

'We'll see, Merek. We'll see.'

After saying their goodbyes, Montgomery used his keycoin to call down the lift and the two of them stepped inside. The door slid closed, cutting off the view of the tunnel and their seven companions, and opened again a few minutes later onto the stark, concrete confines of the third floor of Montgomery's apartment block. One of the electric lights flickered.

'Right. I will catch *you* later!' said Merek, the evergreen smile back on his face. 'Off you go and face the parents.'

Montgomery shrugged, causing his bag to slip off his shoulder again. 'They think I've been at school,' he said. 'Everything'll be fine.'

But no sooner had the apartment door clicked closed behind him, than he realised everything was not going to be fine after all. He could hear his parents talking in the lounge. And just before they fell silent, he was certain he heard his headmaster's voice.

21. "I've Turned Into The Invisible Man"

Montgomery froze in the hallway. 'Hello?' he said, his voice sounding more like Gabriella's than his own. There was a pause before his dad's voice answered from the lounge.

'Could you come in here, please?' Montgomery didn't like the sound of that "please". Nor the fact that his dad was home before four o'clock again. On entering the lounge, the first person he saw was his headmaster, Mr Pemberton-Drake, standing by the sofa and sipping at a cup of tea.

'Ah, speak of the devil,' said the headmaster, clattering his cup onto its saucer, and Montgomery wondered briefly where his mum had found the fancy crockery. 'Not that you're the devil, of course. Hah! No. It's just a... a thing. You know. A saying! Speak of the devil and he... er, does something. Yes, no, a bit of truancy doesn't make you the devil. Who hasn't skipped off school now and again? I was thinking of pulling a sickie tomorrow, myself. Quite fancy a long weekend.' He hesitated, either musing on the suggested weekend or because he'd forgotten what he was supposed to be talking about. Montgomery suspected it was the latter. Mr Pemberton-Drake cleared his throat. 'But, of course, I am the headmaster. However, I'm sorry to say that truancy by pupils is somewhat frowned upon. Which is why I'm here. Hello.' He smiled at Montgomery and, though it was a friendly enough action, the looks his parents were giving him were firmly in the not-so-friendly category. At least, the look Pepper was giving him was a proper angry-mum glare. Victor, who was looking distracted and tired again, was staring out of the window.

Montgomery opened his mouth to speak, but instead he just glanced from the headmaster to his mum and back.

'Well?' said Pepper, hands on hips in the way that mums do when things aren't going to go well for whichever child it's directed at. At least she didn't call him "young man", that would be even worse. 'What have you got to say for yourself, young man?'

Montgomery stared up at the ceiling, as though he might find some handy excuse up there, or maybe a means of escape from this awful situation.

'Sorry?' he mumbled. His bag was slipping of his shoulder and he dumped it by the sofa.

'How about explaining where you've been since yesterday morning,' she suggested, eyebrows raised into perfect, black arches, 'since you clearly weren't at school or at this Julian Poore's house? And while you're at it, Mr Pemberton-Dr-'

'Oh, please, call me Trevor,' said Mr Pemberton-Drake. 'Or Trev, if you prefer.' Victor let out a snort, which he tried to disguise as a cough.

Pepper paused, forcing the edges of a smirk back into a properly stern expression. 'Your *headmaster*,' she continued, gesturing to Trev, 'also tells us you weren't in school last Thursday morning. So where have you been?'

Montgomery's brain went blank. All the possible explanations, which he had toyed with for just such an occasion as this, had vanished from his head and the only thing he could come up with was a shrug. And, 'Um...'

'Um?' said Pepper. 'Is that it? Um?

He tried out, 'I was with *friends*,' stressing the word

"friends" in an attempt to communicate to his mum that he was referring to people in the Underworld and therefore couldn't discuss it in front of his dad or his headmaster.

'Well, they're obviously not very good *friends* if they encourage you to play truant and lie to us. To say nothing of staying out overnight!'

Mr Pemberton-Drake set his cup and saucer on the coffee table and turned to Montgomery. 'I understand, lad,' he said, tucking his hands into his tweed jacket pockets. 'You may find it hard to believe, but even *I* was young once - hundreds of years ago, obviously - and I had a friend called Paul Bransleigh. We used to call him *Porker* Bransleigh what with his fat fingers and everything. Hah! Big as sausages they were! Well, me and old Porker used to play truant all the time. We'd hide out on the common or play at being soldiers round at his uncle's garage that stank of petrol and pig muck.' A far-away expression spread across his face and Montgomery got the impression the headmaster had entirely forgotten where he was. 'There was one time when we built ourselves a bivvi up in Runfold woods and spent the night sleeping in the wretched thing. Well, I say *sleeping*, but poor old Porker fell fowl of the midges and didn't get a wink. He was killed in the end. Not by the midges, of course. No. Silly fool accidentally shot himself out in the Sudan. Probably those massive fingers of his.' He lifted a hand to his face, as if to check his own fingers weren't too sausage-like. 'Yes. So, there you have it, lad,' he said, suddenly fixing Montgomery with a steely gaze. 'Probably best if you come and see me for after-school detention on Monday. It'll give you a chance to catch up on some of the work you've missed. That okay with you, Vic?'

Detention? Montgomery closed his eyes as a feeling of resentment washed over him. After all, he had spent the last two days risking his life to save people, people he cared about in the Underworld, and this was the reward he got? A stinking detention? He wished he could just disappear, make himself invisible like when Bressalan Cealed himself.

Victor blinked and looked away from the window. He hated being called "Vic". 'Er, sure,' he said, his voice not at all sure.

'Tell you what though,' said the headmaster, 'it's not like it used to be. When my father found out about Porker and me sleeping in the woods like a couple of gypsies, he brought me in and gave me a damn good thrashing. But, like I said, that was back in the olden days, when everything was in black and white.' He started laughing at himself, then stopped. In the silence, Montgomery heard his mum gasp, and Mr Pemberton-Drake said, 'I say, where the devil has he gone?'

Montgomery opened his eyes and looked up to see the headmaster peering around the room, even down the side of the sofa. Victor was also frowning around at the lounge, his eyes sweeping straight over his son.

Montgomery opened his mouth to ask what was going on, when he realised he couldn't see his own hands. Worse than that, when he looked down he couldn't see any of his body at all. He staggered backwards, bumped into the wall, narrowly missing the dresser, and was about to shout in alarm, when Pepper spoke.

'He, er… hurried off to his room. He looked a bit upset about you giving him detention.' Though the words were meant for the two men, she keep her eyes fixed on Montgomery, or rather a point about a foot to his left, giving the empty air there a warning look.

'Did he, by Jove?' said Mr Pemberton-Drake. 'Bit of a soft touch, eh? Poor lad. You know, if I had my way I'd encourage a bit of truancy now and again. Helps to get it out of a boy's system, if you know what I mean. But the law's the law and all that.' He nodded at the Vanes for while, clearly not sure what to do next. 'Right!' he said at last, all business-like. 'Best be off. Mrs P-B doesn't like it when the troops turn up late to the mess hall. Not that it's anything more than her, me and a pot of stew, you understand, but that's the way it is. Mrs Vane.' He nodded. 'Vic.' And with that he set off towards the front door, with Victor trailing behind him. Pepper, however, stayed where she was, still wearing her stern face.

She paused, just long enough to ensure the others were out of earshot, before speaking.

'How exactly are you doing that?'

'I don't know,' he said, his voice an alarmed whisper. 'What's happened to me, Mum? I've turned into the Invisible Man and I don't know how to stop it!' There was a small mirror on the kitchen wall and he headed across the room towards it, to check he really had vanished. But as he rounded the kitchen table, it was as though he stepped through some kind of visibility field and reappeared. 'I'm not invisible!' he said, peering at his relieved face in the mirror.

'What's going on?' asked Pepper. 'How on earth did you do magic in our apartment? It shouldn't be possible - the sun destroys magic!' She narrowed her eyes at him. 'What have you been up to?'

'I-' he began, but Pepper raised a hand to cut him off.

'Later,' she said, as the sound of Victor's footsteps echoed down the hallway. 'We'll talk when your father takes Gabriella to her dancing class.'

'Well, that's *Trev* gone,' said Victor, as he stepped through the doorway. 'I should probably-' He stopped, as though he'd walked into a forcefield, and stared at Montgomery, who glanced back into the mirror to check he hadn't accidentally done any more magic. 'What?' said his dad, looking at Montgomery, then bending backwards to peer down the hallway towards his bedroom door. 'How?' He stood there for an uncomfortably long time, pulling the sort of face Gabriella made when trying to work out whether she preferred fairies or the colour pink. Then he shook his head and his weary expression returned. Pulling out a chair from the dining table, he sat down and stared into the distance.

Montgomery grabbed his bag, and hurried off to the safety of his room.

'Watch!' said Montgomery, once he and his Mum had the apartment to themselves. He had spent the intervening time trying to do magic in his bedroom and had managed to do some simple Moving, like picking up a book across the room and placing it down on his bedside table. Or at least *near* his bedside table; he was still finding more precise Moving a bit difficult and a number of the pages lay crumpled across the floor.

Pepper watched as, sitting on his bed, he raised a hand towards his desk. At first nothing happened, then one of the drawers began to slide open ever so slightly. He frowned in concentration and tried to urge the drawer to open a bit quicker.

The drawer shot out from the desk as though someone had kicked it from the other side, knocking his chair over and scattering its contents all over the floor.

Pepper shook her head at the mess. 'So *that's* where you've been "tidying" everything,' she said. 'Stuffing it into your drawers, and hoping I wouldn't notice.'

'Well, it kind of worked,' said Montgomery. 'Anyway, that's not the point. The point is,' he swept a dramatic arm towards the drawer and its contents, 'I can do magic in my bedroom! You try it, Mum.'

She flashed an arched eyebrow at him, a warning

about giving her orders, but then raised her own hand towards the mess on the floor. The jumble of items rose into the air and, to Montgomery's delight, the pens and other items of not-so-stationary stationery settled into the drawer along with his books and a calculator, before it slotted itself back into the desk. At the same time, the screwed up bits of paper, old sweet wrappers and other rubbish dropped into his bin.

'Nice!' he said. 'Tidying with magic would be way more fun than-'

'-just jamming everything into a drawer?' Pepper finished. A single, inside-out sock, which had been hidden away amongst the other items bobbed away out of the door towards the bathroom, but it only got a couple of metres along the corridor before it dropped to the floor. 'What happened there?'

'I'm not entirely certain,' said Montgomery, jumping to his feet and hurrying off to fetch it. 'But for some reason, the magic only seems to work in my bedroom.'

'But you Cealed yourself out there, in the lounge.' She frowned around the room. 'It's like there's some sort of local, magical field.' She stopped as her gaze fell on Montgomery's bag. 'Is there something in there?'

Montgomery patted the bag. 'Lots of really heavy school books.'

'That's it? You didn't bring anything back from the Underworld? No magical amulets that might cast a magical sphere of influence?'

'A sphere of influence?' Montgomery tossed the sock onto his desk, where he would no doubt sweep it into a drawer later, and snatched up his bag. 'Yes, a sphere!' He rummaged around in it, heaving out the text books and dumping them onto his bed.

'Careful with those,' said Pepper. 'They belong to your school.'

'Look!' he said, lifting his hand from inside the bag. In it, casting its dark-purple shadows onto his bedroom walls, sat the Trypasphere. 'Granddad gave it to me.'

Pepper's eyes, already wide at the sight of the glowing sphere, bulged. 'Granddad? Granddad gave it to you?' She took a deep breath and sat on the edge of his bed. 'I think it's time you tell me what's been going on, don't you?'

With the sigh of a teenager being grilled when the answer "Stuff" just won't cut it, Montgomery sat in his chair and explained what he had been up to during his time off school - his visits to Lundarien, Salistra and Yarnock.

'Dinosaurs?' she said, as he relayed the story of his journey on the Transak. 'What was Wyndham thinking, letting you go in there? You could have been hurt, or buried in a pile of rocks.'

She was not pleased to hear that he nearly had been! Nor that Merek had been involved.

'What do you mean you two have been meeting up after school?' she said. 'He was one of my sister's evil henchmen!'

'Everyone keeps bringing that up,' said Montgomery, feeling defensive for his new friend. 'But not only did he think he was saving my life in the Diamond Mines, he also stopped the school bully and his gang from beating me up.' A shadow fell across Pepper's face at the mention of bullies, but she didn't make any comment. She nodded for him to continue his story.

'...after the long walk back down the tunnel to the lift,' he said, coming to a conclusion at last. 'The others carried on to Lundarien, while Merek and I came up in the lift. That's when I found you talking with Trev-'

'That's Mr Pemberton-Drake, to you!'

'-who is clearly insane!'

'True, but he's still your headmaster. Talking about

which, you know I'm going to have to ground you for at least two weeks.'

'But mu-um…'

'But nothing. It may seem unfair to punish you when you were doing what you felt was the right thing. But that's no excuse for lying to us. And when I say "ground", I mean here, on the Surface - not *under*ground! It will be good to have you at home, for dad's sake.'

Montgomery rolled his eyes. 'You keep saying that, and I've been home loads over the last week. But dad doesn't even seem to notice I'm there. He just sits and stares at nothing. He's no fun anymore.'

'Like I told you, work is very stressful at the moment.'

'Why? What's so stressful about making beer?'

Pepper sighed, getting to her feet. 'That's not the problem. The brewery has been laying people off.' Montgomery shrugged, uncertain what that meant. 'People have been losing their jobs. Like Alan, the man who owned Lizzy. And since dad only started there a couple of weeks ago, he's worried he'll be next. Not only that,' she continued, as Montgomery opened his mouth to comment, 'but his boss is not a very nice man, and… well, he's been bullying dad.'

'Bullying?' It was Montgomery's turn to get to his feet, outraged. He held up the Trypasphere. 'Let's do something about it!'

'Shhh!' Pepper waved shushing hands at him. 'Please don't say anything to dad. He doesn't want you to worry about him.' She eyed the glowing orb for a moment, the edge of a smile tugging at her lips. 'I might need to borrow that sometime, though.' She looked at Montgomery and smiled properly. 'And while there will be no more solo forays into the Underworld for you, from what I've seen of your magic, I have a feeling you may be needed to help in the defence of Yarnock.'

Montgomery brightened up considerably at this. 'Thanks, mum,' he began.

Pepper held up a hand. 'So, *I* will be coming to Yarnock with you.'

22. "I'm Picking Up A Fridge!"

'There's no such thing as a ball that lets people do magic on the Surface. It stands to reason. If it's magical, the sun will destroy its power. There's no way... Whoa!' He leapt to his feet as a number of the seed helicopter that were spinning down from the sycamore tree slowed in their descent, until they hung, motionless a few feet above the ground. A couple of nearby pigeons did that funny little half-hop half-flap they do when surprised, though this may have been a reaction to the simple fact that the grass was still green and clouds were moving overhead.

Merek's mouth hung open as the sycamore seeds began to rotate slowly around them both, then picked up speed, spinning faster and faster, until they were little more than a brown blur. Without warning they jerked away, spinning towards the boating lake before dropping, lifeless, to the ground. Merek's turned to look at Montgomery, still sitting on the park bench.

'Someone's been practising!'

Montgomery grinned, pleased at his friend's reaction. 'I have,' he said. 'All weekend, though I still find my Moving difficult to control. I didn't mean them to shoot off over there.' He pointed to where the seeds had landed.

'So, when have you been doing that? You said you were grounded.'

'I am.' Montgomery fished around in his school bag and drew out the small, glowing ball. 'Like I said, this thing we found in that cave in Yarnock makes it possible to do magic on the Surface. As long as you're not more than a few feet away from it, that is.'

Merek reached out a hand to touch it, but stopped short, his fingers poised. 'Can I give it a go?' he asked, his voice hardly more than a whisper.

'Go for it!' Montgomery stood up to check there was no one around but, except for the pigeons, who were busy being startled by the continued existence of a nearby bin, this area of the park was quite empty, well-concealed by the surrounding plants and bushes. Merek beamed. He took the Trypasphere and held out his other hand towards the bench.

Immediately, the screws that held its wooden slats in place started spinning round, undoing themselves, before clattering onto the tarmac of the path, leaving the iron sides and wooden slats to collapse unsupported. Just before they crumpled to the floor, however, they leapt up into the air and gathered in the shapes of a giant stick man, the sides forming his head and chest, the slats filling in the rest.

'Check this out,' said Merek, and Montgomery enjoyed hearing the excitement in the older boy's voice. 'Care for a dance?' The stick man started leaping about, his arms waving and his legs jerking in time to some rhythm in Merek's head. Even Merek himself was dancing on the spot, though with surprisingly less coordination than the bench-figure he was controlling. 'What?' he said, not turning to look at Montgomery, who was snorting with laughter at Merek's ridiculous attempt at dancing. Even the pigeons had bobbed over to see what was going on, seemingly unbothered by the pieces of bench spinning around over their heads.

'Nothing,' said Montgomery, between snorts.

'This is amazing!' said Merek, joining in the laughter.

'Magic on the Surface. I never thought-'

'Quick!' said Montgomery, spying movement between the bushes. 'Someone's coming.'

In an instant, the dancing figure had folded in on itself, forming a normal bench shape once again, the screws spinning themselves back into place. By the time the man rounded the corner and stepped between the bushes, Montgomery and Merek were both sitting on the bench, chatting as though nothing out of the ordinary had happened.

'I've seen that guy before,' said Montgomery, as the man walked past. 'Always carrying around that really skinny briefcase. I think he lives in my apartment.'

Merek shrugged. 'Who cares about him? What about *this*?' He held up the Trypasphere, cupped in his hand, its light reflected in his eyes. 'It's awesome! Just imagine being able to do magic up here on the Surface any time you fancied.'

'I was hoping to use it to practice my Moving and other magic, since I've been grounded from going to Lundarien.'

A shadow passed across Merek's usually cheerful face. 'Not nice being exiled, is it?' He paused, then brightened up suddenly. 'Here's an idea. How about *I* give you a hand with your magic? Well, with your Moving, anyway?'

'When?' asked Montgomery. 'I'm grounded, remember? And I don't think my mum would be keen on you coming to our flat.'

'Apartment,' Merek corrected him. 'We'll just have to grab whatever time we can when you're on your way home after school.'

'That won't give us much time. The only reason I've got time now is because the headmaster let me out of detention early. I think he forgot what I was still doing there!'

'I've got it!' said Merek, jumping to his feet again. 'Just tell your parents your headmaster decided to extend your detention to every day this week. After all, you did skive off for three days. You'd have got that and worse at my old school.'

'It was only two and a half days, actually.' Montgomery considered Merek's suggestion. It was pretty good as far as plans went, and would give them at least three-quarters of an hour each day to work on his Moving. And after watching Merek's dancing benchman, he wanted more than ever to improve his skills. But that would mean lying to his mum again, and he didn't feel comfortable about that. Not after last Friday. 'I'll think of something,' he said, picking up his bag and hooking the strap over his shoulder. 'Now I should get going.'

'Don't forget this,' said Merek, tossing him the Trypasphere. Montgomery had never been much of a catcher, and he was sure it was going to smash on the ground. But the glowing orb never even made it to his fumbling fingers. Instead it hovered in front of him. He reached out to take hold of it, but it bobbed away out of reach.

'Funny.'

'Sorry,' said Merek. 'I couldn't resist'. The Trypasphere floated back and Montgomery went to grab it. It bobbed away again, much to Merek's amusement. 'Here,' he said, the orb floating into Montgomery's outstretched hand. 'And you'll be wanting this too.'

Montgomery looked up to see Merek holding out a keycoin. It was the spare one that sent his lift into the Underworld.

'Nah,' he said, shrugging his left shoulder as she stuffed the Trypasphere into his bag. 'Why don't you keep hold of it for now? My mum and I can share. Anyway, I'm grounded, remember? At least you can go back down if you want.'

'And be welcomed into Lundarien with open arms, no doubt!'

Pepper was busy washing up in the kitchen when Montgomery walked in and, since Gabriella was sitting with her nose almost pressed against the television screen with the volume turned up ludicrously high, he decided to tackle the issue of the after school Moving lessons. *Without* lying. Instead, he'd just come straight out and ask if he could meet up with Merek on his way home. There just might be a chance she'd agree.

'Not a chance,' said Pepper, not even bothering to turn round from the sink.

'What? Why not?'

'Because you're grounded, which means that, if you're not at school, you're here. At home. Where I can keep an eye on you.' She turned briefly, pointing to her eye and getting bubbles on her cheek. 'And anyway, I don't trust that Merek.'

'I know you don't, but he is amazing at Moving, and the more practice I can get in before Saturday,' he checked quickly that his sister couldn't hear, but she was still gripped in the television's colourful claws, 'the better, surely? *You* haven't got time to teach me, have you? You're always super-busy before dad gets home, if he actually turns up before midnight, and then… well, dad's around.'

'Your father likes to have the dinner under way and the house looking nice and tidy when he gets in from work.'

Montgomery, who didn't really care right now about what his dad did or didn't like, banged his bag down on the table. 'I was going to lie to you.' He paused to let this sink in, and Pepper turned to face him, a dripping pan in one hand. 'I was going to tell you that the headmaster had given me detention after school all week, so I could sneak off to have lessons with Merek.' Pepper frowned, but didn't interrupt. 'And it would've worked, too. But instead I decided to tell you the truth, to ask for your permission instead sneaking around behind your back. And once again you don't even bother to listen to what I'm saying, because you've already made up your mind. You and dad are always going on about how lies just get you into trouble, and that the truth is always rewarded. Well, go on then. Here's your chance. Why don't you *prove* it?' He stopped, his heart thumping after this outburst.

Pepper continued to frown at him, while in the background the television filled the air with the sound of cartoons.

At last, after what seemed to Montgomery like slightly longer than forever, Pepper pushed a stray strand of black hair away from her eyes with the pan handle, getting bubbles on her forehead, and spoke. 'I want you back home no later than half past four, do you understand?'

Montgomery almost hugged her. But he was thirteen years old, so he just smiled instead. 'Yes. Thanks, mum.'

'Don't thank me,' she said, turning back to the washing up. 'Instead, you can get on with tidying up the toys from in front of the sofa. And turn that telly down!'

On Tuesday, after school, Montgomery and Merek hung out in the yard of one of the local churches, one of the old ones with a steeple and walls like a medieval castle. Tall, dark windows glared, unseeingly, from the stonework, and water dripped from leaking gutters, green with moss and overgrown with ferns. A sign on the door said there were coffee mornings every Tuesday, but it looked to Montgomery as though no one *ever* went there. It was the perfect place for practicing magic as the yard was blocked from view by the church and an overgrown hedge.

Merek turned out to be a good teacher, explaining how he did various Moves to Montgomery in a way that actually made sense.

'Marlah and Vala,' said Montgomery, ignoring the accidental rhyme, 'both told me I have to *will* the object and see it Moving in my mind.'

Merek shrugged. 'Did it work?'

'Not really. I accidentally blew up a pot and then turned one of the cobblestones into a diamond while trying to Move a button.'

'A button?' Merek laughed. 'Why didn't they just get you to try a grain of sand?' Montgomery made a *huh* sound. 'That's no way to build up your confidence. Start big, that's what I say. Like Moving *that* thing!' He pointed to the corner of the churchyard, where someone had dumped a broken fridge.

Montgomery stared at it, eyebrows raised. 'Well, it's certainly bigger than a button!'

'You bet it is! Right, this is how you're going to Move it, okay? Firstly, take a good, strong stance.' He demonstrated, planting his feet shoulder-width apart, his shoulders square, facing the fridge. 'Get a good fix on it.' He narrowed his eyes. 'Reach out your hand to hold it, like the fridge is right here in front of you.' He did so, as if wrapping his fingers around a small item nearby, rather than a large one a long way off. 'Then pick it up. Don't *think* about picking it up. Actually pick it up!' The fridge rose into the air, a foot or so off the ground. 'Once you've got it you can do whatever you want with it.' It started spinning across the yard, faster and faster, causing the door to swing open and a broken drawer to fly out. There was still an old milk carton jammed inside the door. 'Your go,' said Merek, dropping it back into the corner onto a handy mattress.

Montgomery stood next to him, his school bag with the Trypasphere in the middle of the yard, its sphere of influence just wide enough to cover them and the fridge.

'Stance!' said Merek. Montgomery took up a similar posture to Merek's, though he felt a bit silly. 'Now, get a fix on it!' He focussed on the dirty, cream-coloured object, trying to block out everything else in the yard. 'Take hold of it!' He reached up to where the fridge sat in his line of sight and curled his fingers around it. There was a pause. 'Well, go on then, you numpty. Pick it up!' Montgomery raised his hand as though lifting the fridge from the ground and, to his amazement, the fridge moved with it, scraping noisily up the far wall.

'I'm doing it!' he said, his eyes wide. 'I'm picking up a fridge!'

Beside him Merek nodded his appreciation. 'Give it a spin, then.'

'How…?'

Merek lifted up a hand as though gripping something invisible. 'Imagine I've got a ball in my hand. I'd spin it like this.' He flicked his wrist as one would when spinning a real ball. 'You could do that, right?'

'Ye-es.' Montgomery was hesitant, wondering what was coming next.

Merek pointed at where the fridge was floating, halfway up the wall. 'Do it then. Just spin that fridge like it's a ball in your hand.' Montgomery hesitated, steeling himself. 'Don't think about it. Just do it!'

The fridge pin-wheeled across the churchyard and smashed into the hedge.

'I did it!' he shouted, pointing at the fridge in case Merek had missed it.

Merek dropped a hand on his shoulder. 'It's a good start. Now let's see you do it again.'

As they sneaked back out onto the street half an hour

later, Montgomery had a big grin all over his face.

'That was amazing!' he said. 'Who taught you how to do all that?'

Merek laughed. 'Would it annoy you to know it was your aunt?' Montgomery shrugged, his mood untouchable, even by the mention of Payton. 'She just had a knack of explaining magic. All I did was teach you what she taught me. Same time again tomorrow?'

'You bet!' said Montgomery. He gave Merek a quick wave and headed home, beaming all the way.

23. "It'll Be Over Before You Know It"

Every day for the rest of the week, Montgomery met up with Merek after school and practised Moving in the churchyard. It was by far his favourite lesson of the day, especially on Thursday, when his school timetable consisted of double French, Maths and PE, which Montgomery reckoned stood for "Painful Endurance" as it consisted almost entirely of running about in the chilly sports field in shorts and a t-shirt, followed by a burning hot shower.

The best bit about Moving was seeing how much he progressed. On the Wednesday, they worked on lifting and turning not just one object, but five at once, even objects of different sizes. On the Thursday, he Moved the fridge around in more difficult motions, opening and shutting the door in mid air, even slotting the shelves and the drawers in and out, though the first few times he accidentally punched the shelves straight through the back of the fridge. And on the Friday, he performed these complex movements with other objects, such as opening his bag, lifting out his text books one by one and stacking them on the fridge, opening a pack of cards Merek had brought along and arranging the cards by suit, and even attempting to move a few things with his eyes shut and without using his hands, though that was much more difficult.

And all the while, Merek spurred him on, reminding

Montgomery of the amazing Moving he'd done so far, and occasionally shouting at him, startling him into action, like starting a car by giving it a good shove.

'You know what?' said Merek, as the two of them emerged from the churchyard on the Friday. 'You've picked up this Moving stuff about ten times faster than I did, and everyone told me I was proper quick.'

'Everyone?' asked Montgomery, realising he must be talking about Payton's other rebels, the ones whose defeat he had caused.

Merek flapped a hand as if the "everyone" were there in front of them. 'You know - Payton, Tolliver, that lot. Whatever happened to him, by the way?'

'Tolliver? *My aunt* happened to him, that's what! He ended up with a broken arm, fractured ribs and a bust up nose after Payton dropped him onto the cobbles from about ten metres in the air. Luckily for him, the Healers were willing to fix him up before they exiled him. After that…?' he shrugged to show he didn't know, 'I don't know.'

They headed across the square together, lost in their own thoughts, before Merek spoke again. 'You looking forward to going back to Yarnock tomorrow?'

'I'm not sure I'm "looking forward" to it,' said Montgomery, who had told Merek about Vala's appearance on his television the night before, insisting he and Pepper be ready to leave by the fourth hour of the day. 'In fact, I feel a bit nervous whenever I think about tackling these Atlanteans. They sound proper evil.' He stopped and turned to Merek. 'You're coming though, aren't you?'

It was Merek's turn to shrug. 'If your mate the Watchman lets me.'

'I'm sure Wyndham will be glad of the help.'

'We don't need your help, Merek!' Bancroft jabbed a finger into Merek's leather-jacketed chest, pushing him back towards the Town Hall doors.

Montgomery had left the apartment at half past eight, early for a Saturday morning, after Pepper had informed Victor they were going out to "spend some time together".

'Isn't that a bit like lying, mum?' said Montgomery as the lift slid down into the bedrock beneath London.

Pepper gave him one of her looks, the one with the raised eyebrows and pursed lips. 'That's enough cheek from you, thank you.'

When the lift opened, they found Merek waiting for them in tunnel. He smiled lopsidedly, looking slightly nervous to see Pepper.

'I don't know whether to thank you or thump you,' she said, snatching the keycoin from the air as it shot from the lift panel.

'Might I take the first option?' asked Merek.

Pepper fixed him with another of her looks, the one that always made Montgomery feel like she was reading his mind. 'How about I do neither and instead, let's try to leave the past in the past. Okay?' She gave Merek a brief smile and he nodded his agreement. 'Come on, then.'

The Lundarien Town Square was already crowded by the time they arrived, and the three of them wove their way through the press of bodies towards the Town Hall, faces turning to watch them, conversations dying in their wake. And then, as they mounted the steps to the Town Hall, Bancroft almost launched himself at Merek.

'Come on, Bancroft,' said Pepper. 'I know Merek didn't get off to a good start here, but he's only trying to make up for it.'

Bancroft stared at her as though he thought she'd gone mad. '*Didn't get off to a good start?* This boy,' he jabbed

Merek again, 'was one of your sister's right hand men. Or have you forgotten that he,' another jab, 'and his cronies attacked our people, including almost cracking my wife's head open with a rolling pin? Is your memory so short?'

Pepper opened her mouth, but Wyndham got in first. 'That's enough, Bancroft. Remember what I told you, the lad was acting under Payton's spell. We can't blame him for that any more than we could blame the hostages for being kidnapped. Don't forget that Merek saved Montgomery here from being crushed to death in the diamond minds. Or, at least, he believed he did. Risking his own life in the process!'

'But you can't seriously trust him to join us in our battle with Atlantis?'

'Trust?' Wyndham turned to Merek, who was wearing a suitably innocent expression. 'I'm willing to give the lad a chance. He can hardly make the situation any worse than it already is.'

'Well I say he shouldn't go!' said Bancroft, folding his arms to make the point.

'And *I* say he should,' said Montgomery, stepping forwards and surprising even himself at the force of his statement. 'Not just because of the Diamond Mines or because he scared off a gang of bullies who were going to beat me up. I say he should go because he's proved himself to be a friend. A *good* friend.' He paused, concentrating on a number of objects nearby before continuing. 'Plus, he's been teaching me how to do *this*.'

Wyndham flinched as the short sword hooked through his belt whipped out and swung around in the air above him. At the end of the steps, the small, iron statue of a Lundarien lion leapt forwards into the crowd, while from the lake a snakelike column of water burst from the surface, reaching out towards the crowd. In the middle of the Square, the wooden bench shot up into the air, sending birds flapping from the trees above, before smashing into splinters on the cobbles.

Pepper placed a hand on Montgomery's shoulder. 'I think you've made your point,' she said.

Montgomery nodded, returning the water to the lake and the lion to its plinth, while the short sword floated gently back down to Wyndham.

'If Merek doesn't go,' said Montgomery, jabbing his own finger in Merek's direction, 'I don't go!'

Wyndham plucked the sword from the air as it hovered in front of him and slid it back into his belt. 'Well, I'm glad that's settled,' he said at last. 'But while I'm happy to give you another chance, know this.' He turned to fix Merek with an impressive glare. 'If you set one foot out of line or put any of our people at risk, you'll know about it. And fast!' He looked back at Montgomery. 'Happy?'

'Yep,' said Montgomery. 'And sorry about the bench. That was an accident.'

Wyndham nodded while, behind him, Bancroft muttered something cross-sounding under his breath and stalked away.

'Well, *that* went much better than I expected,' said Merek, stepping away from the wall. 'Imagine how much worse that would have been if I *hadn't* saved you in those mines!'

The Lundarien army soared along the Great Tunnel towards Yarnock on an assortment of various objects, including two iron beds, without mattresses, a circular dining table which had lost most of its varnish, a strange contraption that looked like a pile of bicycle parts strapped together, and a broomstick, which Montgomery was keen to point out to Marlah. And, of course, Lockley's boat. Montgomery reckoned there were about seventy people in all, half as many people as had raided Payton's lair in the Labyrinth; the Novaristee hadn't made the mistake of leaving the city unprotected *this* time!

Although they were heading to battle against a fearsome enemy, the people chattered excitedly, voices raised as they shouted across the Transak, calling out taunts and challenges to each other, more like children on a school outing than adults heading to war. Despite the slightly sick feeling in his stomach, Montgomery enjoyed telling his Underworld friends about his Moving lessons in the churchyard, with occasional interruptions and corrections from Merek. Jarfin seemed surprisingly uninterested, while Marlah just rolled her eyes and looked annoyed. Even Pepper joined in the chatter, though the snatches of her conversation that drifted across to Montgomery were mostly having a go at Wyndham for taking Montgomery to Yarnock overnight without her permission.

The party became more subdued as they neared their destination and, when they pulled over about a quarter of a mile from the cavern, where a handy side tunnel offered a place for the Transak vehicles to be hidden, they were almost silent.

Wyndham led them to the entrance to Yarnock, where two of the Salistran policemen were standing on guard, accompanied by Garrick.

'About time too!' he called, beckoning furiously. 'Come on. Everyone else is already here and our scouts have reported that the Atlanteans are less than an hour away.'

As soon as they were all inside, the policemen turned and headed into the Yarnock cavern. Garrick strode along after them, snapping his fingers with a loud click as he did so. Behind him, the entrance to the Great Tunnel folded in on itself, becoming a solid rock wall.

'Show off!' whispered Merek, as he and Montgomery followed Garrick across the cavern. Despite his mounting nerves, Montgomery grinned.

'We're sticking to the plan, I take it?' said Wyndham, striding along next to the Arister.

Garrick nodded. 'Of course. Anselm and I will give the signal and open portals, but not until the whole Atlantean army is in the main cavern. That is imperative. We don't want any to escape our little trap. Quickly now, get your people inside.'

They had reached the nearest entrance to the Crescent Tunnel and Wyndham held Montgomery, Pepper and Merek back as he waved the other Lundariens through, patting some encouragingly on the shoulder as they went past. Montgomery spotted many of the usual adults, like Favian and Catrain, but also some he hadn't seen for a while, like Yedda, Marlah's mother, and the bearded figure of Medway Soames, the man he'd seen kidnapped the night he first came to the Underworld. Emony Ellendrie was also there, her purple eyes narrowed in concentration. Clovis waved at him as she followed her mum.

'Right,' said Wyndham, as the last of the Lundariens made her way inside. 'Merek, I want you here at the front with me. Pepper, you head through to the centre of the tunnel with Montgomery. Hopefully the Atlanteans will be dealt with before they get that far, but you'll be able to use your Moving and whatever else you've got from there.'

Montgomery looked at Merek, who was peering over the heads of those behind. 'Good luck!' he said.

Merek punched a fist into the palm of his other hand. 'We don't need luck,' he said. 'It'll be over before you know it!'

Montgomery turned and followed Pepper through the glittering sea of diamonds that hung from hundreds of necks, the combined might of Salistra, Lundarien and the western colonies whose cities had been taken over by the people of Atlantis. The silence of the assembled army was eerie and, as Montgomery watched Garrick use the keycoin to seal up the entrance, a wave of panic washed over him. This was it! The ambush was really going to happen and here he was, a school kid from London stuck right in the middle of it. What was he doing?

He was distracted by a strange, bluish glow coming from the rock wall that separated this tunnel from Yarnock. The glow spread outwards to the left and right, and seemed to be eating its way through the wall.

'What's that?' he whispered to Pepper.

She shook her head. 'I'm not sure. I've not seen anything like it before.'

'It's a One-Way-Window,' said a voice from nearby, and Montgomery was surprised to see Marlah giving him one of her know-it-all looks.

'Know it all!' said Montgomery. 'What is it then?'

'I'd have thought that was obvious.' She pointed to the One-Way-Window which now just looked like a big hole cut through the rock. Montgomery could see the city cavern spread out beyond. It reminded him of the thick glass of the viewing area at an aquarium he had visited a couple of years ago - one of Victor's surprise family outings.

'But won't the Atlanteans see us?' he asked.

Marlah gave him the look again. 'Um, it's called a *One-Way-Window*, so...?' Montgomery raised expectant eyebrows at her. She sighed. 'It only lets us see from this side. From the other side, it's just a rock wall, same as ever.'

'Oh! Like a one-way mirror? We have them on the Surface.'

'A one-way mirror?' Marlah gave him a pitying look.

'You do talk rubbish sometimes.'

To Montgomery's relief, someone shushed them. He looked around again at the hundreds of diamonds. It was like standing inside a clear, night sky, or at least the sky in the country, not in London where the street lights eclipsed the stars. Time seemed to move much slower in the silent tunnel. Either that or the Atlanteans were taking their time getting to Yarnock. But then, just when Montgomery had decided they'd either gone straight past and headed to Salistra or they'd decided to leave the attack until another day, he heard Garrick whisper.

'Here they come.' After the eternal silence it sounded as loud as one of Gabriella's television programmes. For a moment, the diamonds shimmered and danced as people shifted into position, getting ready for the moment when the entrances were opened and they stormed into the cavern. Then silence and stillness fell once again.

Montgomery stood on tiptoes to see through the One-Way-Window and, with a start, he caught sight of a single, black-clad figure as it emerged from among the buildings on the far side of cavern, its robes swirling around it like shadows. The figure crept stealthily through the silent streets, its head constantly shifting to peer in all directions as it passed the lake, heading towards Montgomery. As it neared, the Atlantean's hood slipped back, and Montgomery looked, for the first time, on the face of the enemy.

It was a man, and he was every bit as fearsome as Bressalan had claimed. Every inch of his face was covered in a network of tattoos, but not like any that Montgomery had seen before. These were more than lines of ink; they glowed a deep red, as though the man's skin was cracking, breaking apart to reveal a sea of fiery lava below. Worse than the tattoos, though, were the eyes. They didn't even *look* like eyes - more like yawning pits in the man's face, holes that bored through to the dead, empty darkness of space, made all the more monstrous by the bone-white pallor of the man's skin. And, as Montgomery's heart started beating faster, pumping what felt like ice around his body, the man turned his head and those eyes were suddenly looking straight into his own.

Montgomery stepped backwards in alarm, pushing his way towards the rear wall of the tunnel. Sweat prickled his forehead and he nearly cried out as he backed into one of the stalagmites. Around him others also stirred and Garrick's whispered voice cut again across the tunnel.

'Hold still! There's only one, so far. The rest will be along soon enough.'

Montgomery tried to steady his breathing. The narrow tunnel stretched away in front and behind him, filled with the hoards of men and women crouching in the dim glow of the diamonds that hung from their necks. Not one of them made a sound, they barely seemed even to breathe, as they poised, waiting for the signal. Montgomery leant back against the stalactite, one of the many that lined the cavern wall, jutting up from the ground like the fossilised teeth of some vast Underworld monster.

'How long?' he whispered into the darkness, barely audible over the rapid thundering of his heart. There was no reply. There was only the expectant silence of the waiting army.

He sensed a movement behind him, as though the rock had shifted slightly, and he turned to look, to peer into the shadows beyond, but there was nothing there, only the solid tunnel wall.

Again, he felt something move against him, and he stepped back in confusion, unable to make sense of what he was seeing. The rock was moving, coming to life, unfolding itself like a waking troll, human features melting into its surface. From somewhere fingers snatched at him, at his clothes, his arms, his face. He opened his mouth to cry out, to warn the others, but a hand clamped across it, stifling not only the words but his breath as well. Black, sunken eyes looked into his own. White lips drew apart to reveal sharpened teeth.

'I have you!' said a woman's voice and, as Montgomery struggled in her grip, he saw more figures emerging from the darkness. He stared so hard at the shifting shadows that it hurt his eyes, and he could see far more of the pointy rocks than there had been the week before. And then he realised the truth. They weren't rocks at all.

It was the army of Atlantis.

24. "We Bring War"

After the long silence, the roar that echoed through the Crescent Tunnel was deafening, sending shock waves of confusion and panic through the waiting armies of Brytellian. Their focus had been on the Atlanteans in the cavern beyond, but they were suddenly and startlingly aware that the enemy was already here in their midst.

Montgomery, still locked in the clutches of the Atlantean woman, struggled to make out what was going on in the diamond-strewn darkness behind him, but it didn't sound good. The frightened yells and panicked screams were all coming from the Brytellian side, while the soldiers of Atlantis swept through their midst, weaving their magical armoury as they went, binding, stunning, blasting.

'Enough of this struggling,' said the Atlantean, baring her pointed teeth in Montgomery's face. Her voice was harsh and heavily accented, though Montgomery couldn't place it. 'Any more and I will make sure you don't struggle no more!'

From the corner of his left eye, he saw light flooding into the tunnel, and he twisted his head to look. The tunnel entrances had been opened, and the Atlanteans that were now massing the main cavern were flooding in, blocking any escape and forcing the Lundariens and their allies back into the tunnel. They were surrounded.

Montgomery tried again to wrench himself out of the

Atlantean's grip. If only he could get an arm free, he could try Moving something, maybe even the real stalagmites themselves, but the woman's grip was too strong. Releasing Montgomery's mouth, she raised her hand, a strange blue light pulsing in her palm.

'I warned you,' she said. The woman pressed her hand against Montgomery's forehead and he was swallowed up by a sea of blue.

He was floating, suspended in something like, but not quite, water. It was warm and soothing. Turning his head in a slow, lazy arc revealed nothing but the blue, above, below and all around. In the back of his mind, a small voice was shouting about something, something that was wrong, but he ignored it. There were no troubles here. Let others worry about the wrongness, he would just hang around here, drifting in the warm whatever it was. Something nudged at his arm, but when he peered down, he saw nothing, only the blue. Again the nudge. Maybe it was the blue itself, nuzzling up against him. Yes, that would be it.

Somewhere in the distance, beyond his limited vision, he could hear someone saying his name - quiet at first, but then louder, over and over again, invading the calm tranquillity of his warm, blue sea.

'Montgomery!'

The urge to breathe blossomed in his chest, uncomfortable and alien. Looking up he saw no end to the blue. It stretched away into the distance, and he was desperate for air, his lungs pleading with him to give in and breathe.

'Montgomery!'

His chest felt like it was on fire. He began thrashing around, trying to get away, but it made no difference. In all directions, the blue was total.

'Montgomery!'

He could hold his breath no longer. He couldn't fight it. He had to breathe. He opened his mouth and sucked in...

'Montgomery!'

...air! He burst awake, jerking into a sitting up position, coughing and dragging air into his aching lungs.

'Thank goodness!' said a voice, and he turned to see Pepper sitting next to him. She put her arm across his shoulders, hugging him to her. 'I was afraid you were never going to wake up.'

'Mum!' said Montgomery, shrugging off her arm, embarrassed at who might see. He was breathing heavily, confused by the strange surroundings and absence of the blue world he had been trapped in.

It took him a moment to realise he was back in Yarnock's cobbled square. Clustered around him, sitting or lying on the ground, was the rest of the Brytellian army.

'What...?' he began and paused to catch his breath. 'What happened here? Did we win?'

'Have a look around,' said Marlah, sitting on his other side. 'What do you think? And you can let go of my arm, now.'

He glanced down at his hand, surprised to find he was gripping her quite hard, and let go. It was then, as he turned to look around the cavern, that he noticed the ranks of black-robed Atlanteans that surrounded the square, strange looking weapons at the ready, dark eyes fixed on their prisoners. Prisoners?

'Ah!' he said. 'I guess we lost.'

'Exactly. We didn't stand a chance.'

'They knew we were coming,' said Jarfin, who was sitting cross-legged behind him, leaning against Wyndham. 'They ambushed us in the tunnel. Someone must have told them!'

'Really?' said Marlah, in her usual sarcastic tone. 'You think so, do you? Well, at least they didn't actually kill anyone.'

'They *didn't?*' Montgomery turned to look at the others sitting behind him. The faces he could see all looked miserable and, in some cases, as though they were going to be sick, but most of them seemed unhurt. Medway Soames had a nasty-looking gash across his forehead, a line of blood trickling down to his huge beard, but he appeared not to have noticed. Montgomery blinked as he caught sight of the person sitting behind Medway. It was Garrick and, unlike everyone else around him, he had a serene, almost pleased, smile on his face, as though he'd just recalled some pleasant memory. 'Have you ever seen that Garrick bloke smile?' asked Montgomery, turning back to Jarfin, his voice hushed. Jarfin shook his head.

'He doesn't seem the smiley type,' said Marlah.

'Well he's smiling now!' Montgomery jerked his head in Garrick's direction. The others peered round. 'You don't reckon *he* was behind our ambush being… ambushed, do you?'

'What?' Jarfin frowned and spread out his hands, palms upwards. 'Why would he do that? It makes no sense.'

Montgomery scratched his head. 'I don't know. Maybe he made a deal with Atlantis so they wouldn't attack Salistra? I wouldn't put it past-'

'You!'

Montgomery span round to see who had spoken. A few yards away, the ring of Atlanteans parted and the most aggressively-dressed man he had ever seen stepped through the gap into the Square. Or rather his bearers stepped into the Square. The man himself lounged in an enormous, black seat, which they were carrying. Montgomery decided this had to be Kuruk, the leader of

Atlantis, since he wore a crown of twisted, golden spikes, and his night-black robes were especially ornate, laced with purple and gold, with plumes of dark, peacock-like feather woven into his hair. And that seat definitely looked like a throne. Its sides were a mass of carvings depicting medieval-looking weapons interspersed with faces in various states of rage and terror. Its two arms ended with the heads of snakes, their fanged jaws open as if caught in mid-strike. It appeared to be made of stone and Montgomery was amazed the four bearers could hold it up, until he realised their hands weren't actually touching it. Instead it floated a couple of inches above, reminding Montgomery of the floating plank that had let him spy on the Novaristee.

On the throne, Kuruk stirred, leaning forward to peer down with his pitiless, black eyes at the defeated crowd. He smiled a mouthful of teeth, all of which had been sharpened, and lifted his hand to point a single, inch-long fingernail directly at Montgomery. The mouth opened and barked out a sound that didn't sound quite like a real word, and a woman stepped out from behind the throne.

'Yes,' she said, and Montgomery started as he recognised her as the woman who had attacked him in the Crescent Tunnel. 'You! Come here!' Montgomery swallowed and, his mouth suddenly very dry, began to climb to his feet. 'Not you, chid!' shouted the woman, stepping aside to point past him. 'You!'

Montgomery turned to see someone else, a couple of metres behind him, getting to his feet.

It was Merek.

'No!' said Montgomery, standing up fully and turning back to face Kuruk. 'Not Merek! What do you want *him* for? Take me, instead.' He looked at the woman. 'Tell him!'

Kuruk, still leaning forward in his throne, made a

swatting motion with his hand. He opened his mouth again and more, dog-like sounds erupted.

The woman spat out a command. 'Sit down, little boy! I will not tell you again.'

Montgomery opened his mouth to argue, but a hand fell on his shoulder and he turned to see Merek, shaking his head, a look on his face that Montgomery couldn't quite work out, a mixture of sadness, resignation and relief.

'It's okay, my friend,' said Merek, pushing him down gently. 'Trust me. All is not as it appears.'

Glowering at the woman, Montgomery sat down as Merek stepped past and headed towards the Atlantean leader. Kuruk gestured to one of the nearby guards, growling out more of his strange sounds at the man. The guard hurried off, returning, to Montgomery's amazement, with his school bag. Kuruk snatched it from him and peered at the bag, turning it over in his hands as if looking for a way in. He paused, slipping a sharp-looking knife from his sleeve and slashed it open. Stuffing his hand inside, Kuruk rummaged about, flinging an occasional school book out onto the cobbles. When eventually he withdraw his hand, he was clutching the Trypasphere. He held it up to the light of one of Yarnock's diamonds, studying it, before turning to Merek. He didn't look impressed. Nor did his voice.

'This is the thing?' the woman translated. 'His Lordship asks what it is.'

'It's nothing really,' said Merek. 'Just a bauble, nothing more. But it's precious to me, you understand? It belongs to someone I care about.'

Kuruk narrowed his eyes, still turning the Trypasphere over in his hand, and looked for a moment as if he was about question him further.

Merek looked at the woman. 'We had a deal,' he said,

a note of concern edging into his voice. The woman made no response. Suddenly, Kuruk laughed, a grating, unfriendly sound, and tossed the Trypasphere to Merek, who caught it easily and slipped it into his jacket pocket.

And then it dawned on Montgomery what as going on. With a sick feeling in his stomach, he understood what "deal" Merek had made with Kuruk and the Atlanteans. He had betrayed him.

Merek had betrayed them all.

'No!' he said, his voice barely more than a whisper, while the growled murmurs of the Lundariens grew around him. Loudest of all was Wyndham. Montgomery peered over his shoulder at him and was worried that Wyndham would launch himself at Merek.

Kuruk's eyes snapped back round to Montgomery, and he murmured something, which the woman, again, translated.

'Now you have your payment,' she said, directing her words at Merek, 'his Lordship suggests you get away from here. If these people get hold of you, there will not be enough left to fill this puny sack.' Kuruk held up Montgomery's bag again, before tossing it aside with a snort. A Chemistry text book flopped out, falling open on a diagram of the periodic table.

Merek glanced briefly at the sea of hostile faces, said, 'Remember what I told you!' to Montgomery, and hurried away towards the northern portal and the Great Tunnel beyond, the growls and murmurs of the crowd chasing him all the way.

'And as for you,' said the woman, as Kuruk directed his words at them again, 'we have for you a message to take to Salistra. *Join us,*' Kuruk placed a hand on his chest, his nails digging into his skin, *'or we will destroy your precious capital.*' He paused and looked across the seated crowd as this sank in before his jagged words continued, followed by the woman's translation. 'Do not look so surprised. You are aware we gave this same message to these other cities. Even to some of you who are sitting here.' Kuruk waved one thin, white hand. 'Do not make the same mistake *they* have done!'

'Excuse me?' Montgomery peered around for the source of the voice and caught sight of Anselm creaking slowly to his feet. One of his eyes was half closed, surrounded by a fierce-looking bruise. Kuruk glared at him, but said nothing. 'May I ask for a point of clarification? Only, it wasn't clear if you were expecting us to join you *now*, or that we should take your message back to Salistra first.'

Kuruk turned and nodded at the woman, and she took a few steps towards Anselm.

'Just for you, old man,' she said, her black eyes narrowed, 'I will explain once more. You are to take our message back to your capital city, to your chiefs and clan leaders. Tell them you must join us in the Great War that is to come... or you know what must happen next.'

'Thank you.' Anselm nodded graciously, then fixed her with an equally calculating glare. 'And who are you, exactly?'

'I am Rayen, Supreme Chancellor to his lordship, King Kuruk, Master of the Sceptred-'

'Yes, we are aware who your master is, Rayen. And how long will you give us to make our decision?'

Rayen and Kuruk exchanged a few brief words in that same harsh language, before she turned back to Anselm, looking him up and down slowly. 'We will give you time, old man. Time enough to drag your old bones to Salistra and speak with your people. And I suggest you make the wise choice; you cannot hope to beat Kuruk's mighty army.' She swung out an arm to indicate the guards and, in terrifying unison, they barked out a single, unintelligible shout. 'Nor can you hope to face the coming war without us.'

Again Kuruk spoke from his throne, his bony fingers gripping the carved serpent heads, and Rayen continued, 'To help you make the right choice, we will of course take a couple of hostages.'

'Why?' asked Anselm. 'If you come in peace, why take hostages?'

Kuruk laughed again, and Rayen said, 'What makes you think we come in peace? We come with the sword, with fire and with magic. We bring war and none will stand against us!' Again a great shout went up from the assembled Atlanteans, and as their shouts died away, Kuruk raised a finger, directing it at Montgomery. 'His Lordship,' said Rayen, 'will take this boy here, since he has proved so keen to offer himself up.'

Montgomery froze, his stomach turning to ice. Next to him, Pepper's hand tightened around his arm and she was about to speak when another voice spoke up from behind them.

'*This* boy?' it said, and Montgomery turned to see Garrick had got to his feet and was gesturing towards him. 'Do you mean to insult us, Kuruk? He is nothing more than some western urchin. He is of no worth either to Salistra or to Atlantis. Forget about this boy. If you wish to take a hostage, *I*,' he pressed a hand to his own chest, 'am the perfect choice. I am an Arister, of the Salistran Aristane, ruler of the City of the Seven Caverns. Take me, and only me, rather than some nobody from the filthy outskirts of Brytellian.' He turned as he gestured to Montgomery and, for the smallest flicker of a second, he winked. 'I, Garrick Vospen, am all the hostage you require.'

Kuruk leaned forwards, fixing his dark eyes on Garrick, his lip curling back in a silent snarl. 'Very well,' said Rayen, at last, and she waved a hand to one of the guards. 'Take the Arister away and put him with the others.' The guard strode forward and made to seize Garrick's arm, but as his sharp nails drew near, there was a sound like the fizz of electricity and he snatched his hand back.

'I can walk perfectly well, thank you,' said Garrick, stepping imperiously past the guard, who was still clutching his smoking fingers.

Kuruk laughed again, then waved a hand at the others in the Square.

'The rest of you may leave,' said Rayen, as she advanced on Garrick, her palm glowing with a bright, blue light. 'We will meet again soon.'

25. "What's The Opposite Of Not A Complete Moron?"

It was a wretched-looking group that trudged through Lundarien's Westerly Portal later that day. There was none of the laughter and bravado that had accompanied them on their journey to Yarnock, when they were the Lundarien Army. Now they were just a bunch of losers, worn out, beaten and, worst of all, betrayed. They barely exchanged glances, let alone goodbyes, as they headed to their homes to break the news to their families. Atlantis had won. What hope was there now of holding them back as they swept across the Underworld, threatening to consume Salistra and, inevitably, Lundarien?

Montgomery and Pepper followed Wyndham to the Town Hall, where Jarfin had already been sent ahead to gather the rest of the Novaristee.

'You kids wait out here,' said Wyndham, nodding to Jarfin, Marlah and Montgomery, then he turned, threw the Town Hall doors open, and stormed into the building.

Pepper glanced up at the Chronolith. 'We won't be long,' she said, looking at Montgomery. 'It's already after five. Your father will be starting to wonder where we've got to.'

Montgomery just shrugged and, as she followed Favian and Catrain into the Hall, he trudged towards the bench. It was still lying in a splintered heap on the floor, so he headed down to the shore instead. Jarfin and Marlah followed him and they slumped on the ground, staring out across the water.

None of them said anything, but occasionally Jarfin sighed.

'Alright, you lot?' said a voice, and Montgomery glanced up to see Alcott rowing along the shore towards them. 'How did it go today, out in Yarnock? Did you give Atlantis a good sorting out?"

'Not exactly,' said Jarfin.

'Not unless you include Merek "sorting them out" with our plan to ambush them,' said Marlah. 'And using one of Montgomery's keycoins to help them ambush *us* instead.'

'Merek?' Alcott gawped at them in amazement, then heaved on the oars a couple more times, pulling up in front of them. 'But how did Merek know? And where did he get one of Montgomery's keycoins from?'

Marlah gestured to Montgomery. 'Why not ask his bestest buddy over here?'

'I'm not his bestest *anything*!' said Montgomery, who had been forced to put up with comments like these all the way back on the Transak. 'He betrayed me too, you know.'

'Whatever.'

'I'm astounded you gave him a keycoin though,' said Jarfin, shaking his head to show just how astounded he was.

Montgomery took a deep breath, trying hard not to get angry. 'I didn't *give* him a keycoin. He must have stolen it when we were practicing Moving on the Surface or maybe even back last week in Yarnock.'

Next to him, Jarfin kicked at the water with his foot, not meeting Montgomery's eye. 'Well, what about the keycoin that brings you down here in the lift? Merek showed it to me. He said you gave *that* one to him.'

'I might have *lent* it to him…'

'Huh!' said Marlah. 'Doesn't look like he'll be giving it back any time soon.'

Montgomery craned over Jarfin's head to glare at her. 'He was helping with my Moving, unlike *some* people. He was actually a really good teacher!'

'Huh!' said Marlah again, even more mocking than the first.

'Sounds like the two of you have been having a lovely time up there on the Surface,' said Jarfin, kicking the water harder now, causing Alcott to duck back from the splashes. 'No wonder you haven't been hanging out with us down here!'

'I already told you about that. I've been grounded all week!'

'Well, maybe if you'd given one of *us* a keycoin, *we* could have come up and hung out with you on the Surface.'

'Hanging out on the Surface?' said Alcott, awed at the suggestion. 'That would be amazing!'

'Except it'd never happen,' snapped Marlah, splashing him properly, 'because Montgomery here was too busy playing with his bestest buddy Merek and didn't want us coming up and spoiling their fun.'

'I couldn't take you up to the Surface.'

'Couldn't?' asked Jarfin. 'Or wouldn't?'

'Pick one!' said Montgomery, his voice almost a shout. 'Your dad already made that quite clear, remember? He threatened to pull my arms off. With my own teeth! Merek lived up on the Surface for years, anyway. He's used to it. You aren't.'

Marlah jumped to her feet. 'That's because we've never had the chance. We've never been up there. Maybe if you took us with you sometime, we could *get* used to it.'

'Yeah,' said Jarfin, also standing up. 'At least you could have given us a chance! You know we want to see what the Surface is like, but you chose Merek over us. Merek! *Who betrayed us all.*'

'Oh, this is ridiculous!' It was Montgomery's turn to get to his feet. 'How was I supposed to know Merek was going to betray us?'

'Er, because he tried to kidnap me and helped your aunt take over the city?' suggested Marlah. 'He's evil! And thanks to you, we not only lost the battle with Atlantis today, but you've also managed to lose two keycoins and that Trypasphere thing. Maybe you should think a bit harder before making friends in future.'

Montgomery stepped towards her, jabbing a finger into her shoulder. 'Maybe I should!'

'What's that supposed to mean?' said Jarfin. His cheeks were flushed and he was scowling just like his dad.

'It means I'm leaving.' He stepped back from them to see how they would react, hoping they would relent, maybe even say they were sorry and ask him to stay.

'Fine!' said Marlah. 'You're such a… a… what's the opposite of *not* a complete moron?'

'A complete moron?' suggested Alcott, looking confused.

'Exactly!' she turned away from Montgomery, her arms folded. Next to her, Jarfin opened and closed his mouth a few times, clearly at a loss for what to say, before he too turned away.

Montgomery looked at Alcott, who was gripping his oars with white knuckles, a look of utter dejection on his usually cheerful face. 'I guess this means we won't be going to the Surface, then?' he said.

Montgomery sighed and shook his head, then turned and walked away across the cobbles towards the Town Hall. He was barely half way there when the large doors opened and Pepper emerged.

'Ready?' she asked. Montgomery just shrugged. 'Have you said goodbye to your friends?'

He paused and twisted round to look at Jarfin, Marlah and Alcott, hoping to find them all watching him. Instead, Jarfin and Marlah were sitting down again, their backs towards him, while Alcott was already rowing away across the lake.

'Yes,' he said, turning away and glaring at the ground. 'We've said goodbye.'

26. "Time To Break Into Prison"

It rained all day on Sunday, the sky a single dark-grey cloud, so heavy it was a wonder it didn't just flop down and drown the whole city. Montgomery almost wished it would. At least then he wouldn't have to put up with this terrible empty feeling that gnawed away inside him. Everything had been going so well. Jeff was keeping clear of him at school, he had made great progress with his Moving magic thanks to Merek and the Trypasphere, and he had his "second home" in Lundarien, with his friends and his apparently important role in city life. And then, in a single day, it had all changed. He'd lost Merek's protection and teaching, he'd lost the Trypasphere, he'd lost his place in Lundarien and, worst of all, he'd lost his friends.

He wanted to be cross with Jarfin and Marlah at the things they had said, but he simply didn't have the strength. That, and he thought they were probably right. After all, he *had* been spending more time with Merek than them. He alone had told Merek about the visit to Salistra. He alone had spoken up for Merek, when the others didn't want him to join them in Yarnock. He alone hadn't noticed, until too late, that Merek had taken one of the keycoins that opened the Crescent Tunnel. And he alone had taken the Trypasphere along in his now-ruined school bag. Atlantis had defeated them and it was all his fault.

He slumped on the sofa next to Victor, who looked every bit as miserable as Montgomery. Side by side, they stared blankly at the television screen, neither of them really watching it, both lost in their own miserable thoughts: Montgomery about how rubbish his life was, and Victor no doubt thinking about whatever was going on at the brewery. Even Pepper seemed glum rather than her usual stern self, and spent most of the day sighing in the kitchen. Only Gabriella seemed entirely unaffected by the sullen mood in the apartment, but for all her skipping around and waggling dolls and toy horses in their faces, she only made Montgomery sink further into his misery.

'This is a rubbish programme, daddy!' she declared. She faced the television, on which a church service was in full flow, pipe organs and all, and put her hands on her hips in the way Pepper did when she was cross. 'I want to watch the Wobble-Bobbles. They're my favourite! Please can I, daddy? Ple-e-ease?'

Victor grunted something without opening his mouth, felt around on the sofa and handed her the remote. Neither he nor Montgomery shown any signs of noticing as bouncy music blared from the speakers and the bulbous, multi-coloured figures tumbled around the screen.

In the kitchen, Pepper let out a loud sigh.

The rain continued into the week, accompanying Montgomery on his walk to and from school each day. On Wednesday afternoon, it cleared up a little, or at least the sky stopped its incessant dripping, though the clouds still hung dark, heavy and low. As Montgomery wandered home, he stopped by the church and, checking no one was watching him, ducked into the churchyard. It was as deserted as every other time he'd been there, though it felt even more so without Merek's presence.

In the far corner, the now severely-dented fridge leaned against the hedge, its door lolling open on a single hinge, the milk carton still jammed in it. Montgomery held out his hand to it, trying to make it Move, but without the Trypasphere to overcome the magic-destroying effects of the Sun, nothing happened.

'Stupid magic!' he said, walking over and giving the fridge a good kick, but instead of making him feel any better, it hurt his toe and he had to limp the rest of the way home.

During school hours, he avoided Jeff and his gang as far as was possible, taking detours through corridors he wouldn't otherwise go down.

'Ah, young Montgomery,' said the unmistakable voice of Mr Pemberton-Drake as Montgomery sneaked along the Geography corridor during lunch. He turned to see the headmaster emerging from one of the classrooms. 'Glad to see you still soldiering along, coming into school and all that. Got all that truancy out of your system, for now, eh?' Montgomery shrugged, but had nothing to say. 'Good show, good show. Well, keep it up, that's right. Well done.'

His avoidance of Jeff was not one hundred percent effective. There were occasions when they did come across each other around school or during Maths, as they were both in the same set, but the worst Jeff did was scowl at Montgomery and, during a particularly dull lesson on quadratic equations, he kept catching Montgomery's eye and running a finger across his own neck in the *You're dead!* fashion. Montgomery ignored him, not as a show of bravado or to make any particular point, but simply because he couldn't be bothered with it. Instead, he spent his time at school looking blankly at nothing, not taking anything in, not making any effort. It was nothing more than passing the time until he could go home.

But home was no better. His dad, at least, wasn't around much during the week, having to work late into the evening most days, but when he did come home he looked super-tired and grumpy, which made Pepper irritable and snap at the children.

Gabriella, of course, blissfully unaware that the rest of the family weren't dancing for joy around her, was her usual self and nattered away happily through dinner each evening, while everyone else sat in silence, pushing the untouched food around their plates.

Thursday's history homework was on Egypt. Montgomery had decided, from the little he had learned so far, that the Egyptians were magicians. They had to be. How else could they have made the pyramids, had chariots and boats, and done all the crazy things they did, while the rest of the world were still hiding in caves, eating raw mammoth and trying to invent fire?

Hieroglyphics were this evening's topic and he had to write a short message using Egyptian letters for the others in class to decipher. Montgomery had settled on, "LONDON STINKS", which pretty much summed up how he felt, especially since it had started raining again.

'The lion shape is an "L",' he muttered, trying to copy the image from the photocopied sheet. '"O" is... What? Some kind of flower?' He was starting to regret choosing a message with twelve pictures to draw and he wondered if any of the Ancient Egyptians ever managed to write more than a few words at a time. Certainly they couldn't have written any books - they'd never finish them in their lifetimes.

As usual, the thought of old writings brought his granddad's notebook to mind. Maybe that had been written in some sort of hieroglyphics? And he was about to have a look, but the thought of the random, unrelated scribbles changed his mind.

With a start, he suddenly remembered that strange vision he'd had about his granddad, just before going into the Diamond Minds. He'd forgotten about it in all the excitement... and misery.

'You need to be prepared,' Dalton had said. 'Darkness will rise.' He'd also written that in the note he'd left with the Trypasphere, but what did it mean? Was it something to do with night time? Or winter, maybe? And how was he supposed to prepare for it, when he had no idea what it was?

He glanced across at the old framed photograph of his granddad, as if the young man in the image might spring to life and explain everything. But Dalton didn't move. He just smiled lopsidedly back at him from behind the glass, looking up from where he had been reading a notebook.

A notebook? Montgomery leaned forwards. Why hadn't he noticed that before? Pulling open the desk's middle drawer, he riffled through the piles of blunt pencils and crisp packets and pulled out his magnifying glass. It was only small and wasn't particularly powerful, but it was sufficient to enlarge the image of the notebook.

It was lying flat on his granddad's desk and looked very much like the one he had given Montgomery. Dalton was reading it by the light of, not a diamond, but a glowing sphere. Montgomery stared. He'd seen it before, hanging from the wrists of his aunt. His granddad was reading the notebook using the Heliorb! Maybe *that's* what he needed in order to make it readable. And maybe, just maybe, there was something his granddad had written in there that would help them to defeat Atlantis. Why not? After all, he'd known Montgomery would find the Crescent tunnel in Yarnock.

Too excited now to concentrate on his homework,

Montgomery jumped up and headed out of his room to find his mum. Half way to the kitchen, however, he changed his mind. There was no way she was going to let him go down to Lundarien, especially not just to test out whether he could read an old notebook or not. No, he would have to sneak out when everyone else was asleep. And since he would have to somehow get into the Lundarien prison cells, he would need to be prepared. If only he still had the Trypasphere so he could practice his magic skills.

By eleven-thirty that night he was ready, and the rhythmic snoring of his dad finally signalled that the coast was clear. He crept down the hallway to the door, eased it open and checked his pockets one last time: key to the apartment, keycoin for the lift, three marbles he managed to find under the bed and his granddad's notebook - everything he needed to test out his theory. Across his shoulder, he also had the shadow lion hide he had been given after his victory over Payton.

'Right,' he murmured, pulling the door closed. 'Time to break into prison.'

Ping!

The sound of the lift doors opening rang out along the brightly-lit walls of the Lift Tunnel. Catching the keycoin as he stepped out, Montgomery paused by one of the piles of rubble to check the shadow lion hide covered him properly. Everything relied on him being able to blend in with the shadows, which is exactly what this was designed to do, originally for the lion, but now for him. Finally, happy that he was properly covered and grinning with excitement at the thought that he was actually doing something productive, if rather risky, he set off along the tunnel towards Lundarien.

The lights were down, the huge city diamonds

emitting only the slightest hint of a glow, but as Montgomery crept near the Town Hall, hugging the shadows as he crossed the bridge over the Timbris, he saw that the lights were on in the building and could hear faint voices from inside. Sidling up the steps, ducking behind the pillars and scurrying across to the wall, he peered quickly into the darkness of the Square behind him before turning the handle and pushing the door open just enough to squeeze through.

The voices were louder in here, coming from the Novaristee Meeting Room. The door to the room was ajar and light spilled through the crack.

'I don't care, Berinon,' said Wyndham's voice, sounding angry with the Bardle leader. 'You are in no position to make a judgement.'

Berinon's response sounded every bit as acid. 'All the same,' he said, 'I am a member of this council and I will have my say.' There was a thumping sound, which Montgomery reckoned was either Berinon's cane striking the wooden floor, or Wyndham punching him out. He hoped it was the second.

'Get on with it, then,' said the voice of Vala. Montgomery, having noted a patch of shadow in the corner of the vestibule in which to hide if necessary, crept to the crack in the door to see who else was in the room. To his surprise, there were just the three of them, Wyndham and Vala, standing by the large table, Berinon close to the door, his back to Montgomery. 'Some of us need to give our old creaking bones a rest.'

'Of course,' said Berinon, with a nod.

Vala smiled. 'I was thinking of poor old Wyndham, actually.'

'My point,' continued the Bardle leader, ignoring this, 'is that we should at least *consider* Kuruk's demands.' Behind the door, Montgomery stifled a gasp, and checked he was still properly covered by the shadow lion hide, just in case.

'Consider?' Wyndham spat the word as though it was something horrible that had landed in his mouth. 'You suggest we *consider* Kuruk's demands? After he's ploughed a furrow through half the cities in west Brytellian?'

'That's exactly *why* we should consider them, man. It's either that or get run out of our *own* city.' He struck the floor with his cane again.

'So what do you propose?' asked Vala. 'Should we throw open our gates and let them walk all over us?'

'We don't have gates,' Wyndham pointed out. 'Though considering recent events, it might be time we did.'

'From what you and that Bressalan fellow said,' continued Berinon, 'Kuruk is looking for people to join him. He wants to unite the Underworld, doesn't he?'

Wyndham folded his arms. 'As long as it's on his terms.'

'I'll take that as a "yes",' said Berinon. 'So, what's wrong with uniting the Underworld? Isn't that what Calibre's prophecy was all about, after all?'

Montgomery glanced at the picture of Calibre Morricote, the deceased leader of the Mansers, hanging on the wall by the door. The old man grinned merrily out of the frame, his hand clutching the scroll of the prophecy Berinon was talking about. Most of it was too small to read, but he recalled the part about the someone who would unite "those above and those below". Payton had claimed the prophecy was about her, which Montgomery thought unlikely. But could Berinon really think it was a prophecy about Atlantis? Wyndham didn't seem to think so.

'You do come out with some rubbish, Berinon! Do you really think that, if we give in to Kuruk's demands, life in Lundarien will just carry on as usual?'

'You forget, Wyndham, that I have-'

'That you've been to Atlantis,' interrupted Vala. 'That was over twenty years ago, back when Ujarak was in charge. This Kuruk is a completely different ruler altogether. No, Berinon.' She tapped her staff on the floor, to emphasise her words. 'It is *you* who forgets. You forget that you have not seen him. We have, and there is something... evil there. You mark my words.'

'But shouldn't we at least-'

'Good!' interrupted Wyndham. He stepped forwards and Berinon backed against the door, blocking Montgomery's view. 'If you've nothing sensible to say, I suggest it's time to head to our homes.' Montgomery heard heavy footsteps heading for the door and leapt backwards towards the shadowed corner, only to find Berinon had trapped the shadow lion hide in the door. Before he could grab hold of it, it slipped from his shoulders and tumbled towards the ground, settling in folds as the door burst open and Wyndham stepped out.

'What's going on here?' he said.

27. "I Will Help You Escape"

Montgomery screwed up his eyes and stood as still as possible, like a child learning to play hide-and-seek who hadn't yet grasped the idea that if you couldn't see people, they could still see you.

'Who left this here?' said Wyndham. There was a pause and Montgomery opened his right eye just a crack to see the Watchman bending down to pick up the shadow lion hide. 'Doesn't this belong to your nephew?' he asked, turning to Vala who hobbled out of the room behind him.

'That it does,' said Vala. Her eyes narrowed as she peered around the vestibule.

'What's it doing here?' said Berinon, his voice accusing as he jabbed at the hide with his cane. 'Has that Montgomery boy been spying on us?' He too looked around the room, leaning back to look behind a large display of flowers. Montgomery frowned, wondering what was going on. He was right in front of them. Why couldn't they-?

And then it dawned on him. It was a strange sensation to look down at his body and see only the dark wood of the floor, but his invisible face cracked into a grin. He had Cealed himself again.

'Well, if he was,' said Vala, 'which seems unlikely, he's not here now. You can search the place if you want, but I'm going to take this smelly thing,' she tugged the shadow lion hide from Wyndham's grasp, 'and head off to my nice, warm bed.'

'Fine!' Berinon gave up his gazing around and headed towards the main doors. He missed bumping into Montgomery by barely an inch as he spun back to face the others. 'But, I will be putting my proposal to the Novaristee, tomorrow, all the same. Maybe *they* will be more willing to see sense than a jumped-up policeman and an old witch!' And with that he stormed out of the Town Hall, his cane striking sparks from the stone threshold.

'Good luck!' called Vala, then patted Wyndham on the arm. 'I wouldn't call you an old witch,' she said. 'Hardly past your fiftieth year, are you?'

'I'm forty-two!' he said, in mock outrage. 'But he was on the nail with you, though. Jumped-up policeman to the core.'

'Police*woman*, I'll thank you. I am a woman, after all.'

Wyndham laughed, stepping out through the doorway. 'Don't be ridiculous,' he said. 'Of course you're not!'

Vala was just about to walk out behind him, when she stopped suddenly and turned to look directly at where Montgomery was standing. She stared for so long that Montgomery, holding his breath, felt she must be able to see him and had to look down at himself to check. But he was still completely invisible as far as he could tell.

'Something wrong?' asked Wyndham, popping his head back round the door.

Vala shook her head. 'No. Just thinking, is all' she said, heaving the lion's hide up onto her shoulder. 'I reckon it's time I gave my niece and her son a call, to make sure they're coming with us to Salistra next week.'

'Really?' asked Wyndham. 'You still think the boy should come after the disaster in Yarnock?'

Vala frowned at him, as though he had asked if she

needed legs. 'Well, of course he should! A gullible ninny, he may be,' she glared across towards Montgomery again, 'and a terrible judge of character, but Montgomery's role in the future of our city is vital. He, more than any of us, must be there next Tousday, if he's to fulfil his role.'

'His role?'

Vala nodded. 'He's our secret weapon, remember?'

Wyndham paused a moment, looking thoughtful. 'Very well,' he said at last. 'He's your squire. I'll leave you to deal with him.' Then he vanished back out of the door.

Vala peered around at the vestibule, as though she had forgotten something, then turned to the open door. 'There's only the one guard on the cells tonight, I believe,' she said.

'What was that?' asked Wyndham, as Vala joined him outside.

'Oh nothing,' said Vala, pulling the door closed, and their voices drifted away into the darkness, leaving Montgomery alone with the flowers. What was all that about his future in the city? What did she mean about him being a secret weapon? What did Vala know that she wasn't telling him? He was so confused by everything he'd just heard, it took him a moment to remember what he was even doing here.

The only other time Montgomery had been in the Town Hall courtyard, he had entered it through a drainage hole in the wall that opened onto the lake. That had been last month, when he and Marlah had rescued the children locked up in the prison by Payton. This time, it was Payton herself who was in the cells.

Montgomery slipped through the rear door of the hall and into the silence of the courtyard, empty except for a number of large pots with scraggly, bush-like plants in, and a few stone benches dotted around. There was also a man standing by the steps that led down to the cells. "Only one guard," Vala had said and, even though it suggested she was somehow aware of his presence in the vestibule *and* what he was up to, he was glad of the information.

Montgomery, checking first that he was still Cealed, approached the guard, tiptoeing his way across the earthy ground of the courtyard. Unlike the Hunters, he couldn't walk without making a sound, but the man looked half-asleep and showed no sign that he noticed Montgomery's footsteps creeping towards him.

Peering past the guard, down the steps to the gate at the bottom, Montgomery could see the solid iron gate with its rusty lock and noisy hinges. Through its bars, the glow from the prison corridor cast a stripy light onto the steps, a strange glow that seemed yellower than the usual white of the diamonds. Last time he'd been here, Wyndham had given him the key for this gate, but he'd given that back after his fight with Payton. Thankfully, he had a plan for getting this open, which relied on the guard opening the door *for* him.

He slipped a hand into his pocket and pulled out one of the marbles. Then, taking careful aim at the gate below, he threw it. The marble arced through the air and dropped between the rungs of the gate, landing almost without a sound in the corridor beyond. He pulled out another, took aim and tossed that one straight between the bars as well, certain he couldn't have done it if he'd tried. He held out his hand, its palm towards the gate, and tried to Move the marbles back again, but nothing happened. Whatever it was that stopped magic being used in the prison prevented him.

Cursing himself for not bringing something bigger, he drew out the last of his marbles and took aim again. This one *had* to hit one of the bars! He couldn't possibly miss three times in a row.

The marble sailed between the bars, dropping silently onto the floor of the corridor.

'No!' he whispered.

'Hello?' said the guard, suddenly and completely alert. He gripped the hilt of his sword, though he didn't draw it, peering at a point a few inches to the left of Montgomery's ear. 'Is someone there?'

Despite being invisible, Montgomery ducked down instinctively and, as he did so, his fingers brushed against a broken piece of pottery that lay on the ground by one of the plant pots. He waited for the guard's gaze to move away, then picked it up. With a swift flick of his wrist, he tossed pottery shard at the gate, and this time it clattered against the iron bars with a satisfying clang.

The guard span round and hurried down the steps, tugging at the keys on his belt. In seconds he was inside the corridor, the gate still swinging open behind him.

'What's going on?' he called. 'Is someone there?' No one answered, so the guard strode away along the left hand corridor. Montgomery, who was familiar with the layout of the Lundarien prison, waited for him to return and start off along the corridor to the right before he slipped in through the gate.

As he expected, as soon as he stepped across the threshold, he became visible again, so he hurried quickly to the left before the guard returned and spotted him.

In the third cell from the end, Montgomery found what he was looking for. There, lying on a wooden board that hung, shelf-like, from the wall, was Payton. She was asleep, a thin sheet of cloth covering her body. He paused, watching her for a moment as she slept, and was struck by how much she looked like his mother. Much more than before, when she'd been the proud, fierce woman who had tried to seize control of Lundarien.

The silence was broken by the screaming of the gate's hinges as the guard pulled it shut. The noise echoed down the corridor and around the rock walls of the cells, followed by the sound of the key scraping in the lock, and Montgomery felt a stab of panic at being locked inside the prison.

'No!' he whispered, wishing he'd thought of that before he came into this wretched place.

'Montgomery?' said a voice, and for a moment, he didn't recognise his aunt's voice. It sounded weaker, broken. 'What...?' She levered herself up onto her elbow, peering past him to see if there was anyone else was in the corridor. 'What are you doing here?'

Montgomery swallowed, worried the guard would hear them or that she might call for him and give him away. He wasn't sure how he would explain his presence here to Wyndham if he was caught. Or to his mother, since she would definitely end up hearing about it!

'I need your help,' he said at last.

She raised an eyebrow. '*My* help?'

'It's just... I need to test something, that's all.'

Payton looked confused, but made no move to get up and her wrists were still hidden beneath the folds of cloth. 'To test what exactly? Me? You want to check I'm not about to magic my way out of these cells?' She kicked at the wall with her heel, letting out a loud thud. Montgomery stiffened, listening out for the guard, but no sound came from down the corridor. 'I assure you, dear nephew, I am very much a prisoner.'

Montgomery paused, not sure whether he should tell her about his granddad's, her *father's*, notebook. 'I just need that Heliorb thing,' he said, pointing to where he thought her hands were. At last Payton pivoted and sat up. But as she did so, the covers slipped off and Montgomery realised her wrists were no longer chained together. The

Heliorb wasn't there. 'Where is it?' he asked. 'Where's it gone?'

'Oh, I am not required to wear the orb in here,' said Payton, smiling at him as she stood up and stepped towards him. Despite the iron bars between them, Montgomery took a step backwards as she approached. 'Not when the whole prison is lit up with the wretched things.' She gestured towards the ceiling and, as Montgomery followed her gaze, he realised why the light in here was different. Those were not diamonds embedded in the roof of the corridor. After all, diamonds wouldn't work in here, would they? The ceiling was covered with Heliorbs.

Montgomery pulled his granddad's notebook from inside his coat and opened it on a random page, holding it out in the light of the Heliorb above him. But instead of becoming readable, the page was now completely blank. No words. No drawings. No scribbles. Nothing.

He turned the page, but the next one was also blank. He flicked through the rest of the notebook. It was empty; there was not even the smallest mark anywhere in the whole thing. It was clean and white, like new.

'Rubbish!' he said. 'Stupid magic!'

'What have you got there?' asked Payton, and Montgomery almost jumped backwards as he realised she was now standing right against the cell bars. 'Is that... Is that one of my father's notebooks?'

Montgomery shut it quickly and slipped it back into his inside pocket. 'Maybe,' he said. 'He left it to me when he died.'

'Interesting.' She was silent for a moment, nodding slowly. When she spoke again her voice was different, urgent almost. 'You must keep that safe, Montgomery. Don't let anyone else know you have it. No one, do you understand?' Montgomery stared, stunned by this sudden change in his aunt's manner. 'Trust me. There will be things in there which other people, *evil* people, would use to gain power.'

He shut his mouth and scowled at her. 'People like *you*, you mean?'

Payton sighed. 'I am sorry, *truly* sorry, for what happened between us,' she said, her voice gentle and full of regret. 'It was an unfortunate way for us to meet for the first time. But I stand by what I told you then: the things I did, I did for this city, not simply to gain power for myself. Not like *them*.' She gazed at the wall beyond him, as though the evil people she mentioned were there, behind him.

Montgomery resisted the urge to turn and look. 'I don't understand,' he said, trying to keep his voice quiet. 'What people? Do you mean the Atlanteans?'

She laughed his mother's laugh. 'Hardly! Atlantis has only a mild affliction, little more than a taste of the darkness. They're little more than children in comparison to the cultists and maniacs I'm talking about. No. The danger - the *real* danger - is from the East. From the East and from the deep. Darkness will rise.'

'I don't-' he began, but she cut him off.

'Promise me, Montgomery. Promise me you will guard that notebook. Guard it with your life!'

Still confused, Montgomery found himself nodding again. 'Alright,' he said and patted the notebook through his clothes. 'It's not like anyone can read the stupid thing anyway.'

'And now,' she said, a smile lighting her face. 'I will help you escape.'

'How?'

'Guard!' Payton's sudden shout rang up the corridor.

'What are you doing?' he said, panicking at the thought of being discovered.

'Quickly,' said his aunt, her voice an urgent whisper through the bars. 'This guard doesn't like me much, he will take his time. But when he opens that gate,' she nodded along the corridor, 'you mustn't be here. Go! And, Montgomery?' she added as he set off back down the tunnel. 'Do not be angry with Merek. I promise you, it's not what you think. All is not as it appears.'

Montgomery hurried along the corridor as quietly as possible and had just reached the gate when Payton shouted for the guard again. A few seconds later, the key scraped in the lock and the gate screeched open, but by then Montgomery was crouching at the other end of the corridor. A very skinny man was in the cell next to him, and he turned his face, peering out with large, miserable eyes.

'Er, hi,' Montgomery whispered. He hadn't seen the man before and he was worried he might call out, but he just spat on the floor and looked away.

Montgomery turned back to see the guard heading towards Payton's cell, then darted back through the open gate and out into the courtyard.

As he made his way back through the tunnels to the waiting lift, he checked his watch. It was quarter past two in the morning. He had to be up to get ready for school in five hours.

'What a failure,' he said, jamming his keycoin into the lift panel. 'What a waste of time!'

28. "You Did That Once - By Accident!"

'What a waste of time!'

Montgomery sprang to his feet as Vala's face appeared, huge and wrinkled on the television screen halfway through his favourite sci-fi programme. He had been looking forward to watching it while Gabriella was at her dancing lesson with his dad, and wasn't around to whine about wanting to put on something else. The programme had just got to a good bit, where the captain of the spaceship had been captured by aliens and was about to be fed to a three-headed monster that lived in a lava swamp with no hope of rescue…

'I was watching that!' he complained.

'Load of old rubbish,' said Vala, cheering up noticeably. 'Where's your mother?'

'I'm here,' said Pepper, emerging from the kitchen carrying a mixing bowl and a wooden spoon. 'What's going on?'

'*What's going on?*' Vala's cross look returned. 'You *know* what's going on! Those pesky Atlanteans are going to attack Salistra next Tousday, that's what's going on! And we need all the help we can get. Which includes you two.' She jabbed a couple of fingers at the screen.

'Montgomery has school,' said Pepper, stirring the bowl's contents. 'He already missed enough days skiving off to accompany you to Yarnock. He can't miss any more.'

'Really?' Vala flickered on the screen, scowling. 'And what would you say was more important: the safety of Brytellian or learning some of that useless Germish?'

'Do you mean German?' said Montgomery.

'Who cares? It's not important enough to bother knowing what it's called.' Vala returned her attention to Pepper. 'Don't forget this is your home we're talking about. Lundarien is under threat!'

Pepper shook her head. 'Lundarien is not my home, not anymore. My home is here,' she pointed to the flat in general with the spoon, dropping a few globules of cake mixture onto the sofa, 'with my family, in London.'

For the first time since Montgomery had met her, Vala seemed lost for words. She stared out of the television as though she couldn't believe what she was hearing.

'I can't believe what I'm hearing,' she said. 'You'd let you own people - the people your father loved and protected and gave the best years of his life for - you'd let them be taken over by Atlantis, just so your boy can go along to school and learn things that are never going to do him any good outside of an exam? Now, I know things didn't work out so well back in Yarnock. Truth be told, we got a proper beating. But that doesn't mean we should give up, does it?' Pepper didn't say anything. 'Your lad there,' Vala's glare flickered to Montgomery, 'may have made a right old mess of things for us, and been more of a hindrance than a help...'

'Thank you,' said Montgomery. 'I'm right here, you know.'

'...but he's got powerful magic. Powerful-er than anything I've seen since my brother was around. And I know *he* wouldn't have turned his back on us when we needed him.'

Pepper jammed the spoon angrily into the bowl. 'My

father knew what he was doing,' she said. 'He had perfect control over his magic. Montgomery is still learning, still trying to work out what he can and can't do, still trying to get some sort of control even with the simple stuff.'

'I have been learning,' said Montgomery, twisting round on the sofa to look up at her. 'I've got much better control than I had when I beat Payton. I can Watch as well as Wyndham. I can Move almost as well as Marlah now. I can even make diamonds light up and make myself invisible.'

Pepper made a "huh" sound. 'You did that *once* - by accident!'

Montgomery opened his mouth to say he'd actually done it twice, but it might mean admitting going to Lundarien last night, so he closed it again.

On the screen, Vala looked like she was thinking about something. 'Yes, yes. Good, good,' she said. 'I need to talk to your mother a moment.'

Montgomery shrugged. 'Go on then. She's just there.' He pointed at Pepper.

'Without you around, you nitwit!'

Montgomery produced a loud sigh and pushed himself up from the sofa. 'Fine!' he said, dragging his feet out of the lounge. He stopped just outside the door, his back against the wall, listening.

Vala's voice blared from the television. 'I said *alone*!'

With another loud sigh, he trudged off to his bedroom.

Ten minutes later, Pepper followed and stood in the doorway looking at him, her head slightly tilted. After a while, she smiled and gave a little nod.

'Firstly,' she said, 'let me make it clear that I do not approve of you skiving off school, okay?'

Montgomery jumped up from the bed. 'You mean I'm going?'

'It seems we're *both* going to be needed to help stop the Atlanteans. Heaven knows what I'm going to tell your father, though.'

A grin spread across Montgomery's face. 'But we're going to Salistra, right?'

The rainy weather continued into the next week, but Montgomery was impervious to its gloom. Even an afternoon of double *maffy-matticks* did nothing to dampen his mood of excitement, and he spent most of the time staring through the page on multiplying out double brackets, whatever that was supposed to be, daydreaming about the coming battle with Atlantis.

Phrases he had heard during his night time adventure in Lundarien kept popping into his mind, about the evil in the East and in the deep, and what Vala said about his vital role in the city's future. A shiver of excited fear shot through him at the idea of being a powerful magician like his granddad and about what could possibly be so terrible it even made Payton afraid.

On his way home, as he pulled up the hood of his coat against the rain that was falling almost horizontally in the blustery wind, he found Jeff and a couple of his friends huddled on the bench, trying to light a cigarette they'd got from somewhere.

'Can we help you?' said Jeff, his eyes narrowing as Montgomery approached the group.

'Aren't those things bad for you?' he replied, slowing his pace only a little.

Jeff narrowed his eyes, but didn't get up. 'There's all kinds of things what aren't good for you, Twinkles. Like wandering about without that big boyfriend of yours.'

'Stupid matches,' said Steve, busy concentrating on the cigarette. 'They must of got wet, bruv.'

'Where is he, anyway?' asked Jeff, ignoring his friend

and peering round Montgomery as if Merek might be hiding behind him. 'Haven't seen him around for a few days.'

Montgomery frowned. 'Have you been spying on me?'

Jeff just flicked a smile at him, then turned back to his friends. 'Give us them matches, you dunce,' he said, snatching the box out of Steve's hand and spilling half the contents onto the ground.

Montgomery walked away, feeling, if anything, in an even better mood.

29. "I Knew It Was A Mistake Letting You Lot Sit Together"

On Tuesday morning, once Victor had set out to work and Pepper had dropped off Gabriella, arranging for her to go round to Daisy's house after school, Montgomery and his mum waited for the apartment building lift to be free.

By the time they arrived in the Lift Tunnel, the Lundarien army had already set off, and the lift doors opened to show a large crowd of people in the distance, all marching towards the Great Tunnel, weapons in hand, grim expressions hardening their faces. The army was much bigger than last time. As they hurried to catch up, it seemed to Montgomery as though all the magic-capable adults of the city had come out to take on Atlantis.

'How many people are here?' he asked as he followed Pepper through the crowd towards the broad bulk of Wyndham at the front.

Pepper shook her head. 'A lot,' she said. 'Easily over a hundred.'

'One hundred and fifty-six, to be precise,' said Favian, appearing on their left. Behind him, Marlah was busy not making eye contact with Montgomery. He ignored her in return and looked at his mum instead.

She raised her eyebrows. 'That's even more than we took into the Labyrinth to rescue *you!*'

Favian nodded, falling in alongside Pepper. 'Can you blame us, after the thrashing we received at Yarnock? We'll need everyone we've got if we're going to stand any chance against those freakish Atlanteans. Don't worry, though. We've left some of the tougher Watchers to guard Lundarien. And Rowan's up and about now, so he volunteered to stay behind with them.' Rowan was Clovis's dad, the most powerful Hunter in Lundarien, though he'd been badly hurt in the conflict with Payton's soldiers. Montgomery was glad to hear he was better.

'So what's the plan?' asked Pepper, slowing down as they drew up beside Wyndham. Montgomery, lagging behind her, found himself wedged between Marlah and Jarfin. Walking nearby, Clovis joined the other two in ignoring him. He was about to mention her dad being well again, but he just scratched his head, not saying anything. Now and then, he glanced at them out of the corner of his eye.

'Nice and simple,' said Wyndham, sounding grim. 'No tricks. No ambush. Just straightforward battle formation. Anselm will be coordinating the city's defence, but we'll probably have to cover a couple of the Salistran caverns ourselves.' He looked over his shoulder for a moment. 'I see you've brought the lad. No sign of that double-crossing Merek, I suppose?'

Montgomery cleared his throat. 'No,' he said, his voice coming out like a squeak, despite the throat clearing. He scratched his head again, feeling awkward.

'Pity,' said Wyndham, raising his voice so it echoed around the tunnel. 'I'd quite like to have had the chance to warm up by giving him a good thrashing. We'll just have to settle for thrashing the Atlanteans instead, then!'

There was a chorus of agreement and even cheers from those in the crowd who heard. Montgomery could almost feel Jarfin swelling with pride next to him. He didn't turn to look.

At the end of the Lift Tunnel, Vala did whatever magic it was that opened the archway onto the Great Tunnel, and they made their way through to the waiting Transak. Montgomery was surprised to see that most of the tunnel, as it stretched away to the east and west, was deserted, and the many stalls that lined it were closed, their wares removed, no doubt, until safer times. But even more than this, he was surprised by the assortment of items that were clustered by the exit, the various Transak they would be riding for the few hours it took to get to Salistra. The main theme today was boats, of all shapes and size, even what looked to Montgomery like a long canal barge.

'What's that thing?' he asked, pointing to it he passed the familiar shape of the Trago.

Lockley glanced round. 'Canal barge,' he said. 'Got three of my cousins operating it. Good lads, but they tend to be a bit reckless for my liking. Risk takers, if you know what I mean.' Montgomery didn't, but he said nothing. 'I think you young uns are travelling with the Scollands,' Lockley spat out the name as though he didn't like it being in his mouth. He pointed across to the far side of the tunnel. 'They're just the other side of that ridiculous tree.'

Montgomery stood on tiptoes to see over the Trago's bow and could just make out some branches poking up in the distance. 'Are you sure?' he asked, trying not to sound too doubtful.

Lockley checked a sheet of paper spread over the wooden goat's head and nodded. 'Yes, you're with Randall Scolland. Isn't that right, Watchman?'

Montgomery turned to see Wyndham approaching. 'Scolland, that's right. Pepper?' he added as Montgomery's mum appeared with Catrain around the side of the boat. 'You're with me on the Trago.'

'Not again!' said Lockley.

Leaving the adults to get on board, Montgomery headed off across the Great Tunnel. Although the tree was hovering a couple of feet above the ground, he decided it was probably safer to walk around it than duck underneath. The branches were long, with dense green leaves, and from within the foliage small, pink and blue birds with long beaks flittered around, chirping happily to each other.

As he rounded the top of the tree, his heart sank. There, clambering aboard what was definitely a magic flying carpet, were Jarfin, Marlah and Clovis. He was about to mention the carpet, when he remembered he was supposed to be ignoring them.

'Perfect!' he muttered, forgetting how good Marlah's hearing was.

'It wasn't our choice to ride with *you* either,' she said, giving him one of her best withering looks. 'You're more than welcome to walk, if you'd prefer. We won't stop you.'

Montgomery said nothing, but waited until they had boarded the carpet before clambering on behind them. It was an odd sensation, both soft and firm at the same time, a bit like sitting on a bouncy castle, but one woven from wool. The other three had their backs to him, so he looked around at the assembled Transak as they began to set off.

The odd assortment of vehicles glided along the Great Tunnel, the sound of conversations echoing from the walls, a mixture of excitement, anticipation and nerves. They had barely gone a hundred yards before Montgomery decided flying carpets were not the best form of transport. Not only was it constantly shifting underneath him, like a lilo on the sea, but it sagged in the middle, causing everyone to lean against each other, no matter how much they tried not to - it was either that or fall off.

'Is there any way you could make the carpet a bit, er, flatter, Mr Scolland?' asked Montgomery, as he banged against Clovis for the fourth time. 'Or maybe a bit less bumpy?'

The young man at the front turned his scruffy-bearded face to him. 'Only if I drop it onto the ground,' he said. 'And the name's Scolland, mate. Just Scolland. I ain't no mister.'

'Why don't *you* fly it if you're so amazing at Moving now?' said Marlah, who was jammed in between Jarfin and Clovis and didn't sound like she was having fun. 'Let's see what your amazing bestest buddy, Merek, managed to teach you.'

'He's not-' he began, but Clovis cut him off.

'Go on! Impress us with your new skills, Montgomery.'

'Montgomery?' said Scolland, fixing him with his watery eyes. 'That's not a name you hears every day. You ain't that Sunner lad people's been talking about, are you?'

Montgomery's eye widened in surprise. 'People have been talking about me?' The man shrugged in affirmation. 'What have you heard?'

'Stuff about you taking down Payton Stroud after she come back from the Surface. And about you being the grandson of the old Omnifex.' Scolland tapped the side of his nose and Montgomery was slightly disturbed to see there was a large boil on it. 'Word travels fast on the Transak.'

'And it travels on a magic flying carpet,' said Marlah.

'Go on, then, mate,' said Scolland with a grin that showed off his crooked, mostly-brown teeth. 'Give it a go. Let's see what you've got.' He lifted his hand off the carpet and it dropped towards the ground, exactly like a normal, non-magic, non-flying carpet.

'What?' Montgomery reacted instinctively, gripping the side of the carpet. The carpet shot up towards the very solid-looking rock surface of the tunnel roof. Clovis, moving in a blur, pulled the others flat onto the carpet as Montgomery fought to get it under control. He brought it to a halt mere inches from his face. Somewhere, someone was screaming and he was embarrassed to find it was him.

He closed his mouth, his eyes still bulging at the rocks above him. They drifted slowly towards a nearby tree.

'Any chance we could go just a touch lower?' asked Jarfin, his voice strained.

Montgomery took a deep breath and focussed on lowering the carpet. As it fell, the screaming started again, but this time the carpet stopped a few feet from the floor, dropping down right next to the Trago.

Montgomery, whose eyes were shut tight, opened one of them, to see Wyndham shaking his head disapprovingly over the side of the boat.

'I knew it was a mistake letting you lot sit together,' he said as he drifted forwards, away from them.

Slowly, like people waking from a nightmare, Montgomery and the others sat up.

'Well,' said Marlah, 'you seem to have solved the problem of the carpet sagging.' And to Montgomery's surprise he realised that they were no long all huddled up together in the middle. The carpet was as flat and solid as though they were sitting on a table. 'All we need to do now is to start moving forwards.'

'And quickly!' said Clovis, peering behind them.

As one, the others turned round to see the canal barge bearing down on them at an alarming speed. It looked much bigger this close.

'Want me to take over again?' asked Scolland, who was looking even more dishevelled than before, if such a thing was possible. Actually, all he actually managed to say was, 'Want me to take oh-', at which point his words were cut off as the carpet shot forwards as though it had been fired from a cannon. A really big cannon, that shoots out carpets full of people really, really fast.

There was more screaming and, though it was little more than a passing blur, Montgomery glimpsed Wyndham still shaking his head at them over the side of the Trago.

'That was the most amazing thing ever!' said Jarfin, leaping off the carpet and walking, slightly shakily, to the Great Tunnel wall, where Clovis was already sitting, her usually neat long hair, transformed into a blonde bush. 'You're Moving is the best ever!'

On the other side of the carpet, Scolland was being loudly and messily sick.

'Huh,' said Marlah, leaning against the still solid carpet. 'It wasn't *that* amazing. And I bet Merek never taught you how to fly carpets, anyway.'

Montgomery, who had managed to bring their rocket-swift flight along the Great Tunnel to a halt a short distance beyond the Diamond Mines and was feeling exhilarated by the experience, didn't really feel like getting into an argument. After his rubbish week on the Surface, feeling guilty and alone, he was delighted at having done some magic - proper, controlled magic, for a change. Well, *almost* controlled. And he enjoyed being with Jarfin and the others again.

'Can we just drop all the "Merek" stuff?' he said, looking sheepish. 'I really don't feel like getting into an argument.'

'That depends,' said Marlah, though her voice was softer. 'After all, you did say he was a better friend than us.'

'Even though he betrayed you,' added Jarfin.

'And stole that Trypasphere thing and your keycoins,' added Clovis.

Scolland added little to the conversation besides the sound of more sick slapping the tunnel floor. Montgomery slid off the Transak, and it flopped to the ground, a normal carpet once again.

'Yeah, I know,' he said, sagging at his acceptance of their comments. 'But life is so rubbish living in London when you don't have any friends or anyone to talk to about magic and the Underworld and stuff.' He sighed and drooped against the wall next to Jarfin. 'So when Merek showed up it was… a relief! I so wanted to trust him, but I guess it blinded me to-'

'So,' interrupted Marlah 'what you're basically saying is that you're sorry, yes?'

'Wow!' said Scolland, staggering across to them and flapping a hand back in the direction he'd come from. 'That was a lot of sick!'

The group sat and chatted for a while, and Montgomery, so grateful at having his friends back again, told them about how he sneaked into Lundarien and made himself invisible.

'Did you really break into the cells?' asked Jarfin, clearly fascinated by the story. 'I wish I'd been there to see it. You should've come and got me.'

'We weren't exactly talking, remember?' Montgomery waved a hand as if wafting away the unpleasant topic.

'Look,' said Clovis. 'Here come the others.' She pointed back along the Great Tunnel to where the other Transak vehicles were small, growing dots in the distance, barely visible to Montgomery's eyes.

'Right,' said Scolland, pushing himself away from the wall, where he'd been munching on a dried sausage, so long and black it looked more like a stick of charcoal. 'Time to go. Mind if I drive?'

They all settled onto the carpet and Scolland raised it into the air again, drifting along at a far more sedate pace than before.

Montgomery grinned at the others. 'I'm glad we're friends again,' he said. 'Even if we are about to go and fight against those scary Atlanteans.'

Jarfin swallowed. 'They are scary, aren't they?'

'Huh!' Marlah sounded indignant. 'They're just people with stupid tattoos and pointy teeth.'

'Don't forget those creepy black eyes,' said Montgomery.

'And their creepy black clothes,' added Jarfin.

Marlah huffed. 'That's all just for show - trying to trick us into being afraid. Just like they tricked us with that ambush in Yarnock.'

'Well, they won't trick us again this time,' said Clovis. 'My mum said they've had scouts posted along all the major and minor tunnels that lead out of Salistra. We know exactly where Kuruk's army is and when they'll reach the city. It's going to be a straight fight - no ambushes or anything. Just us against them.'

Montgomery glanced at Jarfin, who didn't look quite so confident as the girls.

'Don't worry,' he said. 'I'm sure it's going to be fine.'

30. "They're Coming At Us From All Directions"

'Of course it's not fine,' said Anselm, directing his displeasure at a young member of the Salistran Watch. 'That's over two hundred people we've lost, and the battle hasn't even begun!'

'That doesn't sound good,' said Wyndham, as he led the Lundarien army to where Anselm stood, in front of the same tower as before. 'What's happened?'

Anselm turned a harassed face to him. 'Thank goodness you've arrived. I was beginning to think we would have to face Atlantis on our own.' Wyndham raised his eyebrows, but said nothing. Anselm sighed. 'Honeytown and Ethenside have deserted us.'

'Deserted?' A deep crease formed between Wyndham's eyebrows. 'When did this happen?'

'During the night,' said Anselm. 'They slipped away while the rest of us were asleep during their watch. No one raised the alarm until this morning. We sent scouts to track them, but we fear they have hidden in the Southern Tunnels. There's no time to find them now.'

Wyndham growled something about cowards under his breath as Anselm led them to the large archway that led to the main, central cavern of Salistra. According to Jarfin, who had visited Salistra before, each of the seven caverns had a name, the one they were in being

'Pentalane'.

'Do they *all* have stupid names?' asked Marlah.

Jarfin counted them off on his fingers. 'There's Pentalane, Duventim, Trinta, Quartico-'

'So that's a *yes*, then.'

'What's wrong with calling them cavern one, two, three, four and so on?' asked Montgomery, who couldn't help agreeing with Marlah. 'They'd be much easier to remember.'

'And this,' said Jarfin, as they stepped through the archway, 'is the Primatectum.'

Despite the silly name, even Montgomery had to admit it was impressive. Like Lundarien, Salistra had a lake, not quite as large as Lake Altis but by no means small, and it sat in the centre of the Primatectum, its shoreline a perfect circle. A number of boats were moored around the edges, but there were none out on the lake itself. Not today. Surrounding the lake were blocks of grassy, open spaces and of buildings, the blocks arranged alternately like the sections on a dartboard, twelve in all. Overhead was a veritable forest of trees, whose leafy canopies were broken only by the six massive diamonds that flooded the cavern with light.

Montgomery was distracted by Anselm waving his hand about. He wasn't distracted by the hand itself, though, but by what appeared in the air in front of it. It was a series of glittering lines that looked like they'd been etched into glass, showing a central circle with six oval shapes extending from it like petals from a flower. It took him a moment to work out what it was.

'It's a map,' he said.

Anselm nodded at him. 'Indeed it is,' he said. 'A map of Salistra.' He turned to the group and announced, *'Our* people are going to cover the Primatectum, together with Pentalane and Hexander.' He pointed to two of the petal shapes, before gesturing to their real-life counterparts, the entrance they had just come through and the one immediately left. 'The other forces are smaller, so Cloister and Blayston-Braddock are joining to cover Quartico,' he pointed to another petal and to the first entrance on the right, 'while Munn and Yarnock are in Trinta.' The next entrance round. 'I need you,' continued Anselm, enlarging the final two petal-shapes with a flick of his fingers and pointing to the entrances in question, 'to split up and take Duventim and Cavern Seven.'

'Cavern Seven?!' Montgomery tried to cover up his laugh as a cough, but Pepper gave him one of her looks.

'So what's the latest news?' asked Wyndham. 'Where do you think Atlantis will strike?'

Anselm puffed out his cheeks. 'It's hard to say. Each of the outer caverns have portals and a system of tunnels through which they could enter. Since they're coming from the north-west, my guest would be either Cavern Seven or Hexander, but we can't say for sure. I have Hunters posted half a mile out in each of the tunnels beyond the city, so we should at least get some warning before they attack.'

As the words left his mouth, there was shouting from across the cavern and a woman darted out of the entrance to Hexander. She sprinted across the cavern at a speed that showed she was a Hunter.

'They're coming!' she called, and more shouts joined her own as other Hunters burst from entrances around the cavern. 'They Atlanteans are attacking!'

'By the sound of it,' said Anselm, turning to Wyndham with a look of concern. 'It appears they're coming at us from *all* directions.'

A hand gripped Montgomery's sleeve and he turned to see Jarfin staring at the woman, wide-eyed, clearly alarmed by this news. Montgomery was surprised to find he felt quite relaxed, almost excited, by the prospect of the coming battle.

He patted Jarfin's arm awkwardly and whispered, 'You'll be okay. Just stick by your dad. He'll keep you safe.'

Jarfin opened his mouth, but was evidently too nervous to speak. Instead, he nodded, took his hand away and inched closer to Wyndham.

'Time to go,' said Anselm. 'One way or another, I'll see you when this is all over.'

'Come on!' Wyndham shouted over his shoulder as he headed down the slope towards the lake. 'Catrain, your group take Duventim. I'll take Cavern Seven.'

Catrain, running effortlessly next to him, nodded. 'Seconds!' she called. 'With me!'

Half the Lundarien army peeled away and headed for the entrance directly opposite. Montgomery turned as someone gripped his shoulder, and he was surprised to see Marlah looking *anxious*.

'Clovis and I are going with this lot,' she said, nodding to Catrain's group. 'We'll see you later, okay? Be safe!'

'Er, yeah,' said Montgomery, even more astonished by this display of genuine concern for his safety. 'You too.'

'Remember,' she said, as she let go of his shoulder and started to moved away. 'You're powerful enough to beat them all on your own. You just have to trust yourself.' And with that she was swallowed up by the ranks of those flooding past, leaving Montgomery staring after her, open-mouthed.

'Keep moving!' said Pepper, grabbing his arm and yanking him along towards the archway into Cavern Seven.

Together they burst through the entrance and found

themselves standing in the equivalent of the Lundarien Agra. Fields of golden wheat and tall maize plants swept away in front of them, lit up like a summer's day by the diamonds overhead. From somewhere, a faint breeze stirred the plants. It was hard to believe, looking out across this serene scene, which reminded him of the fields around his old home in Steepleford, that he was not only in the Underworld, but that this place was about to be attacked by the people of Atlantis. It was like some crazy dream or something from a film. This couldn't really be happening, could it?

'Course it's happening!' Montgomery span round to see Vala hobbling towards him.

'Were you-?' he began

'Listening to your thoughts? Course I was. Now, are you going to stand their gawping about or are you going to make yourself useful?' He was about to suggest the first option, but she beat him to it. 'Yes, very witty. Come along.' She struck out through the nearest field and he hurried along next to her with Pepper a few yards ahead.

In the distance, Montgomery could just make out the portal to whatever tunnel it was that led away from here to the west. He wondered how close to it the Atlanteans were.

'On me!' bellowed Wyndham from up ahead, his voice a deep boom that echoed around the cavern, and by the time Montgomery and Vala arrive, the Lundariens had formed a solid defensive wall in front of the portal.

'Stay close,' said Pepper, as he drew up next to her. 'And remember, they may look fierce and scary, but they're just people.'

'People with powerful magic!' said Montgomery, whose heart was beating so fast it felt like it was trying to bore its way out through his chest and run away.

'Hah!' Vala spat on the ground in disgust. 'Bunch of

lightweights, the lot of them! They won't have the advantage of surprise this time, so we'll see what they're really made of. And you can bet it ain't half as powerful as what *we've* got!'

There was a sudden shout from somewhere deep in the tunnel ahead, but it was too dark in there to see what was going on.

'Lights, please, Bancroft!' said Wyndham, and immediately ten brightly-glowing diamonds shot through the portal, illuminating the tunnel beyond. For a while there was nothing to see, but then, forcing their way towards the light, were the dark figures of the Atlanteans, hammering down the tunnel towards them. 'Movers,' shouted Wyndham. 'Cealers. Positions!'

About a third of the people in the defensive wall stepped forwards, forming a new front section, a mix of dark green and yellow. From somewhere they had gathered rocks and other heavy objects, which hovered in the tunnel mouth. In the centre stood the lofty figure of Bancroft and, next to him, Montgomery recognised the broad, stocky shape of the Cealer leader, Bryce Goye, one hand outstretched towards the tunnel mouth.

'On my mark,' said Bryce, looking around briefly to check everyone was ready. 'Three. Two. One. Now!'

With a wave of Bryce's hand, the diamonds Bancroft had Moved down the tunnel blinked out, plunging the approaching Atlanteans into darkness. At the same moment, the Movers' arms shot out, sending their various missiles - Montgomery noticed a kettle and a couple of boots in amongst the rocks, sticks and other items - rocketing down the tunnel. For a moment there was silence as ears strained to listen. Then the yells of pain began as the missiles struck home.

'Lights!' bellowed Wyndham and, with another wave of Bryce's hand, the diamonds along the tunnel burst back into life. Montgomery could make out a number of Atlanteans lying in crumpled heaps along the tunnel floor. 'See!' said Wyndham, 'Like I said, they're only human!' The rest of the Atlanteans took no notice of their fallen comrades, trampling over them in their frenzied dash towards the cavern entrance. Those at the front had their arms extended and it took Montgomery a moment to realise what they were doing. And then he saw. They were Moving the objects back along the tunnel, straight towards the Lundariens.

31. "You Nearly Punched Me In The Face"

'Incoming!' Wyndham's voice echoed around the cavern and the Movers closed together, arms raised. Vala jostled forwards, slamming her staff into the ground, and the air across the tunnel mouth shimmered like the surface of a vertical pond.

The missiles burst from the tunnel and slammed into the forcefield, rocks bursting apart, sticks shattering to splinters. There was a yell to Montgomery's left as something, a boot he thought, burst through, hitting one of the Changers on the side of her head, and further along, a rock bounced beneath the forcefield and slammed into Bryce Goye's shin. He sank to one knee, gripping his bleeding leg, his face screwed up in pain as hands pulled him back into the ranks, towards the cluster of Healers on the far right.

Montgomery turned back to the tunnel to see the Atlanteans almost at the entrance, their eyes bottomless pits, their lips pulled back open over sharpened teeth. Their dark clothes billowed around them and he recalled Bressalan's description of them as wearing the darkness. He was suddenly struck with a strange feeling, a certainty that it was not them wearing the darkness at all, but rather it was the other way round.

'Brace!' shouted Wyndham, snapping Montgomery out of his daydream. And then the fighting began.

At first the forcefield held them back but, as more

and more Atlanteans poured into the cavern, they broke through, forcing the Lundariens back. Movers on both sides blocked, struck out and hurled objects at their opponents, while Cealers added to their numbers and arsenal with illusionary fighters and weapons, while concealing real ones. Hunters darted snake-like among the fighters, striking out with ferocious speed and force, while Changers wrought havoc, turning the solid floor into quicksand and transforming weapons into harmless toys or into venomous creatures that turned on their holders.

Dazed by the speed and bizarreness of what was going on around him, Montgomery found himself backing away through the press of bodies into the field behind. Something struck him hard in the ear and he flinched round to find the tall maize plants thrashing around wildly, striking out at any of the Lundariens they could reach. He lifted his hands to protect his face and felt the sting of a cob whipping across his knuckles. Out of the corner of his eye, he caught sight of six Atlanteans who had worked their way along the cavern wall and were evidently controlling the maize plants, their mouths set in vicious smiles.

Another cob struck Montgomery, this time on his side and he was amazed and how much pain a bit of sweetcorn could produce. But more than that, he felt cross, a sudden surge of all the frustration and anger that had been building up in the last few weeks - the hurt of being betrayed by Merek, the resentment at his Underworld friends for blaming him, the annoyance at his mum for being unfair and punishing him for helping others, and the irritation at Jeff and his gang for making his life at St Kevin's so rubbish. All of it boiled up inside him, giving him knifelike focus and direction.

'Stop it!' he yelled, his arm sweeping out at the plants, and he could feel the force of the magic bursting out of him, flattening the maize, and even the wheat beyond it, as though a plane had landed on the field, the stalks scythed to the ground until not one was left standing. Against the cavern wall, the Atlanteans stared in bewilderment, their smiles frozen on their faces.

'Fall back!' Wyndham bellowed from somewhere in the press of bodies. 'Fall back!' and Montgomery turned to see things were not going in Lundarien's favour. Many of them, easily spottable in their coloured jerkins and bodices, were having to be helped along or even carried by others, while the Atlanteans pressed their advantage, leaving their own injured untended behind them.

Again and again the black-clad soldiers threw themselves at the Lundariens, hurling missiles into their midst, until the retreat became little more than a chase across the cavern, the Atlanteans in hot pursuit.

Pepper burst out of the press of bodies and grasped Montgomery by his arm.

'Come on,' she said, half-pulling, half-dragging him away from the skirmish. 'We need to get back to the main cavern. There'll be others there to help.'

They were almost at the entrance to the Primatectum when one of the Atlantean men burst through the ranks on Montgomery's left, a spear gripped in his hand. His eyes met Montgomery's and the man drew back his spear-holding arm, his pointy teeth glistening in the diamond light. The spear lanced forwards and, as Montgomery raised an arm to protect himself, his view of the weapon was suddenly blocked. He blinked as Wyndham threw himself in front of the spear and it burst through his right shoulder. The Watchman roared in anger and pain, his body turning sideways with the force of the blow. Wyndham reached up and grasped hold of the shaft of the spear, snapping it off as though it was nothing more than a tooth pick.

The Atlantean's eyes widened in surprise, as Wyndham swung the shaft round, making contact with the man's head, the wood shattering into splinters. The Atlantean dropped to the wheat-strewn ground. He didn't get back up.

'Keep moving!' shouted Wyndham. 'Head towards Lake Nova!'

As they began to file through, it was clear that the entrance was too small for more than a handful of people to get through at a time, leaving those behind to face the soldiers of Atlantis.

Again Wyndham's voice blasted out above the noise of fighting. 'Medway! Clear the perimeter. Bancroft, get a shield set up. Buy us some time, man, so we can all get out of here.'

Montgomery was almost bowled over as Medway and the other Hunters streamed past, heading for the front line, where they began to beat back a space between the Lundarien and Atlantean forces. The familiar shimmering in the air signalled that the Movers had erected a forcefield around the perimeter, and an Atlantean woman, who had been on the wrong side, suddenly found herself surrounded by an angry mob of opponents and began scrabbling at the inside of the invisible wall in an attempt to get away.

Again, Pepper tugged at Montgomery, this time pulling him through the archway into the Primatectum, the flow of fleeing bodies carrying him along.

The archway was at the top of the rise from the lake, and from this vantage point, Montgomery could see across the cavern and his heart sank. From every side, he saw people flooding into the cavern from the other portals. It appeared Atlantis was more powerful than they had imagined, even the combined forces of the Brytellian colonies were being forced back. From somewhere horns were blowing.

'That's the signal to regroup,' said Pepper, still clinging onto his arm. Sure enough, across the cavern, people were streaming down towards the lake, falling in behind Anselm and the soldiers of Salistra. With a quick glance over his shoulder, Montgomery saw Bancroft and the last of the Lundarien Movers rushing from Cavern Seven, the Atlanteans in pursuit, sending volleys of missiles, all of which clattered startlingly against the still-operational forcefield. All, that is, except for the kettle, which broke through, striking Medway in the face. The big man shrugged it off and kept on going.

Montgomery ran, resisting the urge to look back and expecting, at any moment, a rock to slam into him or one of the Atlanteans to seize him from behind. As they headed down the grassy slope, past the block of houses to their left, Catrain's party joined their ranks and Montgomery was relieved to see Clovis running next to her mother, though he couldn't see Marlah or Favian in the stampeding crowd.

'Fall in behind!' shouted a Salistran, who Montgomery recognised as the tall policemen he had seen on his first visit here. He waved the Lundariens through a break in the defensive line and they piled through. Montgomery was doubled over, his heart pounding and his lungs aching almost as badly as when he'd been drowning in Lake Altis.

'Are you okay?' asked Clovis, who had nipped through the crowd to join him. Like the rest of the Hunters, she seemed unaffected by the exertion of both fight and flight. Even her hair looked okay, or at least better than it had after the high-speed journey on the carpet.

Montgomery tried to catch his breath, peering around past her. 'Where's Marlah?' he asked. 'Wasn't she with you?'

She shook her head. 'We got separated. Isn't she here?'

Straightening up painfully, Montgomery scanned the assembled army of Brytellian, and used his Watching to search for Marlah. He could see a couple of Healers busy removing the broken spear from Wyndham's shoulder. He could see Vala and his mother, their faces set firmly towards the advancing enemy. Here and there were others he recognised, too, but Marlah and her dad were nowhere to be seen.

'Close ranks!' shouted the policeman. The cry was taken up around the central lake, where the army had gathered for its last stand. 'Brace!'

And then Atlantis was upon them.

Montgomery stared, open-mouthed at the magic around him. It was like being at the cinema, except there was no CGI here - this stuff was *really* happening. He watched a woman pulling rope from empty air and weaving in around the legs of a cluster of Atlantean soldiers. Nearby a man, wielding a short sword, lunged with it at one of the dark-robed woman of Atlantis, only to find it turn into water and wrap itself around his face. He clawed at it, struggling for air and the woman stepped forwards and struck him with a nasty-looking club. A tall Atlantean man with long, knifelike fingers, seized a girl of about Montgomery's age by the shoulders and bent forwards as if he was going to bite her. As he drew near, something like a bolt of lighting burst from the girl's eyes and the man was catapulted backwards, over the heads of his comrades and onto the grass beyond, where he lay, unmoving. The girl brushed at her shoulders as though removing some unsightly crumbs.

Drops of what felt like rain fell on Montgomery's head and he looked up to see a swirling tube of water, like the long neck of a brontosaurus or possibly a diplodocus, towering over him from the lake, controlled by a group of Brytellian Movers. He watched in amazement as the water monster leaned over the gathered army, opened its mouth and plunged forwards, swallowing up one of the Atlantean soldiers and sucking him down into the lake, like a vacuum cleaner dealing with a particularly unpleasant spider.

And still Atlantis fought on, their numbers barely dented. Montgomery looked around him at the thinning line of the Brytellians and the densely packed hoards that faced them, and could see it was only a matter of time before the Atlanteans overpowered them. There were just too many of them. He paused as his eyes passed over the heads of the black-clad fighters, his attention drawn to a patch of air behind them, which shimmered slightly, like hot air. As he watched, the view of the Salistran houses beyond it flickered and vanished, replaced by an entirely different view altogether: a herd of what looked like goats, cowered on a grassy hillside, trees dangling down around them. And then people began streaming through. Montgomery stared in amazement. It was the people from Dursehaven, with Bressalan at the head. They looked different from the last time he'd seen them. Gone were the ragged, travel-worn clothes, and the dirt smeared across their arms and faces. They looked well-fed, fit and ready for action. And they looked angry.

'Look!' said Clovis, pointing at them. 'It's Kolter. They must be teleporting from of the outer caverns.' She looked around at the distant entrances.

Montgomery watched as the teleport closed behind them and the people of Dursehaven formed a ring surrounding the Atlanteans, who found themselves suddenly fighting a battle on both sides. One women turned and hurled herself at this new enemy with a shriek, her pointed claws outstretched, but she didn't even get close. Another shimmering teleport opened in front of her and she vanished from view. A loud screaming made Montgomery look up towards the roof of the cavern and he saw the women dropping between the branches overhead. She burst through them and fell, crashing through the tiled roof of one of the houses, her cries abruptly silenced.

'Yes!' shouted Montgomery, punching the air.

'Watch out!' said Jarfin from right next to him. 'You nearly punched me in the face.'

'Jarfin! You're okay!'

'Of course I am,' he said, and though his voice was shaking, for a moment he looked like he was actually enjoying himself. 'I kept close to my dad, like you suggested. No one's got past him yet!' Montgomery looked over his friend's head to see Wyndham, his teeth gritted and his wounded shoulder evidently forgotten, slam a fist into the chin of an Atlantean, who was about to grab a Changer girl Montgomery hadn't seen before. The blow lifted the Atlantean about a metre into the air before he dropped to the ground in a crumpled heap, out cold.

Montgomery nodded at Jarfin. 'I'm glad I'm on *his* side! Have you seen Marlah? Only, Clovis said they got separated back in that cavern, whatever it's called.'

'Hold on,' said Jarfin and, as the battle raged around them, he put his fingers in his ears and closed his eyes.

A loud crack sounded overhead and Montgomery looked up to see a flock of purple and gold birds erupt from the tree above as one of the large branches was torn away and began to fall straight towards him. Instinctively, he raised his hands to shield himself, and realised what he had to do. Merek wasn't here to protect him this time, but he had trained him well.

Montgomery focused on the branch and pictured catching it in mid-flight. For a moment nothing happened, then, as if hitting an invisible wall, the branch jerked to a stop amid a shower of leaves. Checking first that it wasn't about to start falling again, Montgomery glanced down for a target and caught sight of a group of Atlanteans, standing between two cottages on a small hill. They were weaving their claw-like hands in creepy, synchronised motions, their gaze fixed on the lake. Montgomery turned to see what they were doing to find a huge wave billowing up from the far side of the water, raging towards the allied forces. Several rowing boats had been ripped from their moorings and were riding on its crest.

He breathed slowly, concentrating on the still-suspended branch. Then, with a flick of his wrist, he sent it hurtling towards the cluster of Atlanteans. It bounced on the ground in front of them, sending out a shower of leaves and dirt. At the last moment, they dropped their hands and tried to leap out of the way, but it was too late. The branch crashed into them, sweeping them off their feet. One Atlantean, who had been standing in front of a cottage, was knocked headfirst through the window. Montgomery didn't wait to see what had happened to the others. He turned back to see the wave, which had almost reached his side of the shore, fold in on itself, losing both height and speed until, when it finally broke, it did little more than wash up around his feet, leaving one of the boats jammed up on the sand nearby.

'Found her!' said Jarfin, straightening up and pulling his fingers from his ears. 'She's-' he stopped and peered down. 'Why are your shoes all wet?'

Montgomery eyes flicked down and then back. 'It doesn't matter. Where's Marlah?'

'I spotted her and her dad between the building over there.' Jarfin pointed up the hill to their left, but Montgomery could see nothing but fighting and buildings. 'It was only a glimpse, a couple of minutes or so ago, but

Kuruk and that Rayen woman were with her.'

'Kuruk?'

'I think she's been kidnapped.'

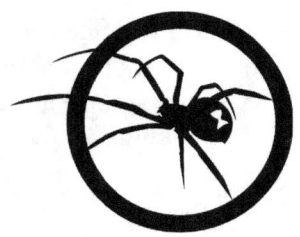

32. "And That's How We Fight On The Surface"

'What?' Clovis turned to look at Jarfin in disbelief. 'Why would Kuruk kidnap Marlah?

'It doesn't matter why,' said Montgomery. 'We have to rescue her!'

'But how're we going to get through this lot, though?' asked Jarfin, gesturing at the densely-packed ranks of the Brytellian and Atlantean fighters. As Montgomery turned to look, a spear rose up over their heads and arced down towards a group of Changers but, just before it struck home it exploded into a shower of golden glitter.

'Do you think you could Move us out of here on *that?*' Clovis pointed towards the boat that had washed up on the shore.

Montgomery eyed it. It was bigger than the carpet, but he didn't see why it should be any harder to Move.

'I'll give it a go,' he said and stepped towards it. As he did so, Vala hobbled out of the crowd in front of them, with Pepper at her side. They climbed into the boat and sat down as though waiting to go for an afternoon's fishing or just enjoying the view.

'We'll join you, if you don't mind,' said Vala.

'What?' said Montgomery, slowing as he drew near. 'How did you-?'

Vala just tapped the side of her head. 'You and your

loud thinkings, again,' she said. She did flapping motions with her arms. 'Come on, let's get this old thing up in the air.' Montgomery tried not to think about Vala being the *old thing* in question. 'Thinkings!' she said, giving him a pointed look.

He quickly took his place in the boat, Jarfin squeezing in next to him.

'Try not to crush us against the roof again,' said Clovis, as they shoved up to make room for her.

'I'll try,' said Montgomery. 'I think goes like this…'

The boat rocketed into the air, the force pushing them all down into their seats, and it took him a moment to get it under control.

'Well, that's a start,' said Vala, peering out between the branches of a tree and brushing some bird poo from her shoulder. Montgomery couldn't help noticing the twisted stump, where the branch had broken off earlier, only inches from his face.

'Don't look down,' added Jarfin, from the leafy canopy. Montgomery decided this was good advice as he peered over the edge at the sprawling mass of the battle below, bands of colour around a thick ring of black. After all he was sitting on what was little more than a few planks of wood hanging about fifty metres above the ground.

He gripped the side of the boat. 'We're going to die!' he said, his voice little more than a squeak.

'Don't talk rot,' said Vala. 'I think we need to head that way.' She pointed down towards the Pentalane cavern. Montgomery took a deep breath to steady his pounding heart and Moved the boat down and across the cavern, high over the heads of the seething masses below.

The boat felt much heavier than the carpet had and it weaved around through the air, in the general direction of where he meant it to go.

'We're going quite fast, dear,' said Pepper, talking

through clenched teeth. 'Perhaps it might be worth going a *little* slower?'

The boat did not slow down and hit the ground in a shower of sparks and splinters, spilling its five occupants out onto the turf.

'Thank goodness you aimed for the grass and not the buildings!' said Clovis, on her feet in an instant in true Hunter style. Montgomery, who had in fact been aiming for the entrance to Pentalane some way off, decided not to say anything. Jarfin scrambled to his feet, brushing himself down and pulling a large chunk of the now destroyed boat out of his tunic.

'That was fantastic!' he said.

Together the five of them hurried towards the nearby entrance. Behind them, the sound of the battle echoed around the cavern.

'Where do you think *you're* off to?' shouted Vala as they entered Pentalane. Apart from the four figures ahead of them, and a few unconscious bodies lying around, the cavern was deserted.

Kuruk looked over his shoulder, then stopped and turned to face them. He looked exactly as he did before, though without the throne and the bearers. And a couple of his black feathers had snapped off.

'It's the little boy,' said Rayen, who had also turned to face them, 'who volunteered for his so-called friend, no?' She laughed, gesturing towards them. 'I trust you chose your companions better this time, little boy. They make a fearsome-looking group!'

Between the two Atlanteans, Marlah and Favian looked as though they could hardly stand up. Marlah's eyes were closed and her head lolled around as though half-asleep. Blood was dripping from a nasty gash over Favian's right eye.

'What have you done to them?' demanded

Montgomery, his fists clenched at his side as he strode past the tower towards Kuruk, still some fifty metres or so away.

'This girl here is a fighter,' said Rayen, who was holding Marlah by the arm. 'I had to send her into the blue, but she is okay. You are okay, aren't you, girl?' She gripped Marlah's chin, her fingernails digging into her cheeks, and nodded her head up and down. 'This one,' she added, thumbing at where Favian was slumped next to Kuruk, 'is not so good. Kuruk had to smash a table into his head.' She shrugged, still smiling at Montgomery and the others.

'Let them go!' shouted Pepper, now only twenty metres away.

Kuruk let go of Favian, who flopped to the ground, and stepped towards them. He started barking at them in Atlantean again.

'These are now prisoners of Atlantis,' Rayen translated. 'Which means they are none of your business. They belongs to his Lordship!'

Kuruk took another step forwards, barring his sharpened teeth in a snarl as he pointed to the group and, in faltering English, he growled, 'Now *you* also belongs to me, I think.'

'You seem very sure of yourself, boy,' said Vala, her voice soft and icily cold. 'But there's only two of you, and there's five of us.'

Kuruk, no longer smiling, raised his arms. 'Not no more!' He brought his hands down hard, crouching as he did so, his fists crashing to the ground. In front of him, the cavern floor burst apart and continued outwards like a ripple in a pond, the ground surging up to engulf Montgomery and the others in a crushing wave of rock.

Montgomery closed his eyes, shielding his face with an arm as though that might somehow protect him. He could hear himself screaming again, barely audible over the rumble of the approaching death... and then it was silent. Except for his continued screams.

Opening one eye, he peered up at the wave of rock, which towered motionless above them. Vala was standing in front of him, her staff raised in the air. With an almost casual motion, she swept the staff to the left and the rocks cascaded across the tunnel, landing in a noisy heap on the grass.

'Glad it won't be me clearing up in here later,' she said, then hobbled towards Kuruk, who was blinking at her in evident astonishment. 'You were saying?'

Kuruk laughed, but it sounded ever-so-slightly nervous. 'But you is just a little, old lady.'

Vala clicked her fingers and the end of her staff burst into flame. 'I prefer "experienced",' she said, tilting the staff forwards. The fire burst from the end, heading straight for Kuruk, who stepped backwards, caught off-guard for a moment. He recovered quickly, though, and met it with a sheet of water, magicked out of thin air, that wrapped itself around the flames, extinguishing them in a burst of steam.

Kuruk didn't have long to look pleased with himself as, with a flick of Vala's wrist, she Moved the ground beneath him, like yanking a rug out from under someone's feet. Off balance, Kuruk staggered and was blasted in the chest by a jet of water, the very water he had made only moments before.

'Come on!' said Pepper, distracting Montgomery from the fight. 'Now's our chance to rescue Favian and Marlah. I'll deal with Rayen while you get them to safety into the Aristane Tower.' She pointed back to the building in question, then, moving with Hunter speed, she and Clovis raced towards Rayen.

Montgomery and Jarfin followed at a more normal

running pace.

The Atlantean woman dumped Marlah against a house and turned to square up to Pepper. 'Why are you dressed like a woman from the Surface?'

Pepper gave her a cold smile. 'Because I *am* from the Surface. And that means I've learned to fight with *and* without magic, as you're about to find out.'

Rayen laughed. 'What chance do you have against a real Underworld woman, like me?' Without warning, she leapt forwards, the blue already glowing in her palm. She looked certain to make contact but, at the last instant, Pepper, moving in a blur, ducked below Rayen's arm and slipped behind her, elbowing her in the back of the head and sending her sprawling on the ground.

'You sound like my sister,' said Pepper. 'Only not so tough. Now get up!'

'You get his other arm,' said Jarfin, struggling to lift Favian by the shoulder. 'We'll have to drag him.'

'I could trying Moving him instead,' suggested Montgomery, tearing his eyes away from the fighting.

Jarfin looked up, still holding Favian's jerkin. 'He's already pretty bashed up. I'm not sure he'd survive one of your crash landings!'

Montgomery nodded, taking hold of his other arm, and together they began to drag him away towards the Aristane Tower.

'Why are adults so heavy?' said Montgomery, straining as he heaved on Favian's arm. 'It's like trying to drag a sofa with horse on it.' He turned his head to see Clovis already entering the doorway of the tower with Marlah. Still pulling on the arm, he looked back at the fighting.

Pepper was running circles around Rayen, literally, spinning her around by one arm until the Atlantean was little more than a blur. Rayen managed to lash out with a foot, catching Pepper on the side of her knee, which sent her staggering into the wall of a nearby building. But while Rayen was trying to get her balance back, Pepper recovered and flicked a hand towards the ground beneath Rayen's feet. The ground began to swallow her like quicksand.

A short distance away, Vala had produced an axe from somewhere and was in the act of throwing it at Kuruk. He, in turn, had created a wall of what look like crystal around himself, but as the axe struck it, the wall shattered into thousands of jagged fragments. They didn't drop to the ground, however, but turned their razor sharp edges towards Vala. Kuruk thrust his hand forwards and the pieces shot towards her.

Montgomery gasped, dropping Favian's arm and causing his head to thud on the floor, but by the time the shards of crystal had reached Vala, they had transformed into...

'Are those jelly babies?' said Jarfin.

'I think so,' said Montgomery, quickly picking up the arm again as Favian groaned. 'Nearly there.'

Once Marlah and Favian were safe inside the Aristane Tower, Montgomery and the others ran back out to see how Vala and Pepper were getting on.

Somehow, Rayen had freed herself from the quicksand and, brushing her blue-black hair out of her eyes, she began forming great lengths of chain to wrap around Pepper, trapping her arms. Pepper wasn't beaten yet, though, and kept kicking out at Rayen as the chain worked its way round and down her body.

Vala seemed to have the upper hand against Kuruk, whose body looked as though it was encased in ice. While he was trapped there, she kept striking him over the head with her staff.

Montgomery decided to try and help his mum, and

sprinted towards her.

'Get away from her!' he yelled as Rayen stepped closer to Pepper, who was now so chained up that she was unable to move her arms or legs. Rayen raised her hand, the palm glowing blue. 'I said leave my mum alone!' Rayen turned a triumphant smile towards him.

'Hey!' shouted Pepper, and Rayen looked back just in time to see Pepper's head blurring towards her. Rayen tried block it with her hand, but she was far too late. Pepper's forehead connected with her nose with a sound like someone snapping a dry branch, and the Atlantean crumpled to the floor in an unconscious heap, the light in her hand winking out. 'And that's how we fight on the Surface!' said Pepper. 'Not that I want to see you doing anything like that,' she added, noticing Montgomery staring at her, open-mouthed.

He turned in alarm at the sound of Vala shouting in pain. Somehow Kuruk had managed to break free from his ice-prison and was now twisting Vala's arm up behind her back in one hand. His other hand was held over her head, its palm also glowing, but not blue like Rayen's. Kuruk's palm glowed black. Vala lashed out at him with her staff, but Kuruk ignored it as he lowered the black light onto her forehead.

'No!' shouted Montgomery and, from where he stood, thrust out a hand towards Kuruk with that same, sweeping motion that had flattened the maize in Cavern Seven.

Kuruk was knocked off his feet and sent bowling across the cobbled street. Vala, however, was also struck by the force of Montgomery's magic and span through the air, slamming into the wall of a house and sending up a cloud of plaster dust.

'No!' Montgomery said again, his voice barely a whisper, as he stared at her motionless figure slumped on the floor. He ran towards her, calling over his shoulder to where Clovis and Jarfin were helping Pepper untangle herself from the chains. 'Vala's been hurt!'

Skidding to a stop, he dropped to his knees beside her and tried to roll her onto her back. She looked twisted, somehow, as though her old body had been taken apart and put back together wrong.

He leaned over, his ear near her mouth, listening for any signs of breathing, but could hear nothing. Sitting up again, he tried shaking her by her shoulder. 'Vala?' he said. 'Auntie? Wake up! Please!' But still there was nothing. No movement. No sounds. Nothing at all to suggest she was still alive.

'The old hag is dead!' said a voice, and Montgomery turned in surprise to find Kuruk leaning over him, covered in dust, the blood from cuts and scratches on his face mingling with the red lines of his tattoos. His hand hovered above Montgomery's head and, as he looked up at it, Montgomery saw the strange, dark light glowing in his hand.

And then the darkness consumed him.

33. "I Am The Darkness"

Montgomery opened his eyes, but it hardly made a difference. There was light here, wherever *here* was, but it was a faint, washed out kind of light, like it had been used up and worn out and did barely more than add shadows and outline the darkness.

He was flat on his back and, though the ground beneath him was hard, it didn't feel like rock. It was smooth and, as he pushed himself up, it felt warm against the skin of his hands. He climbed, somewhat unsteadily, to his feet and looked around, trying to work out where he was. The last thing he could remember was Kuruk's glowing palm descending. What had happened after that? Had the Atlanteans dragged him off to some cave? And if so, why? Was this a prison?

The cave, if indeed it was a cave, was domed, like a huge blister, with no visible doors or windows. Its roof was twice Montgomery's height in the middle and the circular floor only slightly wider than the lounge in Montgomery's apartment. As he thought of his home back in London, anxiety gripped his insides like a fist. Where was his mum? What was his dad going to think when they failed to come home? He'd have no idea that they were in the Underworld. It would seem as though they had simply vanished off the face of the earth ... which they had, in a sense.

Montgomery leaned forward, trying to steady his

breathing and the pounding of his heart. He was just getting his fear under control, when he felt something brush past his ear. He span round, peering into the half-light, but could see nothing.

Again, something touched him, moving across the skin on the back of his hand as though someone had breathed on it. He looked down and could just make out something moving, like a fine, dark mist, an almost indiscernible shadow. And then he sensed it, like a dawning certainty. There was a monster in the dark.

He couldn't see it, but he felt it all around: its anger, its hatred, its malice. In the blackness of the cave something was stirring and Montgomery leaned forwards to peer into the shadows, panic rising as he strained to make out what it was.

And then he understood. The monster *was* the shadows. Around the cave, they began to shrink and thicken, taking form like smoke being drawn backwards into a fire. But there were no flames here, there was barely a suggestion of light, only the gathering darkness drifting towards him.

Montgomery turned to move away, to run, but there was nowhere to go, no escape, just the bare wall on every side. And behind...

Little by little the creature emerged, its arms, its legs, its body, a skeletal form woven from darkness and night, all skull and ribs. It was tall, far taller than a man and, as the last wisps of shadow fell into place, it leaned its face down almost touching Montgomery's. Its eyes opened, two holes red with fire, and then it spoke, its voice an echo from an ancient cave.

Three words: 'I know you.'

Montgomery stepped backwards. 'What?' he said, his mouth dry, his voice little more than a whispered croak.

'I know you,' repeated the creature, tilting its head to

one side as if to examine him better. 'I have watched you through more mortal eyes than these.' The fire in the dark sockets flared up for a moment, lighting Montgomery's face. He stepped back again, and could feel the downward curve of wall behind him.

'Who... who are you?' he stammered.

The creature smiled, or at least its mouth widened and something like teeth, black as midnight coal, glittered. 'I am the darkness,' it said, spreading out its bony arms. 'I am the footstep in the night that wakes you in your sleep. I am the breath that whispers in the wind and murmurs through your windows. I am the creaking of your house when no one else is there, the one who watches you from the shadows where no light can reach. I am the darkness,' it said again, 'and I know you, Montgomery Vane.'

Montgomery opened his mouth and was about to ask the creature how it knew his name, when a thought struck him. 'The prophecy!' he said, his voice a little stronger. 'I remember. The prophecy spoke about you. You're... the Creeping Darkness?'

The creature stepped forwards, towering over Montgomery. 'I have been known by many names and at many times. But that is as good as any. I am only a glimpse of the darkness, however, a shadow once trapped in a cave deep below Atlantis. They released me from my tomb and I have ridden them all this way.'

'*Ridden* them?' Montgomery frowned, his fear giving way to interest. 'You mean you *possessed* them? You forced them to attack Dursehaven and the Brytellian colonies?'

'Hardly *forced*,' said the creature, shrugging its bony shoulders and stepping back. 'I do not *force*. They did nothing they did not wish to do, deep down. The destruction of those colonies was simply a means to an end. For the greater good. The *greatest* of goods.'

Montgomery shook his head. 'I don't understand.

People died today, because of you, and you call that *good?*' He glared at the face that towered above him, but the skull-like features remained blank, unmoved by his words.

'When I am released,' it said, 'I shall fill the world - the world below *and* the world above - and I bestow such a gift! I will give to everyone their deepest desires.' The Darkness bent down again, its glowing eyes level with Montgomery's glowering ones. 'Tell me, boy. What greater good can their be?'

Montgomery looked away, confused. He knew this creature was wrong, that what it had done and what it sought to do was evil, but he couldn't explain it. 'What do you mean, when you're released? I thought you said the Atlanteans released you?'

'I also said I am but a glimpse of the darkness. I am little more than a half-forgotten memory of myself. My *true* self, my *full* self, is still imprisoned, far away and far, far below the world of humanity.'

'And that's what this has all been about,' said Montgomery, comprehension dawning at last. 'This is why Atlantis attacked Brytellian, so you could break yourself free from... wherever you've been trapped? So you could take over the world?'

The mouth above him opened into what Montgomery couldn't help thinking of as a grin. 'I did my best with the tools at my disposal, but the people of Atlantis are blunt, undignified weapons. This is why I have left them. This is why I am here, why *we* are here. What need have I of such people, when I can wield greater power in a single body?'

'A single...?' Montgomery paused, his mouth forming an 'O' of surprise. 'Me?'

'With an Omnifex in my power, who will stand in my way?' And then Montgomery felt it, the force of desire hitting him like a wave, a longing to join with the

Darkness, to serve this creature, to bring about this good. This greatest of all goods. It was like the yearning for water after running on a hot day, almost overpowering, but he fought against it.

'No!' he shouted, stepping backwards to find himself pressed hard against the wall. It's surface vibrated slightly at his touch. 'I won't!' Once more the wave crashed over him, and the desire to let this creature take him was formidable.

'Yes!' said the Darkness, reaching a long, bony finger towards him. 'Let me in. Together we will change the world!' The finger drew nearer, pointing towards his chest, towards his heart, ready to pierce, to consume, to control. Behind him, Montgomery felt the wall of the cave shudder and it jerked him forwards, towards the creature. 'Let me in,' it said again. 'I only-' It stopped, its head snapping up as though looking at something, and Montgomery was sure he saw fear in its face, even though it remained expressionless. It's eyes locked onto his. 'Quickly,' it said. 'Let me in.'

Montgomery gritted his teeth against another wave of persuasion, and hissed, 'No! I will *never* help you.' Behind him the wall was shifting again, forcing him forwards and he noticed that, on every side, the walls were drawing in. The cave, or whatever this place was, was shrinking.

'No!' Again the creature looked around, afraid. 'There is no time! You must let me in now!'

But Montgomery shook his head, forcing himself to focus through the mental onslaught of the waves of desire. Above him, the creature began to bend as the roof lowered and the walls drew in. 'I would rather die than let you in!'

The Darkness said nothing, but continued to bend forwards, until its skull-like face was mere inches from his own. Montgomery found himself staring into its eyes, as the flames within danced and burned, growing and spreading, expanding into an inferno that filled his vision. He glanced from side to side, but the cave was so small now there was barely room for the two of them. He felt a stab of panic at the idea of them both trapped inside place, crushed to death by these shrinking walls.

'It makes no difference,' said the creature at last, its eyes blazing. 'You may have stopped me today, but I *will* rise, Montgomery Vane. Darkness will rise with or without your help.'

'It'll have to be *without*,' whispered Montgomery, lifting a hand to shield himself from the heat of those fiery eyes. But there was no relief, the fire was spreading, even the walls were burning as they continued to close in around him.

And once more, the voice spoke. Three words.

'Darkness *will* rise.'

34. "This Is Not The King I Wanted To Be"

Montgomery burst awake, kicking out against the crushing walls, his hands thrashing at the flames. But there was no fire, no shrinking cave. Instead, he opened his eyes to find a face like wrinkled leather, ancient and worn, hovering only inches above his own.

'Aargh!' he yelled, trying to push himself backwards into the solid rock floor. 'What the...? Where?' He tried to gather his thoughts as he blinked in wonder at the ancient face.

'Ancient?' said the face. 'I prefer *experienced*, as well you know.'

'Vala?' said Montgomery. 'Vala! You're okay?'

'Hah,' Vala drew her face back, which was no small relief to Montgomery. She was smiling. 'It'd take more than some whippersnapper shoving me at an old building to get the better of me. I'm old!' she said, jabbing a wrinkled finger into her chest. 'Means I'm hard to kill!'

'Experienced at staying alive,' suggested Pepper, who was looking at Montgomery over Vala's shoulder. 'How are you, dear? You gave me quite a fright there.'

Montgomery propped himself up on an elbow, looking around. He was still in Pentalane, a short distance from the Aristane Tower. Marlah was sitting on one of its step, leaning against her dad, who was clutching his head as if... well, as if he'd been hit with a table.

'What happened?' asked Montgomery. 'How long was I out?'

'Oh, about five minutes,' said Pepper. 'Though it caused quite a stir when Kuruk Quarantined you.'

Montgomery frowned. 'Quarantined?'

'The thing *she* did to you back in Yarnock.' Pepper turned and gestured to Rayen, who had been dumped, unconscious, against a wall. 'Healers use it if they need to knock out their patients. Anyway, when Kuruk Quarantined you, you weren't the only one who passed out. Look!' She pointed to where Kuruk lay in a black heap on the floor.

'What happened to him?' he asked.

'You must have duffed him up with your magic!' said Jarfin, smiling as he climbed the hill to join them. 'And all that lot, as well.' He pointed back towards the Primatectum and, as Montgomery shuffled round awkwardly, he realised the sounds of battle had vanished.

'What happened to the Atlanteans?' he asked, staring at the distant dark figures strewn around the central cavern. They lay in a wide circle around the lake, having clearly dropped to the ground where they had been fighting. 'Why are they all on the ground?'

Vala shrugged. 'It happened at the exact same moment Kuruk touched you. Or so your mother tells me. I was having a little snooze at the time.'

Montgomery looked down at his feet. 'Um... Sorry about that,' he said. 'Are you okay?'

'Better than ever,' said Vala. 'In fact, you've completely healed the ache in my left shoulder.' She twirled her arm like a windmill, then snatched Montgomery's hand and pulled him up effortlessly. 'See?'

'She's stirring,' called Marlah, and Montgomery turned to see her pointing at Rayen. Sure enough, Kuruk's right-hand woman was trying to sit up. She was groaning in pain, which probably had something to do with the strange angle of her nose. And all the blood.

Pepper strode over and yanked Rayen to her feet, who was now gripping her face, her eyes tight closed.

'Please,' said Rayen, though it sounded more like "bees". 'Wait, please.' There was a glow beneath her hand, where it touched her face, though it wasn't the blue light of the Quarantine she had inflicted on Montgomery and Marlah. This light was white and clean, and for a moment it shone so brightly between her fingers that the others had to turn away. Then it dimmed, fading as Rayen dropped her hand back to her side. 'That is better,' she said, and Montgomery was surprised to see her nose was back to its former shape, only a smear of blood on her lip and cheek to show she'd ever been head-butted. By his mum! He still couldn't quite believe that.

'You're a Healer?' said Pepper, peering at her nose.

Rayen nodded, raising an arm to shield her face from the light of the cavern's single diamond. 'Why is it so bright in here?'

Pepper peered at Rayen's face. 'What's happened to your eyes?' she asked. 'They were… they were black.'

Rayen blinked her now-normal eyes, like a person waking from a dream. 'It is gone,' she said. 'The darkness. It is gone.'

'Where is he?' Wyndham's booming voice roared across the cavern. Montgomery caught sight of him striding up towards them, his face a mix of pain and fury. 'Where's Kuruk?'

'Over there,' said Vala, jabbing a staff at the still-unconscious heap. Wyndham strode over and, with a swift, easy motion, as though he was doing nothing more than picking a daisy, he swept Kuruk up over his shoulder and headed to the Aristane Tower.

'I shan't bother asking who did him in,' said Wyndham, raising a single eyebrow at Montgomery, 'but it seems to have been pretty effective! The whole Atlantean army's been knocked out. Our guys are busying tying them all up, good and tight.' He turned to Pepper and gestured at Rayen. 'Grab that woman, would you? It's time to bring them before the Aristane.'

'It's a bit cramped in here!' said Vala, as the leaders of the various Brytellian communities crammed themselves into the room at the top of the tower. Montgomery was willing to bet it was called the Aristane Meeting Room. It was circular, with six arched windows equally spaced around its stone walls. In the centre of the room was a circular platform of white marble, set into the floor. Most of the people, about forty in all, were standing, but in one of the ornately-carved chairs that surrounded the platform sat Anselm, his eyes narrowed at Rayen, seated opposite. Wyndham dumped Kuruk into the only other chair and moved to stand next to Anselm. The Atlantis leader was still unconscious, but Emlyn stepped forwards and placed the palm of her hand on his forehead. For a moment Montgomery glimpsed a bright blue light shining between her fingers, then she pulled it away as Kuruk jerked awake.

He barked out something, pushing himself back in the chair, and looked round at the assembled faces, a startled look in his eyes. Montgomery was surprised to see that the black holes had been replaced with normal eyes, though the irises were a deep gold colour. He cleared his throat and spoke in jagged English. 'How came I here?'

'We will be asking the questions!' shouted Wyndham, slamming his massive fist onto the marble platform. 'Starting with, what exactly happened to your army out there?' He gestured through the window that looked out towards the central cavern of Salistra, where most of the

Atlanteans were still scattered about the place, unconscious. Montgomery peered out and, amongst the aftermath of the battle, he could just make out the figure of Clovis, flicking her long, yellow plait from her shoulder, deep in conversation with Kolter.

Kuruk leaned forwards, surveying the scene. 'I don't understand. It was…' He raised a hand to his head, but stopped short and stared at his palm, eyes wide. 'It must have been the boy.' He looked around the room and, when he caught sight of Montgomery he pointed a pointy finger at him. '*You*. What did you do to us?'

Montgomery opened his mouth to answer, but Wyndham held up a hand. 'I said *we* will be asking the questions. What happened?'

'I don't know,' he said, shaking his head. One of his black feathers fluttered to the floor. 'All I remember is touching this boy, and then I am here.' He tilted his head a little, as though trying to listen to some far off conversation. 'It is different.'

'What do you mean?' asked Anselm, who had fixed Kuruk with an unblinking stare.

'The darkness. It is gone. After so long, it is a strange feeling.' He glanced back at Montgomery. 'It is something to do with you, no? You have freed us?'

'It is true,' said Rayen. Throughout the exchange she had sat, looking down at her lap, but now her gaze flicked around the room, eager and intense. 'It is like a shadow has been lifted from my mind. The world… the world is warm again.'

'What are you talking about, woman?' said a voice, and Montgomery leaned forward to see Destrian, one of the Yarnock leaders, glaring at Rayen. 'What has this got to do with you attacking us and forcing us from our homes?'

Anselm held up a hand, not turning from Kuruk. 'Tell

us about this darkness,' he said.

The Atlantean leader nodded. 'It started many years ago. You know the old stories of Atlantis, yes? When they let in the waters above? Many thousands of people died and our city was destroyed. But this time... this time is worse. We digged too *deep*.'

'Digging?' said Wyndham, perching on the edge of the platform. 'Digging for what?'

'What does anyone dig for? Gold!'

Montgomery felt Pepper stir next to him. 'But I thought Atlantis was rich?' she said. 'That's why it's known as the Golden City. How much gold does one city need?'

'Hah! When my father died, hardly nothing was left. Little gold, little money, and thousands of hungry mouths to feed. We needed gold and so I digged for it. This is why my people call me the Razor King, because I cut the ground deep to slice out the gold.'

'You said you dug too deep,' said Anselm. 'What did you mean?'

Kuruk shook his head. 'We were following a rich seam, good, clean gold, when we breaked through a wall. It opened onto a small cave. They said it was nothing but an empty pocket - no way in, no way out. But it was *not* empty. Something had been trapped in there and we let it out!'

'What sort of something?'

He shook his head again. 'Something... evil. A darkness.'

'We do not know how,' added Rayen, a look of fear shadowing her face, 'but this darkness spread out through our city, touching people, changing people, taking us over.' Wyndham turned to Anselm, who nodded, not breaking his unblinking gaze on the Atlanteans.

'How did they change?' asked Wyndham. 'What did

this darkness do to your people?'

'It was not only my people,' said Kuruk, dropping his gaze. 'The darkness found me too. It took me. It took us all... until today. Until this boy come along.'

Wyndham glanced at Montgomery, then back to the Atlanteans. 'So what did it do to you? Did it take control of you? Is that why you attacked us?'

Rayen shook her head. 'It was not control, exactly.'

'No,' added Kuruk. 'It is like the darkness takes your desires and twists them.' He mimed twisting with his claw-like hands. 'It uses your own will and bends it to its own.'

'What a load of old twaddle,' said Vala, nudging past Destrian so she could scowl at Kuruk properly. 'Give us an example of this *twisting*.'

Kuruk scratched his head, pausing to look out of the window again at his people being woken by the Healers. Others were leading them away, presumably to the Salistran prison, if there was such a thing.

'This here,' he pointed at the scene, 'is bad. The fighting, the killing, the kidnapping, the forcing people to do what they don't want... This is not the king I wanted to be.' He turned back, his eyes meeting Vala's. 'But what I said about joining together is true. My desire truly was to unite our nations, to help the Underworld prepare for the Great War that is to come.'

Again, Wyndham turned to Anselm, and again the Arister nodded as if in answer to an unspoken question. 'This is a good desire, no?' Kuruk continued. 'But the darkness took it and made it so I did terrible things to get what I want. *That* is the twisting I speak of.'

There was a pause as these words sank in, broken by the creaking of Anselm's chair as he leant back in it.

'He is telling the truth,' he said, stroking his beard with one hand. With sudden certainty, Montgomery realised that Anselm was using magic to find out if Kuruk was lying or not - yet another sort of Conjuring, he guessed.

'You say you've been freed,' said Wyndham. 'So where is this darkness now?'

Kuruk tilted his head to one side. 'If you want to know that,' he said, 'you should ask *him.*' Again he pointed at Montgomery, and all eyes in the room turned on him.

'Don't look at me,' he said. He would have taken a step back, only someone was standing right behind him. 'All I know is that Kuruk tried to *Quarantine* me and I found myself in a weird, shrinking dome, talking with some sort of skeleton smoke monster.'

'Really?' Beside him Pepper looked concerned. 'What happened?'

'What did this creature say?' asked Wyndham, leaning forwards, his hands pressed on the marble surface.

'Um…' Montgomery closed his eyes, trying to use his Watching to recall what the creature had told him, but he was too tired to focus properly. One thing, however, he remembered clearly. 'It said it was going to free the darkness, whatever that means. It didn't say where from, but that was what it wanted the Atlanteans for, to help it free the darkness. That…' He paused, wondering whether to tell them it had left the Atlanteans so it could have him instead, but as he looked at the faces around him, with their looks of alarm and worry, he decided it probably wasn't a good idea. 'That was it. Then it just disappeared and I woke up.'

He shoved his hands in his pockets, feeling awkward, and the fingers of his left hand brushed against something small and hard. As the attention eased away from him, he slipped his fingers round it and pulled it out. The object looked like a black marble, about an inch across, except that it wasn't just black. Instead, it seemed to suck at the light, blurring its surroundings so it appeared to be coated in a layer of shadow.

'So that's it?' said Emlyn, cutting through his thoughts. 'It's over?'

He shoved the marble back into his pocket and looked at Kuruk. Everyone else turned to look at him as well and the Atlantean leader held up his hands, warding off their unspoken questions. 'Yes, yes. We will not make no more trouble for you. Like I said, like the boy said, the darkness is gone. It has no more hold on us.'

'What about our cities,' demanded a woman. Montgomery had seen her when they first went to Yarnock, but he didn't know her name. He assumed she was a leader of one of the other western colonies. 'What about our homes? What about the people, good people, you've killed?' She pointed an angry finger at Kuruk.

He climbed, unsteadily, to his feet and bowed to her. 'I cannot bring back those who have lost their lives,' he said, 'and for this I am truly sorry. But I make this promise for you.' He placed a hand on his chest and his voice grew in confidence, sounding almost kingly. 'Our people will make good the cities we have attacked. We will rebuild what we have damaged. We will restore all we have taken. We will repay for the wrong we have caused your people. This I swear.' He slapped his hand down on the platform and looked the woman in the eyes, unwavering.

'Is that the truth?' asked Wyndham, directing the question not at Kuruk but at Anselm.

The elderly Salistran looked up at him. 'Oh yes,' he said. 'Every word of it since he woke up. Not even the trace of a lie. It would seem Dalton's grandson here,' he reached out and patted Montgomery on the shoulder, 'really was your secret weapon, after all.' Anselm turned back to Kuruk. 'And maybe as your first act of restoration you can show us where you've hidden Garrick and the other hostages. Okay?'

Kuruk smiled those pointy teeth, and somehow they didn't seem quite so unpleasant as they had before.

35. "It's All My Fault"

The Brytellian allies were not easily convinced that their former enemies had changed. After all, the Atlanteans, in their midnight robes and glowing tattoos, still looked pretty scary, even if their eyes were now back to normal. However, after a short speech from Anselm, the return of the hostages and the revelation that many of the Atlanteans were Healers, there was a grudging acceptance of their help.

Tired and still dazed from the morning's events, Montgomery leaned against the entrance to Pentalane, staring out across the central cavern. In every direction, the ground was littered with those who had been wounded in the battle. Next to a large, ornate building that may have been their Town Hall, sheets covered the six still forms of those who were now beyond the power of the Healers.

'How did it come to this?' he wondered. 'How could a whole nation of people be driven to commit such horrors?' The creature in his vision, if indeed it had been a vision, had claimed it did not force people, but instead gave them the power to pursue their deepest desires. But this? He shook his head, still gazing at the lake, where a couple of Atlanteans and a woman in a green bodice were Moving another body from the depths, water cascading from its black robes. 'How could anyone desire this?'

'Want to tell me about it?'

Montgomery span round to find Vala right behind him leaning on her staff. 'About what?'

'Darkness will rise?' She tapped a bony finger above her left ear. 'It's all muddled up there in your head.'

'Where you have no right being!' He glared at her, but it had no discernible effect. Her eyes bored into his and, after a few seconds, he looked away. 'I keep hearing it,' he said. '"Darkness will rise." First from granddad in some sort of vision and again in that note he left with the Trypasphere. Then Payton said it.'

'Payton?' Vala raised a knowing eyebrow. 'Which reminds me. That wretched shadow lion hide of yours is cluttering up my cottage!'

'Then the smoke creature said it as well,' he continued. '"Darkness will rise."'

Vala pulled out her pipe and pointed at him with it. 'So what do you think it means?'

He blew out his cheeks, considering the question. 'It must be something to do with what the creature was trying to do. Like I said,' he gestured towards the Aristane Tower, 'it wanted to use the Atlanteans to free its "true self", so I guess there's more of it out there somewhere. The *real* darkness.'

'Any idea where?' asked Vala, chewing on her pipe and puffing out little clouds of smoke.

'No idea.' Montgomery held up empty hands, thinking back to what the creature had said. 'Somewhere far away, below the world of...' He paused as a thought struck him. 'Payton said something about the danger in the east. Maybe that's got something to do with it? After all, the Atlanteans *were* heading east.'

'So are we!' said Marlah, coming up the slope from the Primatectum. 'Wyndham says it's time to get back home. Most of the wounded have been dealt with, thanks to all those extra Healers.'

Montgomery peered past her to see the other Lundariens heading in their direction. 'What's going to happen with the Atlanteans?' he asked. 'Are they going to be put in prison?'

'Don't worry about them,' said Vala, placing a hand on his shoulder. 'They'll not be any trouble. The battle with Atlantis is over.' She tapped below her eye with the pipe. 'I've seen it, lad.'

The triumphant return of the Lundarien army was spoiled somewhat by the frantic and confused scene that greeted their arrival at the Westerly Portal. As they marched along the road that led down to the Town Square, it became clear that everything was not alright in the city. At first, Montgomery wondered if the people were simply afraid, afraid that Atlantis had won, that Salistra had fallen and that Lundarien would soon become the focus of the Atlanteans' destructive form of unity. But it soon became clear that the problem was more immediate.

Payton had escaped.

'What do mean she's escaped?' Wyndham demanded, towering over Dain Cottle, the Watchman he'd left in charge in his stead. 'That's impossible.'

'Impossible it may be,' said Berinon, striding down the Town Hall steps, his cane kicking up even more sparks than usual, 'but she has escaped nonetheless.'

Wyndham frowned at him. 'What happened to your face, man?' he asked.

Berinon frowned in return as he reached a hand to his eye, swollen and already starting to blossom into a purple bruise. 'What do you think? It seems Payton was none too pleased to see me when she burst in from the courtyard.'

'So let's hear it,' said Wyndham. 'What happened?'

'She punched me in the face.'

'Not what happened to your eye, you idiot. How did

Payton get out?'

Berinon bristled, puffing out his chest, which was about a quarter of the size of Wyndham's. 'Oh, *I'm* the idiot, am I?' he said. 'I am not the one who left the city undefended. *Again!* It was only a few short weeks ago that you dragged all our best magicians off into the Labyrinth, leaving Payton free to take over our -'

'You know why we took so many to Salistra,' said Catrain, glaring at the Bardle leader. 'And even then, I doubt it would have been enough to beat the Atlanteans if it weren't for Montgomery.' Montgomery blushed, glad he was hidden in the press of bodies. 'We won, by the way, in case you hadn't noticed!'

Wyndham raised his arms to silence the excited chatter this comment provoked from those nearby. 'There'll be time for that later. You were saying?'

Berinon paused before speaking, clearly annoyed at having been interrupted. 'An hour or two after you all left the city, Payton's rat, Merek, seized his chance to slink back in.' Montgomery gasped and, behind him, Marlah growled. 'No one saw exactly how he did it, but one of the young Bardles out fishing reported a figure standing in a boat, peering in through one of the drainage holes in the Town Hall courtyard. We believe it was Merek, Moving something into the prison to free Payton.'

'Some*thing*?' said Pepper, with a quick, sharp glance at Montgomery. 'What sort of something?'

Berinon was about to answer, but Montgomery got there first, pushing forward through those in front. 'It was the Trypasphere, wasn't it? Merek sent in the Trypasphere in the prison to counteract the effects of the Heliorbs. And now Payton's escaped. It's all *my* fault.'

'That,' said Berinon, with a nasty smile that caused the tips of his ridiculous moustache to quiver, 'pretty much sums it up.'

Wyndham placed a hand on Montgomery's shoulder. 'Of course it wasn't your fault, lad.' He glared at Berinon. 'So where did Payton vanish off to after she gave you that beautiful shiner?'

Berinon's smile vanished and he touched his fingertips to his bruised face. 'East,' he said. 'She and her rat scuttled off into the Hanging Forest. We sent Rowan and the few Hunters still in Lundarien to follow her and see where she went, but they couldn't find any tracks. It was as though the forest simply swallowed them up. We've placed guards across the eastern entrances to the city, but I can't imagine she'd come back... at least, not until she's gathered herself another following of outcasts and criminals!'

Wyndham nodded, then turned to mount the Town Hall steps to look out over the crowd that had now gathered in the Town Square. It seemed to Montgomery as though the whole city had come out to hear the news, and they filled the cobbled area and the streets around, all eyes looking to Wyndham.

'It's no use worrying about Payton now,' he said, his huge voice echoing across the square. 'We will deal with her, and with Merek, when the time comes, I can assure you. Now, however, it is time for us to celebrate the fact that the threat of Atlantis is no more. Our city is safe and those Lundariens who fought bravely today in Salistra have all returned home!' A cheer rippled across the crowd and Wyndham raised his arms for silence. 'Sadly, not all the Brytellian colonies were so lucky. Good men and women lost their lives in this conflict and, despite our victory, we have a greater need than ever to be vigilant, to be united and to be prepared at all times.'

'What for?' called a woman from the crowd. 'Is there another threat?'

'Not as far as I know,' said Wyndham, taking a step

forwards to look at the woman. 'But in barely a few weeks our city has been under threat from Payton and from Atlantis. Who knows what other powers are out there? So, it is important to be prepared. And for that reason,' he gestured towards Montgomery and, for a moment Montgomery was worried he was going to draw attention to him again, but instead, the watchman continued, 'I have asked Vala to take up her old seat on the Novaristee, as representative of the Lectimentors.'

Montgomery turned in surprise to look at Vala. 'I thought you didn't want to have anything to do with all the political stuff,' he whispered.

'What?' she growled crossly, though she was grinning as she did so. 'Ain't I allowed to change my old mind if I feel like it?'

Montgomery grinned back at her as Wyndham continued.

'Right then, unless there's any other business...?' He paused, looking around at the sea of faces.

'Um... We lost the door to one of the cells,' said Dain, clearly feeling awkward at speaking in front of so many people. 'And the prison gate, as well. Sorry, sir. Payton destroyed them.'

'If that's everything...' Wyndham raised his arms in a dramatic pose. 'I propose we celebrate!' Another cheer went up from the crowd, even louder this time, and then people started moving, getting ready for their celebrations.

'Unfortunately,' said Pepper, placing her hand on Montgomery's shoulder, 'we can't stay. It's almost five-thirty and I haven't even started making dinner yet!'

36. "We Should Teach Him A Lesson"

On Saturday morning, Montgomery was up extra-early. Nine o'clock - early for a Saturday, anyway. He tugged on his clothes and gulped down his breakfast as quickly as possible, because today he was no longer grounded.

Pepper had been to see Mr Pemberton-Drake and, though Montgomery wasn't exactly sure what she'd told him about Montgomery's absence earlier that week, he was fairly certain she hadn't mentioned going to the Underworld to battle with Atlantis! Whatever she had said, it had at least kept the headmaster from giving him another detention, though every time Montgomery saw Mr Pemberton-Drake around school over the next few days, the headmaster had given him an "understanding" look, as though he thought Montgomery might be upset about something.

But today, he didn't care about school, he just wanted to get down to Lundarien and see his friends. He was particularly excited, because he had a surprise for them.

'Where do you think you're off to?' asked Pepper, finding Montgomery forcing on his shoes by the front door. 'I thought we could have a family day today.'

'Not another one,' he said, pulling a disgruntled face. 'Is dad upset about work again?'

Pepper shook her head, her dark hair falling across her face. 'No. That's just the thing. He's been promoted!' She flicked her hair back to smile at her son.

Montgomery paused, one shoe swinging from his toes. 'Promoted? But I thought his boss didn't like him.'

'His boss has been fired. It turns out he'd been up to all sorts of dodgy dealings. And because of all dad's experience at the old brewery, the board of directors has asked him to take on the boss's old job. Dad wants to take us all out to celebrate.'

'Take us out? Where?'

'Have I got a surprise for you!' said Victor, appearing behind Pepper. 'How does an evening in the West End sound? I thought we'd grab a meal together then go take in a show. We can even go on the Underground. How about that?'

'Tonight?' asked Montgomery, suddenly hopeful. 'Does that mean I can go and play with my friends this morning?'

Pepper turned to look at Victor, who stroked his moustache as he considered the request. 'Sure,' he said at last. 'You go along and play. Oh, there was one other thing,' he added as Montgomery returned to jamming his foot into the shoe. 'This arrived for you, this morning.'

Montgomery looked up to see his dad holding a small, square package wrapped in brown paper. It didn't look very interesting - not enough to distracted from his morning's fun, anyway.

'I'll check it out later, dad. Just dump it on my desk.' And with that, he darted through the door before anyone else tried to hold him up. He didn't want to be late.

Ping!

'You're late,' said Marlah as the lift doors slid open, revealing the slightly bored-looking faces of her and Jarfin.

'Actually,' he said, snatching the keycoin from the air as it ejected from the panel, 'I only said I'd be coming *in the morning*. I didn't give you a time.'

Marlah shrugged, already marching off towards the

side tunnel. 'Well, morning started hours ago!'

Jarfin just grinned at him and, together, the three of them headed into Lundarien, to the Melladie Maker, where Clovis and Alcott were sitting at a table, five steaming mugs set out in front of them.

'I feel like I haven't been here for ages,' said Montgomery, squeezing past the table where two old women were nattering away about how foreign people were much more friendly back in their day. He pulled up a chair.

'You haven't,' said Jarfin, taking the seat next to him. 'You've been too busy up on the Surface to hang around with us lot.'

'Hanging out with your *other* friend,' said Marlah, muttering into her mug.

Montgomery ignored her, savouring the Christmas-in-a-mug smell of the Melladie. He took a sip, then smiled up at the others. 'I'd much rather be busy up on the Surface hanging out with my *best* friends.'

He leaned back in his chair, giving the others a meaningful look over the mug cradled in his hands. They frowned back at him in silence.

'Oh!' said Jarfin, his face lighting up in sudden comprehension, his eyes wide. 'You mean…?'

Montgomery nodded.

'No!' said Marlah, a hand darting to her mouth. She looked around the room, as though checking they weren't being spied on, then spoke through her fingers in an excited whisper. 'Really? You mean it?'

Montgomery continued his nodding.

Clovis leaned forwards over the table, her voiced also lowered conspiratorially. 'But won't you get in trouble?' she asked.

Montgomery changed to shaking his head. He looked across at Alcott, whose face was still wearing its original confused expression.

'Sorry,' said Alcott, scratching his head. 'Are we talking about Merek again? Only I thought he'd scarpered with your aunt.'

Montgomery stopped shaking his head. 'No, Alcott. I'm talking about you guys.' He gestured towards the four of them, in case this wasn't clear enough. 'It's about time you saw for yourselves what life is like up on the Surface.'

Fifteen minutes later, they were huddled together inside the lift as it sped upwards towards London, nervous and excited all at the same time.

'It's like the night before Boarstide,' said Alcott, his eyes wide, 'when you're desperate to get your presents, but you're worried you might not get what you wanted.'

Marlah laughed. 'What? Like the wrong colour trowel?'

'What's Boarstide?' asked Montgomery, wondering if it was like an Underworld version of Christmas.

'You don't have Boarstide?' said Jarfin, giving him a pitying look. 'It's like a big celebration we have each year, when we give each other presents and sing songs under the Festing tree.'

'I can't believe you don't have Boarstide,' said Clovis. 'It's the best bit of the year!'

It sounded to Montgomery *exactly* like an Underworld version of Christmas. 'We've got something like it,' he said. 'Now, listen. When we get to the top, we'll need to sneak out as quickly as possible without being seen. And remember, there's no magic on the Surface.'

'So not a massive change for you then, Alcott,' said Marlah, grinning at him. 'And we'll find out what it's like to be useless like you.'

Ping!

Ducking down and looking as suspicious as possible,

they hurried out of the lift and Montgomery led them through the door onto the street. He had decided to take them to the park, but first he had to wait for ages while they stared around in wonder at everything.

And they really were fascinated by *everything*.

'Is that the sky?' asked Jarfin, pointing up to the mottled grey clouds. 'For some reason I thought it would be blue. It looks like it's made of slowly moving rocks!'

'What are those things?' asked Clovis, pointing to a small group of cyclists, who were heading up the road.

'Those trees are ridiculous!' said Marlah. 'Who ever heard of trees growing *up* out of the ground? Don't they get in the way?'

'It's all... so... big!' said Alcott, clinging to a bin as though worried he might float away. 'And bright as well.'

Montgomery, who thought it was a rather dreary-looking day, didn't say anything. Instead he tapped his foot impatiently, waiting for them to stop gawping at stuff. The more he waited, the more exposed he felt. He didn't dare look up at his apartment window, for fear of seeing his dad or, worse, his mum staring down at him. And the longer he stood there, the more he sensed eyes watching him.

'So which of these do you live in?' asked Marlah, pointing at the Victorian terraced houses across the road.

'I live in this place,' he said, thumbing over his shoulder, without turning round.

Alcott gazed up at the apartment building. 'Wow! Look at this massive place. It's like a palace I read about in a story book. It's so beautiful!'

Montgomery sighed. 'Come on,' he said. 'Let's get out of here.' And he walked quickly, almost at a jogging pace, up the road towards the park.

It was a long and tedious journey, with his four friends stopping every few metres to point something out and stare around. When, at last, they entered the gate opposite the boating lake, the first people Montgomery spotted were Jeff and some of his gang, kicking a football around on the nearby grass. He decided to turn back and take the longer route round, but it was too late.

Jeff chipped up the football and caught it under his arm, before strolling towards him, his mates in tow.

'What is all this then, Twinkles?' he said, running his eyes over Jarfin, Marlah, Alcott and Clovis, as if trying to work out what to make of them. They were still wearing their Underworld clothes. 'Who is these weirdoes?' There were a few half-hearted laughs from the rest of his gang.

'These,' said Montgomery, gesturing to them, 'are those "invisible" friends that I told you about, remember?'

Marlah barged past him, squaring up to Jeff. 'What did you just call us?'

Jeff held up his hands. 'Watch out, boys!' he said, half-laughing. 'It's a scary girl.'

Clovis stepped up next to Marlah. 'I think he called us "weirdoes," she said. 'Maybe we should teach him a lesson.'

'Him and all his *weirdo* friends,' added Alcott, joining them. A sliver of sunlight cut through the clouds and, for the first time, Montgomery realised just how huge Alcott's arms were. They were uncovered and the muscles bulged as he tightened his fists. Behind Jeff, Steve swallowed nervously.

Jarfin placed a hand on Montgomery's shoulder. 'Is this that boy you were telling us about?' he asked. 'From your school?' Montgomery nodded. 'Well, let's show him what happens when he messes with one of our friends.'

'Now, hold on, there,' said Jeff. He took a step backwards, bumping into Steve. 'There's no-'

He was cut off by a yell from Marlah. 'Get them!'

Jeff and his gang froze for a moment, but then

Marlah, Clovis and Alcott advanced on them, and, as one, they turned and fled across the grass.

'Come on!' said Jarfin, heading after the others as they broke into a run.

Montgomery grinned and set off to join them.

EPILOGUE

Montgomery turned the package over in his hands, looking for some clue as to who had sent it, but apart from his own name and address, and the stamp, postmarked "London WC2", the brown paper was unmarked. Unless it was his birthday, he never received anything in the post, and he certainly wasn't expecting anything. He lifted it to his ear and shook it. Something bumped around inside.

'Only one way to find out.' He sat down at his desk and started tearing off the paper. Inside was a wooden box, plain except for the brass latch and hinges on its lid. Flicking back the latch, he eased it open and his room was immediately bathed in a strange, but familiar, purple glow. Montgomery stared at it, open-mouthed. This didn't make sense. What was it doing here, delivered to him by the Royal Mail?

He lifted out the Trypasphere, warm and tingly against his fingertips. The shadows it cast on the bedroom wall twisted and stirred like living things.

In the bottom of the box was a square of folded paper. Placing the Trypasphere on his desk, ensuring it wouldn't roll off, he took out the paper and unfolded it. It was a note. A note written in the same neat handwriting that had been on the package. He scanned it, silently mouthing the words as he read.

"Dear nephew," it said. *"I believe this item belongs to you. I am returning it as my father wanted you to have it. He also wanted you to have his notebook, and only a fool would think the two are not connected. Thank you for loaning it to Merek."* Montgomery let out a short, harsh laugh. *"Please do not be angry with him. Remember what I told you: all is not as it appears. Your aunt, Payton."*

He read it through twice more before placing the piece of paper onto his desk and pulling open one of the drawers. There, nestling amongst the sweet wrappers and other rubbish, was his granddad's notebook. Despite everything, he was sure Payton was right, these two things must be connected. After all, something had happened when he exposed the book to the Heliorbs in the Lundarien prison, even though it was just that the pages turned blank. It made sense that this other magical artefact, which could counter the effects of the Heliorbs and even the Sun itself, would do the opposite and make something *appear* on the pages. Hopefully something Montgomery could understand.

Nudging a dirty sock out of the way, he lifted out the notebook and laid it on the desktop, next to the Trypasphere.

'This *has* to work!' he whispered, as he slipped a finger under its cover, hardly daring to breathe, and opened the notebook.

To his astonishment, as the orb's eerie light washed across the paper, the scribbles shifted, dancing like the shadows on his wall. But instead of becoming normal, readable writing, the scribbles settled to form an ornate border around an empty space in the middle of the page. He frowned at it with a rising sense of disappointment... and then gasped.

In that central space, two words formed. They said, *"Greetings, Montgomery"*. As soon as he had read them, though, the words disappeared and new ones appeared in their place. *"Welcome to your lessons"*. Again, as he read them, the words vanished, replaced a moment later by more: *"Watch this space"*.

Each time Montgomery finished reading, the message changed. *"Here you will learn"* gave way to *"all I know"*, which changed to, *"about the world of magic"*.

Montgomery stared in amazement, stunned by what he was reading. He snatched up the Trypasphere and the notebook and lay down on his stomach on the bed, making himself comfortable. Then he opened the notebook again, and started to read.

"Let us begin…" it said.

ACKNOWLEDGEMENTS

It's been an epic voyage writing this second stage in Montgomery's adventures, with all the anguish and elation, the struggling and sauntering, and the long, hard grind that go with such a journey. But I have not always travelled alone.

Accompanying me were my fantastic bunch of beta-readers: Will, Karen, Emma, Steve, June, Mark and Joel. Thank you all for providing such valuable comments and criticism, and so helping to shape this book.

Thanks also to Firedudewraith, who created the cover image, Jon Wotton, who drew the Lundarien map, and my editor, Sharmila. Great work!

GLOSSARY OF UNDERWORLD TERMS

The Agra
Three large caverns to the north of Lundarien where Bardles grow crops and rear various animals for food.

Alboars
Enormous white pigs kept in the Agra, which grow to about the height of a tall man and as long as a large car or a small corridor.

The Aristane
The three Multifexes who oversee the affairs of Salistra, the capital city of Brytellian. *(See also Brytellian)*

Atlantis
An Underworld nation below the Atlantic ocean, to the west of Brytellian. It is known also as the Golden City.

Bardles
Underworld people who have no magical abilities, so do most of the normal, everyday work. In Lundarien, they live mainly in the Vines.
Although not strictly one of the Magic Circles, the Bardles are represented on the Novaristee by their leader, the Lord Chapman. *(See also Magic)*
Symbol: Bee

Brytellian
The Underworld nation below most of the UK, Ireland and parts of France. Its colonies include Lundarien, Yarnock, Honeytown, Blayston-Braddock, Ethenside, Cloister, Munn, Dursehaven, and the capital city, Salistra.

Chronolith and Time

Made of two circular stones, this time-keeping device is mounted on the Lundarien Town Hall.

The twelve hours of the day begin with the first hour (equivalent to 6am) and end with the first hour of the night (equivalent to 6pm).

Lights Down in Lundarien is at the third hour of the night, with Lights Up at the first hour of the day.

The Underworld days of the week are as follows:

Wunday	-	Monday
Tousday	-	Tuesday
Thrieday	-	Wednesday
Forsday	-	Friday
Sichsday	-	Saturday
Sevunday	-	Sunday

Conjurings

These are produced by Multifexes using combinations of their magic. For example, if someone is both a Mover and a Changer, their conjuring is the ability to Summon.

If a Multifex has more than two types of magic they may have a Conjuring for every combination. For example, for a person with Moving, Changing and Cealing may have:

Moving + Changing = Summoning

Moving + Cealing = Teleporting *(within line of sight)*

Changing + Cealing = Creating Fire *(close at hand)*

Moving + Changing + Cealing = Creating Fire
(within line of sight)

The Great Tunnel

A single tunnel that connects the Steppengrads (near St Petersburg in Russia) to Pacifactris (below Hawaii). It runs through southern Brytellian, passing near Lundarien, Salistra and Yarnock. *(See also Transak)*

The Hanging Forest
A vast cavern to the north-west of Lundarien, full of downward growing trees and providing a home for many strange Underworld creatures.

Heliorb
A small sphere that shines with a yellow light and projects a field of non-magic.

Lake Altis
The Lundarien lake which may, or may not, contain tunnels that lead down to other Underworld communities.

Lundarien
The Underworld city below London. For further information see the map at the start of this book.

Magic
Although magic cannot survive on the Earth's surface, due to the destructive power of the Sun, the same is not true of the Underworld. Here there exist eight different types of magic, known as the Magic Circles, as follows:

Moving - the ability to move around an object or objects without physically touching them.
<u>Symbol</u>: Mammoth

Cealing - the ability to create illusions, making others see what isn't there, or not see what is there.
<u>Symbol</u>: Moth

Lectimenting - the ability to read people's minds and even control their actions.
<u>Symbol</u>: Snake

Watching - the ability to remember what is being seen or has been seen with supernatural precision.
<u>Symbol</u>: Octopus

Healing - the ability to cure illness, disease and injury, without using medicine etc.
<u>Symbol</u>: Spider

Hunting - the ability to move with superhuman speed and without making any sound. Also includes supernatural eyesight.
<u>Symbol</u>: Cat (aka Furzlebum)

Changing - the ability to transform physical objects, whether solid, liquid or gas.
<u>Symbol</u>: Frog

Mansing - the ability to see the future and predict what is going to happen.
<u>Symbol</u>: Owl

Melladie
A calming, yet invigorating, drink that is very popular in Lundarien. It is the normal practice to drink it hot.

Multifex
A person who is able to perform more than one type of magic.

The Novaristee
The group of nine leaders who oversee the affairs of Lundarien. Each member represents one of the Magical Circles.

Omnifex
A person who is able to perform all eight types of magic. Such people are very rare, and most Underworld communities haven't had an Omnifex among them for centuries. *(See also Magic and Multifex)*

Sunner
The Underworld term for people who live on the Surface, usual used as an insult.

The Surface
Where the 'Sunners' live: the surface of our planet. Because of the Sun's rays, magic cannot survive on the Surface, hence most people from the Underworld would never wish to go there.

Transak
Objects that are used as transportation along the Great Tunnel. They comes in many different forms, but are all operated by powerful Movers.

Trypasphere
A small sphere which emits a strange purple glow. It also has magical properties.

The Underworld
Far from being the place where dead people go to be tormented by evil spirits, the Underworld is a magical world that exists far below the Earth's surface.

The Vines
An area of densely-packed houses built around a network of alleyways, mostly inhabited by the Bardles. It is also home to the Melladie Maker and the market stalls of Lundarien.

UNDERWORLD MEASUREMENTS

Ear	the width of a barleycorn	1.8mm
Narl	9 Ears	1.6cm
Cob	17 Narls	27cm
Breech	4 Cobs	1.08m
Oar	2 Breeches + 1 Cob	2.16m
Bride	745 Oars	1 mile

If you have enjoyed this book, please consider reviewing it
on Amazon or Goodreads (or both)
Your review makes all the difference for independent
authors like me.

And feel free visit my website for other titles, free books
and to keep updated on Montgomery's adventures:

www.phinhall.net